BESIEGED

He was working on his second cup of coffee in the pearly light of a peaceful dawn when the Blackfoot, Cheyenne and Sioux attacked, sweeping down the steep slope to the west of Fort Washington.

"There's hundreds of them, Preacher!"

Preacher took aim at one. The Injun left the back of his pony for the Spirit World as Preacher popped another at forty yards.

An increased rate of fire told of the arrival of even more hostiles. Eighty-five Lakota warriors, painted and ready for war, rode out of the trees.

"I got a feelin' it's gonna get worse," Preacher said, "before it gets better. Boys, we'd better be gettin' to the walls. Those Injuns ain't here for a bison feast."

BOOK YOUR PLACE ON OUR WEBSITE AND MAKE THE READING CONNECTION!

We've created a customized website just for our very special readers, where you can get the inside scoop on everything that's going on with Zebra, Pinnacle and Kensington books.

When you come online, you'll have the exciting opportunity to:

- View covers of upcoming books
- Read sample chapters
- Learn about our future publishing schedule (listed by publication month *and author*)
- Find out when your favorite authors will be visiting a city near you
- Search for and order backlist books from our online catalog
- Check out author bios and background information
- Send e-mail to your favorite authors
- Meet the Kensington staff online
- Join us in weekly chats with authors, readers and other guests
- Get writing guidelines
- AND MUCH MORE!

**Visit our website at
http://www.zebrabooks.com**

WILLIAM W. JOHNSTONE

THE FIRST MOUNTAIN MAN
BLACKFOOT MESSIAH

ZEBRA BOOKS
KENSINGTON PUBLISHING CORP.
http://www.williamjohnstone.com

ZEBRA BOOKS are published by

Kensington Publishing Corp.
850 Third Avenue
New York, NY 10022

First Printing: February, 1996
10 9 8 7 6 5

Printed in the United States of America

ONE

Preacher had to go east to travel west, he discovered, when he decided to accept an assignment from the U.S. Army. Times had been lean for a while. Trapping was a thing of the past. Only a handful of men clung to the old ways, trapped and traded pelts to a market with little demand. Not so the legend called Preacher. Wisely he had salted away ample gold and silver coin, even invested some, most recently in what sounded to many like a fool's venture; Mr. Fulton's steamboat works.

As the smoke-belching paddle wheelers proliferated, so did Preacher's profits. Although ten years of only investment income had severely drained his reserve, he could no more leave the High Lonesome than many of the mountain men. Which meant he had to take whatever he could get to stay in supplies and keep afloat. Thus it was that he grudgingly considered accepting a commission from the War Department to act as trail guide and scout for a regiment of Dragoons. Preacher read again the letter that had accompanied the commissioning papers that had yet to see his signature.

Word has come out of the Northern Rocky Mountains of the Unorganized Territory that the Blackfoot are gathering in great numbers. The savages are being agitated by some holy man, who claims to have the way to bring back the White Buffalo and drive the white men out of the plains forever.

It is vital in these unsettled times to secure our northern flank. A conflict with Mexico seems imminent and our nation could ill afford an Indian uprising when our attention shall be directed southward. To which purpose, it is the decision of the Secretary to dispatch a battalion of Dragoons to the area of the Bighorn Mountains in the northeast part of the Territory to serve as a presence in the area.

The battalion is to depart Jefferson Barracks in Missouri, and proceed up the Missouri to the North Platte River, and from there into the high country of Wyoming where they will establish a fort. The purpose of this post will be to oversee the Blackfoot from a discreet distance, and to show the flag to the Cheyenne and Sioux.

What a stupid idea, Preacher thought. Then, as was the habit of many men who lived alone in the stunning quiet of the High Lonesome, he spoke his ruminations aloud.

"That'll only cause trouble where there's none now. What's got in ol' Quincy's head?" Preacher was referring to Quincy Vickers, an old friend. "He lived out here, and trapped, and knows the Injuns. Maybe it ain't this idee at all. Might be he needs his irons hauled out of the fire."

Knowing the striped-pants crowd from past experience, Preacher was well aware of their propensity for overreaction and . . . for stupidity. He was to sign the papers and take them to Bent's Fort, where two copies would be sent by fast messenger to Jefferson Barracks and Washington City. There he would pick up the first installment of the fee offered him. After a heavy sigh and an idle scratch of his thick, yellow-brown hair, Preacher picked up a quill pen and dipped it in his ink pot. With meticulous care, he formed the letters of his name.

* * *

Preacher shut and latched the door to his wintering place, careful to poke the latch string back inside. He'd be busy all summer, most like. He curled a dally of the lead rope of his packhorse around the overlarge horn of the Mexican saddle and swung atop his most recent acquisition, a crossbreed Morgan stallion which had a sturdy mountain mustang for a dam. Preacher had named him Tarnation. He shook the reins and drummed heels into stout sides.

"Well, Tarnation, we'd best be eatin' miles. I reckon I can find some companionable fellers down Bent's Fort way to accompany me on this commission as they called it."

In his letter, Quincy Vickers had told Preacher that he was authorized to hire on up to four men, at a rate of three dollars a day. Leave it to the government, Preacher mused, to offer enough money for some men to kill over it.

Big Nose Harper and his sidekick, Algernon Bloore, had gotten roaring, stumbling, falling-down, crap-in-their-drawers drunk the previous night. Now, some seven hours later, they didn't fare much better. Still too soaked in alcohol to suffer hangovers, they nevertheless sought some "hair of the dog." Their source, no matter how ill-advised, was William "Nifty" Bates, who had recently opened a trading post and road ranch saloon at the summit of Trout Creek Pass. Nifty was frankly afraid of Big Nose.

Big Nose Harper was a bear of a man, with a barrel chest, long, thick arms, tree-trunk legs, and his most memorable feature which gave him his nickname, an overlarge nose that had been smeared over his face. He held in contempt all "shopkeepers," to which subspecies he considered Nifty Bates belonged, and he went out of his way to make their lives miserable. Nursing his alcohol fog, Big Nose now went about tormenting Nifty.

"This whisky tastes like frog pee. You waterin' it down again, you cheat?"

"N-n-no, not at all, Mr. Harper," the barkeep stammered. Bates would soon sell out, inspired in part by the events of that afternoon.

Harper slammed his pewter mug on the pine-plank bar hard enough to make dust rise. "I say yer waterin' it. An' m'name's Big Nose."

"No I'm not, Mr. . . . er . . . Big Nose."

Harper's mean, close-set eyes narrowed. "Are you makin' fun of my honker?"

"Oh, no. You— you told me to call you Big Nose."

Big Nose looked offended. "I never said no such thing. Any man calls me that's lookin' for a killin'. A pantywaist like you's good for a knuckle-drubbin'."

A shadow fell across the toes of the boots worn by Big Nose, cast by a figure that filled the doorway. "Why don't you pick on someone nearer your size, Big Nose? Or should I call you blubber ass?"

Harper spun to face his detractor. "Who in hell are you?"

"They call me Preacher."

"Folks say he's a mean one, Big Nose," sniggered Algernon Bloore, who was more than a few biscuits shy of a plateful.

"Shut up, Algie," Harper snarled. He sized up Preacher and found him wanting. Whisky had so clouded his reasoning that he failed to see the hard, deadly glint in the gray eyes of the raw-boned man in the doorway. "Now, if you'll oblige me by gettin' the hell outta here, I'll have another drink. Barkeep, make it snappy."

Emboldened by the presence of Preacher, Nifty Bates took a stand. "No, sir You've had too much. The bar is closed to you."

Harper cut his eyes to Algie. Surprise registered on both their faces. No man ever spoke to Big Nose Harper that way. Growling, Big Nose reached across the plank bar and balled the front of Bates' shirt in both hands. With a yank that looked effortless, and was, he hauled the proprietor off his feet and across the bar.

Taking quick, mincing steps, which caused his long, greasy black locks to churn in protest, Big Nose Harper crossed the room and threw Nifty Bates out into the dusty dooryard. He then dusted hamlike palms together and snarled a reply to Bates.

"I say who drinks an' who doesn't around here."

Preacher took exception to that. "Like hell you do."

Glee brightened the pig eyes of Big Nose. "Mr. Preacher, prepare to meet yer maker."

With that, he came at the living legend of the mountains, arms widespread for his favorite bear hug. It had crushed the life from seven men before this. Big Nose saw no problem in making it eight. Which proved to be a terrible mistake.

Preacher crouched and duck-waddled out of the grasp of those powerful arms. When Big Nose blundered past, Preacher popped up and slammed an open palm into the side of the brawler's head, cupping it over the ear. If not for the thick ropes of greasy hair, the blow would have burst the ear drum of Big Nose. All it did, though, was set up a furious ringing and made him even angrier.

Big Nose whirled and swung at Preacher's chin. Preacher pulled his head back a few inches and let the big knuckles swish past. Then he went to work on the exposed ribs of Big Nose. Soft thuds sounded clearly enough to be heard by Nifty Bates. Dull-witted Algie Bloore decided to get in some licks on Preacher to win favor from his companion. He got a solid kick in the stomach for his efforts, flew backward with a hefty grunt and smashed into the bar. At once he began to spew up the liquor he had consumed.

By then, Big Nose had rallied and again grappled to encase Preacher in a bear hug. Preacher would have none of that. He backpedaled and swung a short, hard right to the face of Harper. Big Nose's most prominent feature got a little bigger when Preacher connected with the much-broken bridge. Preacher followed with a left hook that snapped Harper's jaw shut with a loud click. A second later, arms and legs twined around Preacher from behind.

Always a sneak, though not bright enough to profit by it, a somewhat recovered Algie Bloore had maneuvered to where he could leap on Preacher's back. "I got him, Big Nose, I got him!" he yelled gleefully.

Instead of struggling, Preacher simply flexed his knees and rammed himself backward into a six-by-six upright that supported part of the roof. Algie's shout of triumph turned to a squeal of pain.

"B'god, b'god, I think my back's broke."

"You'll git over it," Harper growled. Then he came for Preacher.

Always obliging, Preacher stepped away from the post and let Algie fall limply to the floor. He met the onrush of his opponent with a series of fast lefts and rights. A small grunt came from Harper with each impact. Half a dozen and he staggered sideways, his vision blurred. Fresh rage welled up inside him and he reached for a knife.

A shaft of sunlight through the open doorway made the keen edge a streak of fire. Harper advanced on Preacher, who produced his Greenriver and took a couple of swipes through the air. When Harper lunged

Preacher cut him across the back of the hand. The knife fell from pain-filled fingers. Preacher kicked it aside.

"Yeaaaaah!"

Preacher whirled to find a revived Algie Bloore hurtling at him, a knife extended in one hand. Preacher parried and sidestepped. He kicked Bloore's feet out from under the slightly built, ferret-faced man and Bloore went sprawling on the plank floor. His face was gouged by the rough boards; his knife skidded across the room. Preacher paused to take stock.

Both men looked fairly well whipped. Big Nose Harper stood, slope-shouldered, his breath harsh and irregular, head bowed. He tried, clumsily, to wrap a bandanna around his wounded hand. Preacher strode to the bar and pulled a beer for himself.

"Look out!" The warning shout came from Nifty Bates in the doorway.

Preacher spun on one heel to see Algie Bloore pull a long, single-barrel, caplock pistol from his waistband. Now, Preacher had been willing to oblige when the pair of frontier trash yanked steel on him, but he figured this was going too far. Recently outfitted with a pair of .44 Walker Colts, Preacher unlimbered one. He smoothly cocked the hammer as the muzzle cleared leather and snapped his elbow inward to elevate the barrel and level it on the target.

For all of his getting started last, Preacher's bullet reached the target first. Algie Bloore's head snapped backward from the impact of the 200-grain ball. A fist-sized chunk of his skull erupted from the left rear and showered the wall with gore. Reflex triggered his pistol and sent a ball into the front of the bar, close by Preacher's leg.

Enraged beyond caution by the swift death of his partner, Big Nose Harper dragged out a pair of double-barreled pistols. He thumb-cocked one awkwardly and swung it in the direction of Preacher. His first barrel discharged and put a ball into the wall beside Preacher's head a split second after Preacher put a .44 slug from his Walker Colt in the center of Harper's forehead.

Ears ringing from the confined detonations, Preacher examined his handiwork. Thick layers of powder smoke undulated in the cool interior of the saloon. Shakily, Nifty Bates entered. He walked over to Preacher and wrung his hand in gratitude and relief.

"I ain't never seen such fancy shootin' in my born days. Drinks are on the house, Preacher. Dinner, too. This pair's been nothin' but a misery and torment to me the past three days."

Up in the Blackfoot Mountains of Montana Territory, a huge gathering of warriors whooped it up around a large fire. The entire carcass of a bison, cut into quarters, turned on green-wood spits over separate cookfires. Off to one side, three Blackfoot braves handed out shiny new rifles from wooden crates at the back of a wagon. Each man gifted with one of these received a bag of a hundred lead balls and a horn of powder. For the time being, they would not be given the percussion caps. Four older men, seated around a large drum, hit the final double beat and concluded their song. The warriors stopped dancing and gathered in a wide semicircle around a startlingly white buffalo-hide lodge.

A young-looking man stepped out of the entrance and struck a pose before them. Although in his mid-thirties, he had the look of a man in his early twenties. His coppery face was elastic and unlined. He wore ankle-high moccasins, beaded and quilled in traditional Blackfoot design, a knee-length loincloth and an abbreviated, soft, pliable, elkskin hunting shirt. Over that was a most unusual item of garb, which lay in turn beneath a second, larger hunting shirt. Hair-pipe bracelets adorned his forearms and a breastplate of bison teeth, hair-pipe beads and brass cones covered his chest. He raised his arms above his head to command attention. The silence, immediate, became profound.

"My brothers, there are many among you who say Iron Shirt is too young to make strong medicine. You say that I have been a medicine man for only ten winters. Yet, I say to you that I have the strongest medicine. I received it in a vision when I visited among the Paiute. My spirit guide appeared to me and showed me a hidden valley. 'Dig here' the spirit said, pointing at a low mound. 'You will find the power of White Buffalo. You will learn the ways of making the medicine that will bring back White Buffalo and drive the white-eyes from our land forever.' I dug there, and I found what the spirit wanted for me. Then I was shown the dance we have just danced, and much more. It makes me safe from any white man's bullets. It will work for you also. The day is coming soon when the white men will fall to the earth like soft hailstones. I bring you rifles, the newest and best. Plenty of bullets, too. When you have finished the ritual of Iron Shirt, you will be stronger than any bullet."

"You say the white man's bullets cannot harm you, Iron Shirt. Prove it and we will follow you," a doubter among the experienced warriors challenged.

Iron Shirt looked at his detractor contemptuously for a moment, then forced an amiable expression on his face. He was, after all, selling something. He pointed with his chin at one of his earlier converts.

"I ask Bent Trees to step to the far side of the fire. Take your gun in hand and point it at my chest." Bent Trees did as bidden. When he was in position, Iron Shirt continued. "When I say so, shoot me."

Gasps of surprise and shock arose among the Blackfoot. "He will not aim at Iron Shirt," one brave stated flatly.

"The gun is not loaded with a bullet," opined another. "It is a trick."

Another convert sought to disabuse them. "No, it is the power of Iron Shirt's medicine. Watch and see."

"Now, Bent Trees."

With a sharp crack, the .60 single-shot pistol discharged. A black hole appeared in the outer hunting shirt worn by Iron Shirt a split second before he violently rocked backward, his face twisted in pain. Several Blackfoot rushed forward. Iron Shirt held up a hand to stay them.

Carefully he reached into the hole and worked his fingers a moment. He came out with a flattened .60-caliber ball. Yips and whoops of victory broke out among the spectators as he held it high and slowly turned full circle. When the jubilation subsided, he spoke again.

"You will be shown the secret of this medicine when you complete the ritual to become part of my Iron Shield Strong Heart Society. Death to all white-eyes!"

Seated inside the lodge of Iron Shirt were three white men, dressed as Blackfoot. One, Morton Gross, with thinning, mousy brown hair and eyes that looked like chips of blue ice, smoked a cigar. All three looked inordinately pleased with the progress being made. The nominal leader of their cabal nodded to Gross.

"It's fortunate that you have important friends in high places, Morton. Nice to get advance warning that a regiment of troops is on the way, and that it would be guided by an experienced frontiersman."

Morton Gross made light of his informant's importance. "He's only a clerk. The really important ones are so high up they don't dare make direct contact with us, but my informant was able to read the letter sent to the former mountain man, Preacher."

Praeger beamed as he bragged to his companions, "And now, if the men we sent to watch the Santa Fe Trail only do their job, our goal is in our hands."

Two

A day's ride from Bent's Fort, Preacher sipped from his first cup of coffee in night camp. Orange shafts slanted over his right shoulder and the night birds and katydids were gradually tuning up for their serenade. They suddenly went silent and Preacher stiffened a moment, then moved with studied casualness as he set aside the tin cup and draped a hand over the butt of his right-hand Walker Colt. A moment later a man's voice rang out from among the trees.

"Hello, the camp. We done smelled coffee."

Preacher looked up in that direction. "Howdy to you, stranger. If you be friendly, come on in. There's plenty for both of us."

"We be two if that's all right by you?"

"Fine as frog hair. Come sit a spell."

Two men entered the clearing on foot, leading their horses. The one in front had a broad, ample girth, chubby arms and legs, and a moon face. The one behind him had a skinny frame, gaunt as a scarecrow's, with flat, dull eyes and big ears. He wore his hair in a boy's "soup bowl" cut, Preacher noticed. The friendly voice came from him.

"They call me Fat Louie, though I can't for the life of me figger why. Ain't put on a single pound since before my voice changed. This lump o' lard be my pard,

Yard-Long Farmer. I reckon you can work out why the name," he concluded with a wheezing cackle.

Yard-Long Farmer joined in the laughter. "Yup. When I was ten I had me the biggest tallywhacker of any kid under fifteen in our town," he offered in the event Preacher could not puzzle through the nickname.

"Name's Arthur," Preacher responded evasively. He had heard of this pair and kept alert. "Sit a while."

He poured coffee around and broke out some cornbread and a pot of molasses. While they munched and sipped, Fat Louie spoke flatteringly to Preacher.

"I tell ya, Arthur, you're the very best we ever saw. We didn't cut no sign of you whatsomeever. We wouldn't have found this camp if we hadn't near stumbled right into it. You been in the Big Empty long?"

"Since before my voice changed," said Preacher dryly, mocking Fat Louie's earlier turn of phrase.

Fat Louie seemed not to notice. "It certain shows. Say, that's a mighty fine horse you've got. Looks like he could go a long ways, rid hard and put up wet, an' not be harmed. Must be worth a pretty penny."

"He's out of a shaggy mountain mustang," Preacher deliberately belittled his sturdy stallion.

Over the next half hour the conversation went much the same way. When Preacher came to his boots to pour more coffee, Fat Louie cut his eyes to Farmer. The chubby thug nodded slowly. Fat Louie agreed. They had this Arthur off his guard. At once, both rogues whipped out pistols and drew down on Preacher.

"Don't get goosey, Arthur. We'll just be takin' all yer gear an' yer horses an' those fancy irons yer wearin'."

Having been credited with inventing the words *gunfighter* and *fastdraw*, this did not faze Preacher in the least. He had known of this pair's reputation for years, knew them to be cowardly trash who would kill him in a hot tick. He slowly turned toward the louts threatening him.

He spoke in a soft, flat tone. "I don't think so."

Fat Louie smirked over the barrel of his pistol. "Oh? What makes you say that?"

"Because you've got yourselves a little problem here. Most folks don't call me by my given name. They call me Preacher."

Yard-Long Farmer's eyes went wide and he let his jaw drop before he gulped out a frightened, *"Oh . . . hell!"*

Between the *Oh* and the *hell,* Preacher unlimbered a Walker Colt and shot Fat Louie in the center of his breastbone. Louie's pistol bucked in his hand and he put a ball through the side-wing of Preacher's long, colorful *capote.* Then his legs went rubbery and he sank to his knees.

Preacher immediately turned on Farmer and put a .44 ball in the hollow of his throat. Yard-Long went down, gargling his blood. His finger twitched and he fired one of the pair of pistols he held, sending the ball into his left calf. Pain sounded through his gurgles.

"Why? Why me?" he managed to choke out.

Preacher stepped over to him and removed the unfired pistol from his hand. Right then he heard the click of a caplock mechanism. Fat Louie had not yet gone off to meet his maker. Ignoring the question for a moment, Preacher turned to his right and fired in an almost casual way. His bullet went in one ear and out the other, ending forever the nefarious career of Fat Louie LaDeaux. Then Preacher dropped to one knee beside Yard-Long Farmer.

"You know, it's too bad you and yer partner chose the wrong path to walk. Best you make your peace with the Almighty. You ain't got much time."

When Preacher reached Bent's Fort, he encountered two old friends, Antoine Revier, a half-breed Delaware, and Three Sleeps Norris. Former mountain men who, like Preacher, could not leave the mountains after the fur trade collapsed, they moved like ghosts from one old haunt to another. Three Sleeps Norris burst out through the stockade gate with such animation that dust boiled up around his moccasins.

"I'll be danged if it ain't Preacher. Still got his hair, if he has growed a little potbelly."

Preacher dismounted and they embraced, then danced around and around. "I don't have a potbelly," Preacher protested. "And I keep my hair by stayin' on the watch for those who would lift it." He stopped their caper and held Three Sleeps out at arm's length. "I will say that you have grown a mite rounder since I last saw you."

Three Sleeps faked a pout. "I ain't no rounder. It's these clothes."

"Sure, sure, of course it is. Anybody else around from the old bunch."

"Antoine Revier is inside now. Also Pap Jacobs is mendin' from a broke leg. Nobody else at home but a couple of stuffy soldier-boys."

Preacher frowned. This was embarrassing. "They're waiting for me."

Three Sleeps cocked his head to one side. "What? Preacher hangin' with soldier-boys?"

"Not exactly hangin'. I got some papers for them. To be delivered. Back in Washington City."

Three Sleeps gave Preacher a knowing wink. "Couldn't be that you're signed up to actual work for the Army?"

Preacher swallowed hard and rushed his words. "We'll-talk-about-that-later. Now I want to wash the trail dust out of my throat."

"Wal, come on. Old Turner has him a new spring house where he keeps his beer barrels. Like to crack yer teeth it's so cold."

The Bent brothers had long since departed from the private fort named for them. Currently a man named Ransom Turner occupied the trading post and saloon, and the immigrant's store. The fortifications had deteriorated badly. The Arapaho were no longer a threat, and the Kiowa raided farther east. Turner, more a businessman than a frontiersman, had not bothered with repairs. One of the gates, Preacher noted, hung from a single huge iron hinge. They strode across the small parade ground to the front of the saloon to encounter another warm welcome for Preacher.

Seated at last at a table in the plank-floored saloon, Preacher drank contentedly from a large stein of beer, which he used to chase swallows of some whisky of dubious origin. He easily saw why his present companions preferred the beer. Across from him, Antoine Revier leaned toward Preacher. Beady, black eyes glittered with merriment under Revier's thick mane of black hair and bushy brows.

"*Sacré nom,* it is good to see you again, Preacher. When was the last time?"

Preacher studied the traces of gray shot through Revier's hair at his temples and in his luxuriant mustache. A lot of time had gone by. "The 'twenty-eight rendezvous, as I recollect."

Antoine slapped a big hand on the tabletop. "You are right. It has been at least that long. What have you been doing of late? Met any of the other trappers?"

"Not in awhile. I did get crosswise of Fat Louie LaDeaux and Yard-Long Farmer jist the other day."

Revier scowled. "Those two are bad business. They rob the dead— people they have just shot in the back."

Preacher's eyes sparkled. "Not anymore. They tried their game on the wrong feller."

Revier and Norris sniggered. "Now that 'wrong feller' wouldn't happen to be called Preacher, would he?" Revier prompted. At Preacher's nod, he went on. "Good riddance."

Three Sleeps Norris tapped the side of his long nose. "I don't mean to pry, but what brings you this far south, Preacher?"

"Like I said, Three Sleeps, later."

Before Preacher could be asked more, the soft thumps of moccasin soles in the doorway drew their attention. A grizzled mountain man, one not known by any of the three. He nodded to the trio and crossed to the bar.

"Whisky," he ordered. "You hear the latest, Ransom?"

"What would that be, Ev?" asked the proprietor.

"There's word on the wind that a wagon train of pilgrims have been led astray somewhere up to the northeast. They was last seen along the Platte River." Evan Butler turned to include Preacher and his companions. "What do you think, boys? I say we've got more than enough flatlanders shovin' in around here. Present company excepted," he added over his shoulder to the relative newcomer, Ransom Turner.

With his tongue, Preacher worried a scrap of jerky that had caught in his teeth. When he freed it he spat it on the floor. "I say half of those who have come into the High Lonesome are more than enough. Why, them that don't want to tear up the sod and plant crops are Bible thumpers and Psalm singers. Most of them can't button their trousers of a mornin' without retraining, nor know which foot their boot goes on. Give me another beer, Mr. Turner," Preacher said in an aside. "Them lost pilgrims out there can rot for all I care." When the beer came, he quaffed a long draught and smacked his lips.

* * *

Quinton Praeger arose from the fragrant pile of pine boughs on which he had slept and stretched his long, lean frame, toughened by years of living out of doors. He was of an age with Morton Gross, yet he knew himself to be in far better shape. Years as a mining engineer had conditioned him to sleeping on the ground, and for him, unlike the rotund Gross, the Blackfoot bed of buffalo robes and boughs was a luxury. He reached down for his clothing and nudged the bare flank of the young woman who had pleasured him the previous night. She turned on her side and opened blue eyes. When she focused on Praeger, her expression registered disgust. But, as a slave to the Blackfoot, this white woman had no choice, Praeger knew.

Although he would have preferred a young, barely nubile Blackfoot girl, his host had offered this one and he would have offended by refusing. She'd been good, though, he had to admit. At least once he had gotten her suitably warmed up. They would be moving on today. Iron Shirt's Traveling Medicine Show, Praeger reflected with amusement. Three more bands of Blackfoot to visit, then they would go to the Cheyenne. Before long they would have the entire frontier aflame.

Over a rack of open pit-roasted bison ribs, Preacher finally acknowledged that his earlier assumption had been correct. He could not nursemaid a battalion of baby Dragoons all the way to the Big Empty alone. He indeed needed someone to come along. So he began to fabricate an elaborate tale to spin for his friends. Licking grease off his fingers, Preacher tossed away one rib bone and cut off another.

"Now that our bellies are full and we're feelin' good, I'll tell you all about what I come here for. Three Sleeps is right, I gave them papers to the soldier-boys. An' . . .

though it galls me to admit it . . . I done signed on for
a job with the Army. You see, there's this new-formed
battalion of Dragoons . . ." Preacher went on to describe
what he expected to find when he reached Jefferson Barracks. After talking of the well-known hazards of the
vastly unforgiving mountains, he concluded with his
sales pitch.

" 'Course I knowed right off that it was gonna take
men of courage and powerful wisdom to shepherd those
green soldier-boys to Wyoming. I'll have to be real careful and choosey as to who I pick."

"Why, that's the stupidest thing I've heard," Three
Sleeps Norris exploded. "Them greenhorns would be
out there all alone. The nearest white settlement is more
miles away than I can count, even if I take off my moccasins. Wyoming, plumb crazy."

"Oh, I agree. No man in his right mind would pick
that wild and wooly country for putting up a solitary
fort. 'Course the government is gonna pay in gold, and
plenty of it. They wrote me that I could pay three dollars,
gold, a day for any who sign on."

"Three dollars?" Norris and Revier chorused.

"Yep. That's right. The way I see it, it'll take the entire
summer to get the job done. That comes to a total of
two hundred seventy-six dollars."

Antoine scratched his head. "Well, now, they sure are
generous. Out here a man can live a whole year on that
and have some left over. And it beats competin' with a
dozen other fellers over every dinky little bit of work
that comes up. If you'll have me, Preacher, I think I'll
come along."

Three Sleeps nodded in agreement. "What you said
about the competition for jobs out here is right, Antoine.
Seems as how Preacher has got himself into a bear cave
the first day of spring. Might be a couple of good fellers,
like ourselves, could save his bacon for him. Count me

in." He extended a hand to Preacher, who shook on the bargain. Then Norris signaled for another round.

Preacher beamed at them with sincere gratitude. "I've done seen the soldier-boys, and they took off lickety-split back east. We can light out first thing in the mornin'."

THREE

Night swiftly came on again at the edge of the Wyoming Bad Lands of the Great Divide Basin. Eve Billings hugged herself with tired arms. They ached from driving a team of six mules all day. Only two days previously had they found a way out of the Medicine Bow Mountains, at least that's the range in which she believed them to have been. Eve teetered on the verge of losing her battle with despair.

How much more must she endure? How much could she ask her children to take in stride? First the loss of her husband, killed a month and a half ago by a war party of Sauk and Fox in Iowa Territory. Next, their captain and his trail guide had led the wagon train into a blind canyon in the Medicine Bow range. There the scoundrels had robbed and abandoned the settlers. When at last the party had found their way out of the mountains, this stark desert rolled over to the horizon to daunt them.

Resolutely she spoke aloud her foremost thought. "We have to move on."

There was scant water for the stock, blistering heat, although it was only the end of May, and terrible chill at night. However could they find their way? In the distance, a coyote called for his mate, to be answered by half a dozen yaps and yelps. Eve shuddered and tightly clutched the barrel of the Model 40 Bridesburg Arsenal rifled musket her husband had so prudently provided as a necessity. A thin sliver of moon hung in the east, while the western sky still was washed in orange and magenta by the afterglow. Her eldest child, Charlie, came up to her and tugged at her apron as he had done as a babe.

"Mom— Momma, I'm hungry. Anna is cryin' again and wants to eat. What are we goin' to have?"

"There's some bacon, and a few potatoes left."

Charlie wrinkled his nose and twisted his ten-year-old face into a mask of repugnance. "Ugh! The bacon's all green and slippery on the outside."

"I'll trim it. That's all we have."

"Why can't we just go back?"

Eve's heart ached at the misery and pleading in the expression of her son. "We can't, Charlie. It's two months' journey back to New York State. In two months we'll be in the Oregon Country. A new home, a new life."

Charlie rubbed one bare foot over the other. "I don't want a new home. I don't *want* a new life. 'Sides, who's gonna lead us to Oregon? Mr. Tate? Mr. Labette? They can't find their way to the outhouse."

A scowl formed on Eve's high, clear forehead. "That sort of talk will get your mouth washed out with soap, young man. You are not old enough to fail to show respect to your elders. Mr. Pruitt seems to know what he is doing. At least he can hitch his mules without someone showing him how to do it."

"Big help that is," Charlie jeered, then dodged the swat Eve aimed at his rump.

"Back to the wagon, Charlie." When she turned back, the stars shone brightly in the bowl of the sky. Maybe tomorrow help would come.

Twenty-four naked Blackfoot warriors stood in a solemn rank on the bank of the Bighorn River. Monotonously, two drummers struck the surface of the big drum with their milkweed and sacred pollen padded buffalo-hide strikers. *Thummm* and *thummm* the skin stretched over a large section of hollowed tree trunk sounded. The close-by walls of the Bighorn Mountains reverberated with the drumming. Before the men stood Iron Shirt, stripped of his loincloth and moccasins. For a man of such ambition and power, he had surprisingly average endowment. He raised his bare arms above his head to capture the initiates' attention.

"My brothers, you are about to learn the mysteries behind my great medicine. First you must be purified. Part of that has already been accomplished in the sweat lodges. Now your fear of the white man's bullets must be washed from you so that you are reborn into the society of the Iron Shield Strong Hearts."

Here he paused and stepped backward into the shallows of the river. His bare feet found purchase among the rocks that lined it. The water was aching cold, though he showed no effect. He beckoned with both arms to the first two in line.

"You two come forward into the water." When they did so, his instructions continued. "Turn around and face your brothers." Once in position, four of Iron Shirt's closest followers joined the Blackfoot. Tipping them backward, they lowered each candidate into the water until fully immersed.

Iron Shirt raised one hand over each in benediction and solemnly intoned, "I command all wickedness and fear to abandon you, for you to renounce the power of the white man's bullets, and I baptize you in the name of the three-faced god, the Father and the Son and the Holy Ghost. Arise my brothers in Iron and go forth to be warmed by the coals."

Obediently, the pair waded clear of the river and walked to where a long, narrow trench had been pre-

pared. The air above it shimmered with distortion from
the heat given off by a deep bed of coals. They stood
near, letting the radiant waves warm their chilled bodies.
While they did, Iron Shirt continued until all the remaining initiates had been baptized. Then he joined them at
the firepit. Again he spoke the ritual words.

"To walk safely through the blaze of the white man's
bullets, you must first walk through this earthly fire. Prepare your bodies and spirits for this ordeal by praying
to the Great Spirit for the strength of the Sky Legend;
Firewalker. When you are ready, I will lead you across
the abyss of flame."

Iron Shirt waited a hundred heartbeats, then posi-
tioned himself at the lip of the trench. He stuck out one
foot and made contact with the bed of coals. With a firm,
unhurried tread, he walked the length of the shimmer-
ing embers. On the far side, he strode ten paces from
the pit and raised first one foot, then the other, to reveal
not the least damage. The candidates had followed close
on his heels and emerged now in the same condition,
until the twenty-second in line.

Suddenly that unfortunate warrior let out a pain-
wracked shriek and leaped to one side. He fell to the
ground to reveal feet of a cherry-red hue, puffed and
badly blistered. He had not enough faith. Iron Shirt
turned to him. He made a gesture of sympathy.

"Go and have Red Elk dress those feet with bear
grease. Know that you did not gain dishonor for your
failure. When your faith grows stronger, come again and
make the sacrifice, that you may join us." When the injured man had been helped from sight, Iron Shirt gestured to the others. "Come, my brothers of Iron Shield,
gather around. It is time for me to reveal the mystery of
my medicine's power."

They did, eager as small boys around a strange animal.
Iron Shirt reached down and pulled up the hem of his

outer hunting shirt. It revealed a complete set, front and back, of chain mail. Although dented in places and rusty in other spots, its sturdy construction and latent protection awed them all. Iron Shirt turned slowly so they could examine the all-encasing war garment, then lowered his shirt and retrieved his loincloth and moccasins. The initiates did likewise, silent throughout. At last, Iron Shirt addressed them again.

"And would you now like to test your new power?" To their enthusiastic agreement, he added. "To the south and west of us, there can be found many rolling lodges of the whites. We shall ride there and kill them all. It is a true thing, I tell you. Not a one of us will fall."

They had circled the wagons for the night. Asa Wharton peered out into the ruddy glow of the setting sun and wondered at what fools they had been. To believe that they could make their way to the Oregon Country on their own should be enough to put them in the asylum, he thought with chagrin. We are too far north, his musings prompted. We always have been. It had been as much his fault as anyone else's. Worse, his voice had been one of the loudest, insisting that the Brothers not bring along any firearms.

"We are the children of God," he had declared. "We must show that we come in peace."

A lot of good that will do. There are Indians out in the hills all around us. He could feel it in his bones. He strongly doubted the savages would spend much time listening to anything they had to say. For the first time since childhood, Asa Wharton wondered what it would be like to die. He shuddered when he recalled the hoofprints he had seen in the loose soil.

He had been riding ahead of the slow-moving wagons when he came upon them. They angled down one slope and crossed the trail. From there, they disappeared over the ridge to the south. By the time the first wagon arrived, a stiff breeze had wiped out any sign of them. *Why had he not told the others about them?*

Because he did not want to create panic. Now it was too late. Asa sighed and turned away. He had taken only one step when the eerie, seething hiss of an arrow registered on him before the projectile winged between a pair of nose-to-tail wagon boxes and buried to the fletchings in Asa's back. The bloody point protruded, dripping, from his chest. Blackness engulfed him.

Iron Shirt led his Strong Hearts silently across the scrub-studded plain. They came within fifty feet and loosed a flight of arrows. Screams of terror and shrieks of pain followed moments later. Young Blackfoot boys, apprentice warriors, held the horses while the braves streamed forward on foot. The only shots fired came from the rifles in the hands of the Blackfoot. They had devastating effect. Seven men fell in the seconds after the death of Asa Wharton.

Whooping Indians broke through the barricade and rushed toward the stunned people. With tomahawks and war clubs they slammed into the helpless whites huddled beyond the fire. Iron Shirt stood back and watched with growing satisfaction. Given another moon, he would have an invincible force. The Cheyenne would join. The Sioux would be next.

Then, he thought, his mind filled with darkness, he would deal with the white men who masqueraded as Blackfoot and run the war against all whites his own way. How good that would be. Beyond him, within the circle of wagons, the slaughter grew terrible. Children, he contemptuously labeled the men and even the women who fell without offering the least resistance.

When the last white died, Iron Shirt came forward. A quick check showed him that there had been no survivors. And better still, the Blackfoot took no losses.

Early the next morning, Preacher and his companions set out together along the north fork of the Santa Fe Trail. Hard-packed and rutted from much past use, it let them make good time. Near mid-morning, they came upon a packhorse trader. He had three animals on lead, their packsaddles heaped with tin pots and pans, shielded tin lanterns; one loaded with patterned pressed panels for ceilings.

He hailed the trio enthusiastically. "Howdy, fellers. good to see a friendly face. I'd be obliged if you'd ride along a spell. You're more than welcome."

Preacher considered it odd the peddler was headed the same way they were. "Don't mind if we do," he responded. "M'name's Preacher. These two are Three Sleeps Norris an' Antoine Revier."

"Pleased to meet you. I go by the name of Tinman, but it's really Morris Lorson."

"If you don't mind my saying so, them goods of yours looks like something bound for Santa Fe," observed Preacher.

"It is— it is. I just came from there. I got turned away, you see."

Three Sleeps gave him a puzzled look. "How's that, Tinman? I thought those Mezkins was all-fire hot for American goods."

"They are, usually. Only lately things aren't so cordial for Americans. Not since the Texicans won their independence back in 'thirty-six."

Preacher furrowed his brow as he thought this over. "That's old news, and didn't have anything to do with us Americans. What's got into 'em now to get riled at our people?"

Tinman Lorson gave Preacher a knowing look. "Didn't you hear? For the last couple of years there's been talk about the Texicans wantin' to join up with the United States. An' the folks in Washington City are pushin' for them to do it. You can see how that don't sit well a-tall with the Mexicans."

"That a fact?" Preacher responded, then tuned out the peddler's chatter.

They made camp late in the afternoon. Around coffee, after ample plates of broiled grouse— provided by Antoine with his delicate, slender-barreled shotgun— fatback and beans, Tinman Lorson studied his impromptu fellow travelers. After several moment's consideration he hesitantly explored a subject of great interest to him.

"If you don't mind, I surely don't wish to pry, but would you tell me how you got that name— Three Sleeps?"

"Wal, it ain't nothin' much. It happened a long time ago."

"No, really, I'd like to know. I . . . ah . . . collect nicknames and the stories behind them. It's something to pass the long hours shared with others along the trading path. Please, indulge me if you will."

Preacher inserted himself in the conversation. "Three Sleeps is too modest to brag on hisself. I'll be happy to enlighten you."

Lorson brightened. "Yes, do."

Preacher thought a while, then began his tale. "Like Three Sleeps says, it happened a long time ago. He was a youngster then, hardly old enough to wet his throat with good whisky. As it happened, he was doin' just that one fine day when this notorious brawler slammed into the tradin' post where young Archibald Norris stood at the bar. As it happened, this bear-wrastlin' lout was spoilin' for a fight. Hadn't thumped on anyone for a couple of days and was feelin' out of sorts.

"So he eyes Arch here and says, 'Who let this skinny little puke in here?' Now Arch happened to be sensitive about his size at the time," Preacher went on with a chuckle. "He turns to face . . . ah . . . what was his name?"

"Travers. Meat Hook Travers," Three Sleeps provided quietly. He gave a little shudder.

"Yep. That's the one. Meat Hook Travers. Anyhow, ol' Meat Hook stomped up to the bar while Archibald formed the words he would say. Meat Hook thumped Arch on the chest and bellowed to the barkeep. 'Somebody answer me.' Archibald had his words gathered by then and decided it was up to him to speak. 'I brought myself in on my own two legs, and I reckon to leave the same way.' For Meat Hook, that was too hard to chew, let alone swallow. So, he rears back and bellows at Archibald. 'You'll go out of here on a plank.' " Preacher paused for a swallow of coffee.

"An' that's where ol' Meat Hook got a big surprise. Young Archie came at him like a buzz saw. He walked up Meat Hook with his fists and down t'other side. He booted that tub of muscle and lard in the butt and when Meat Hook turned with a roar, Arch mashed his lips with a solid left— or was it a right? Never mind, he moved fast as a wasp with a busted nest. Archie was quick and he was sneaky. He landed five punches for every one Meat Hook connected. Then Meat Hook tried to catch Archibald in a bear hug.

"Archie was havin' none of that. He danced back and kicked Meat Hook in the belly. That did it. Meat Hook sank to his knees. Arch here waded in. When he got done, Meat Hook was stretched out on the dirt floor, cold as an iced-over lake. Arch rubbed his sore knuckles and stepped back to the bar. 'You'd best put some distance between the two of you,' the bartender advised. 'Not a problem. I think I'll finish my whisky and have a little brew,' Archibald responded. The fellow in the apron had good advice. 'He'll come after you for sure.' All calm and collected, Archie swallowed down his whisky and gestured for a beer. 'There's plenty time to make tracks. The way I see it, he's good for about three sleeps.' And, by jingo, if the name didn't stick. I know for certain it happened that way because I was the only witness beside the barman."

Slack-jawed, Morris Lorson stared into the fire. He did not know, for all his experience at collecting names and legends, if he was having his leg pulled or not. Then something that had been nagging at him all day went off in his mind. He looked up at the weathered features of the narrator of the tale.

"Are you the same Preacher who single-handed cleaned a nest of thieves and cutthroats out of a trading-post saloon a decade ago?"

"Friend, it's been at least a dozen saloons I've cleaned out by myself," Preacher enlightened him. "Not to count the Injuns I've fit and the personal squabbles with other mountain men. You've got the right one, sure enough, if your claims for me are a mite more modest than some."

Lorson beamed. "Then it's a pleasure to be counted among your associates, if only for a short while. And I have me a new nickname and the story behind it. I'm obliged." He rocked back on his heels.

"An' I'm for gettin' some shut-eye," announced Preacher. "Daylight comes mighty fast in these parts."

Along about what Preacher judged to be ten-thirty in the morning, he and his partners parted company with Tinman Lorson. They spurred their more lightly loaded mounts and rode ahead, to soon lose him from sight over a ridge. Shortly after that, Preacher began to pick up sign of an Indian presence.

A trimmed, decorated eagle feather stuck an inch or two above the ridge to the south. Bird calls, which had been plentiful moments before, had dwindled to a few. Those that came did not sound entirely true. A tiny puff of dust drifted upward suddenly from beyond the swale to the north. Preacher reined in abruptly and dismounted. His friends did likewise.

After a quick look around, they formed a close square with their mounts and the packhorse. Antoine cut his eyes to Preacher. "I noticed them, too, *mon ami.*"

A second later, a small party of howling Kiowa warriors broke the southern horizon and thundered down toward the white men behind the improvised barricade.

FOUR

"Watch our backsides, Three Sleeps," Preacher instructed calmly while he sighted in and cleaned one Kiowa from the saddle with his rifle.

Quickly, Preacher reloaded. He changed his point of aim and put a .54-caliber ball through the shoulder of another warrior. Beside him, Antoine fired his trusty .36-caliber squirrel rifle and plunked a ball through the center of a screaming Kiowa's forehead. His war whoop ended mid-yelp.

Behind them, Three Sleeps Norris downed another warrior with a gut shot. "You were right, Preacher, they're comin' from the north now."

By then, Preacher and Antoine had reloaded. It would be their last rifle shot for this charge, they knew. The Kiowa braves had come within twenty yards now. Preacher fired first. He split a buffalo-hide shield and shattered the forearm behind it. The warrior ignored it, his left arm flopping uselessly amid a shower of blood. Antoine ended the life of another savage with a ball through the throat. Then Preacher drew one Walker Colt. He made a quick check of the percussion caps, found them secure on the nipples. Then he raised the heavy revolver and eared back the hammer.

A fat cloud of smoke enveloped the defenders when the big .44 fired. Preacher quickly recocked the revolver and got off another round. A shout of pain answered him. The light breeze slowly blew the obscuring cloud away. Another round from Preacher's Colt took a warrior in the side. With that, they had enough.

A shrill bark turned the Kiowa and they swung away from their target. They quickly galloped out of range.

"They'll be back," advised Preacher.

Several minutes passed in an eerie silence. Then the Kiowa came again, this time from the east. Preacher had counted twenty warriors at the outset. Now four lay dead on the ground and three had been severely wounded. That left a baker's dozen. Three rifles spoke with deadly authority and reduced the number to ten.

Still the Indians would not leave off. Their blood was up, their friends killed or wounded. They badly wanted these white scalps. Once again they recoiled from the blaze of Preacher's six-shooters.

Running Bull could not understand it. Had they come upon a party of the Texicans called Rangers? He knew of no others who possessed the fast-shoot hand rifles. If so, why did the others not use theirs? From the reverse slope of the rise to the east, he studied the besieged white men with keen eyes.

They are only three, he thought with confusion. How could they kill so many so quickly? A quick glance left and right showed his warriors poised for another attack. He also detected signs of nervousness. They, too, could count.

Running Bull raised his voice in exhortation. "This time we do not turn away. Ride over them, wet your lances in their blood. Are you women that only three frail white men can stop you?"

Blood lust boiled over and the Kiowa set the mounts to a fast trot up and over the ridge, to thunder down the incline. Ahead waited the fiery death of the white men.

Not a one of them lacked fear; yet they knew it to be a good day to die.

"*Sacre-bleu!* Here they come again," Antoine spat out as he raised his rifle to take aim.

At extreme range, Preacher sighted in with his Hawken and put a ball in the chest of a warrior, piercing the right side. Undaunted, the Kiowa raised his lance and charged on. Preacher set aside the .56-caliber rifle and put the slender buttstock of his French Le Mat to shoulder. The finely made .36 sporting arm had served him well before. Now he honed the sights in on the face of his enemy.

Hair-fine, the second of the double-set triggers let off the round with ease. Smoke belched and blew away in time for Preacher to see the black hole that appeared where the tip of the warrior's nose had been a moment before.

At once, his lance sailed skyward and the Kiowa did a back-roll off his laboring pony. He hit with a thud and bounced only once. Preacher reloaded swiftly, only to be caught with the ramrod down the barrel of his Le Mat when the distance between him and the warriors closed to less than twenty feet. He lowered the muzzle against Tarnation's heaving flank and drew the reloaded Walker Colt. With what precision he could muster he emptied it into the mass of Indians in front of them, and yet they came on.

A lance thudded into the ground so close to his leg he felt the pressure of the shaft. Preacher holstered the Colt and drew the second one. He spent two rounds before the Kiowa warriors reined around and beat a hasty retreat. A quick count showed Preacher that only five remained alive.

"Stubborn," he told his companions. "Plain damn

stubborn. They coulda quit a long time ago. I'd been
willin'. What about you?"

"*Oui*. Without a doubt," Antoine panted.

Preacher turned to the horses. "We'd best be movin'
on. We don't want them to work up the spit to make
another try."

One fine afternoon, three days later, Preacher and his
two friends rode along the trail with the sparkling waters
of the Arkansas River to their right. Chubby barrel cactus
and wicked-tipped Spanish bayonet abounded on the
rolling sand hills ahead of them. Abruptly, Preacher
raised his hand for a halt.

From a distance ahead came the dull thumps of gun-
shots. They all had heard them, and had halted to try
to make out what they meant. With the recent Kiowa
attack fresh in their minds, Preacher and his companions
suspected a war party.

It had to be a large group under attack, or both sides
had firearms, Preacher decided a moment later when
the rate of fire escalated. This country did not lack for
human trash that would prey on the law-abiding. He
drummed heels into the ribs of Tarnation and rushed
forward. Antoine and Three Sleeps came right behind.

Over the next rounded dune, the sounds of shots grew
clearer. Preacher drew his revolver. Antoine and Three
Sleeps loosened pistols in the holsters slung over their
saddlehorns. Dust mingled with powder smoke had risen
high enough to be clearly seen before they topped the
grade. Preacher halted them again.

"Let's not blunder in, boys. I'll take a peek first."

He dismounted, removed his floppy summer hat and
approached the ridge in a crouch. Slowly he raised his
head. A moderate-sized freight train came into sight
first. Preacher raised up a little higher and focused on

some twenty white renegades, several of whom fired on the teamsters from an outcropping of boulders south of the trail. Others milled back and forth on horseback, apparently prevented from circling front or rear of the caravan due to concentrated fire at those points. It looked to Preacher like those freighters could use some help.

Quickly he returned to the others and explained the situation. Mounted again, he led the way up and over the ridge. Pistols in hand, they dashed down on the unsuspecting outlaws. The surprise arrival of three more fighting men cleared four of the ten saddles before the bandits knew that help had come for the teamsters. Quick to realize that relief had arrived, the teamsters began to rally. Preacher heard a voice raised over the tumult, singing in a sweet tenor.

" 'At the risin' o' the moon, at the risin' o' the moon, the men and bies will gather at the risin' o' the moon.' Give 'em hell, bies, there's help on the way. C'mon, ye soldier-bies!"

That galvanized the outlaws. Those who could whirled away and ran a murderous gauntlet along the length of the stationary wagons. Those afoot in the rocks turned and tried to make a stand. Preacher sighted in on one and reined sharply to send a .44 messenger on the way. The letter it carried was death.

Shot through the mouth, the highwayman fell backward in an awkward sprawl. Preacher emptied the last round from the Colt into the stomach of another hard case. He changed weapons quickly and sought another target. A ball cracked past close enough that he heard its ominous moan. The shooter died an instant later, shot through the heart by Antoine Revier. To his left, Preacher heard the sound of increased resistance.

Bullwhackers fired and loaded and fired again. Rifle balls snapped through the air, whined off rocks and brought forth screams from human targets. Several more outlaws died in this withering fire. Ahead of Preacher, wounded men crawled toward their horses, desperate to escape. Churned-up dust began to obscure the scene. Preacher fired at a fleeing man and missed. He turned Tarnation and sprinted to the head of the wagon train.

He reached his goal in a growing silence. Gradually the crackle of gunfire had diminished. At the lead wagon Preacher saw half a dozen highwaymen spurring frantically until they disappeared beyond the next swell.

A big, red-faced man came out from between two wagons and walked Preacher's way. He was a bull of a man, with bulging muscles and ham hands. When he spoke, his mouth became a black hole in his heavily bearded face.

"Right on time, lads, that ye are. Good work. Sure an' where's the soldiers you're scouting for?"

Preacher gave him a curious look. "At Jefferson Barracks. We haven't joined up with them as yet."

Momentarily stunned, the lead bullwhacker worked his mouth soundlessly. Words returned with a sputter. "Y-y-you mean there's just the th-three of you?"

"That's right."

"Well, truth is you fight like a whole company of soldiers. They call me Big Tom Lawson. This here is my strong right arm, Brian O'Shea, an' we're obliged to you."

Preacher gave them a nod. "Big Tom, Brian, my pleasure. I answer to Preacher, and these be Three Sleeps Norris an' Antoine Revier. Any idea why those road agents picked your train to raid?"

"None that make sense. What we're haulin' is too heavy to take off on horseback and these wagons would leave a trail a blindman could follow." Finally Preacher's name registered. "Say, you ain't *that* Preacher are you? The one in the penny dreadfuls?"

Preacher's cheeks carmined. "To my eternal torment,

I be. What foolishness them idiot writers can dream up would gag a maggot. What you read in them things ain't true a-tall. Except I may have been in some of those places at the time they said I was, and I may have had something to do with what happened to some of those fellers they claim I done for. Jist may have, mind you."

Big Tom made a wry face. "Sure an' I don't buy none of that at all. Never mind. You are a gen-u-wine legend in yer own time. A living hero, you are. We'd be overjoyed to have you join us in our trading expedition, full share for all of you. Lord knows, you just earned it."

"No," Preacher replied politely. "We have to push on to Jeff Barracks. Gave my word. In writing, at that."

Big Tom looked greatly disappointed. "I understand contracts right enough. The least you can do is stay a spell and take supper with us. We'll lay on a right regular feast. Why, we even have a fruitcake along. All sopped up in brandy." He gave a big wink. "I figgered to use it to mellow the Governor General in Santa Fe. What ya say, Preacher?"

Patting his flat, hard belly, Preacher produced a euphoric smile. "I never could resist fruitcake. 'Special if it's got itself drunk."

Once started out onto the Great Divide Basin, after long, heated debate, the wagon train ran into disaster after defeating disaster. Mr. Ledbetter had three mules die. After acrimonious exchanges, in which accusations of selfishness flew like snowflakes in a blizzard, it was decided to draw straws to see which two wagons would "voluntarily" give up a mule so that Ledbetter could keep up. Eve Billings drew one of the short straws.

No sooner had that predicament been solved than another sprang up. One day five precious water barrels had sprung leaks or broken apart. The next day, three more became useless. With much shouting and gesticulating, the decision was made to turn back. Eve had nothing to tell her children.

"Mom, are we really going home?" Charlie asked eagerly when it became apparent to him that they were retracing their steps.

"Only part way, dear," Eve told him tiredly.

"But why?" His button nose wrinkled in the effort to understand these adult mysteries.

"We aren't ready to go on as yet. We need a guide, someone who can take us out of this wilderness. Without water, the livestock will die, like Mr. Ledbetter had happen." She did not add the obvious, that people would die as well.

"I want to go all the way home."

"Don't start on that again, Charles Ryan Billings."

Charlie instantly lapsed into silence. He always knew when he was in trouble; his mother used his proper first name. When she used his middle name, too, he knew he was up to his neck in it. Charlie heaved a defeated sigh and scampered over the rumps of the mules to his favorite spot on the back of Jake, the lead animal.

Eve watched her son move with agility and assurance and then lifted her gaze to the horizon. She estimated they had another day of travel, back to the old camp.

A storyteller's high, singsong voice rang out across the camp in the Bighorn Mountains. He related an ancient tale of the grandfather times. One in which the Cheyenne and the Blackfoot were allies. It had to be a long time ago, Cloud Blanket thought as he watched the historic meeting from his place in the Cheyenne council circle.

Less than a moon ago, he would not have believed this gathering could happen. The Blackfoot had come under a white belt of truce. They had a great story to relate. About a young medicine man and the power he possessed. When the council gathered, the talk quickly turned to war against the whites. That greatly disturbed Cloud Blanket, though he could not name the reason why. All he could say was this was not the time to fight the white men. Suddenly he found the talking stick offered to him. He took it and came to his moccasins.

"You say that this prophet's medicine is so strong none of you fell in the battle which was described to us?" Two Moons nodded in the affirmative. "That may be so. It could also be that the whites did not carry long guns with them." His eyes twinkled with secret knowledge. He might have seen forty winters, might be past his prime, but he was not helpless or ignorant. Cloud Blanket had his sources of information, and one of them had told him of the attack on the unarmed whites. How odd, he thought, that anyone would not carry weapons. Did they not know there were tribes hungry for war? He suddenly realized the Blackfoot named Two Moons had responded to his jibe.

"The great prophet will come among you soon," Two Moons repeated when he saw the Cheyenne chief's attention had returned. "He will show you his medicine. It is true that he cannot be killed by normal bullets. His medicine is strong, the most powerful. We have been given his shield," Two Moons stated emphatically.

Cloud Blanket remained unimpressed. "I have seen far too often what the bullets of the white men can do."

Too hot in his zeal, Two Moons snatched up a rifle that lay beside a Cheyenne. "If you doubt me, take this, shoot me. Go ahead. I will not be killed."

"If I believed that, I would shoot you." Cloud Blanket shook his head resignedly. "I have heard of such medicine before. It has always failed its user. Leave us now, the council will reach a consensus and let you know. I am but one man, my voice is not listened to as much as it once was. Perhaps you will win an ally after all."

After the Blackfoot delegation withdrew to eat and nap through the afternoon, the Cheyenne spoke heatedly about the issue. Several agreed with Cloud Blanket: it would be a bad idea to make a pact with the Blackfoot. Had they not been enemies for longer than the storyteller could remember? In the end, Cloud Blanket prevailed on that point. He lost on the other. He felt obliged to take the word to the Blackfoot. He found them in the lodge that hosted them.

"Our council has come to a consensus. We will not ally with you at this time. You can send your prophet, Iron Shirt; we will listen to his message."

FIVE

Preacher, Three Sleeps and Antoine spent the night at the Cottonwood Crossing on the Santa Fe Trail. There, they underwent inspection by two disreputable characters, one with wispy strands of mustache that drooped below his jawline in Oriental style. His brown skin marked him as a Mexican. His partner had wild-straw hair that stuck out at all angles, buck teeth and pale, hollow cheeks. The pair slouched into the saloon of the trading post shortly after Preacher and his companions arrived.

Preacher nodded in their direction. "Now there's a pair to draw to."

Three Sleeps sniffed the air. "I wonder if they know what the word *bath* means?"

Antoine nodded agreement. "How about 'soap'?"

Preacher chuckled, a low, throaty sound, and leaned closer to them. "Way I rec'llect it, ain't neither of you could lay claim to bein' in the Every Saturday Night club." He drew in a lungful. "Though I will admit they've got a certain ripeness about them."

For the next hour, the surly pair nursed pewter mugs of beer and paid considerable, though covert, attention to Preacher and his friends. Then they settled their tab and stomped out. Preacher watched them through the open door as they settled down some distance off from the tavern and inn that had sprung up at the crossing to accommodate stagecoach travelers.

"Not overwhelming sociable, are they?" Preacher observed to his partners.

"I ain't gonna lose any sleep over it," remarked Antoine.

Preacher stroked his chin. "I wonder which way they're goin'? That's a pair it would do a body good to keep track of."

Three Sleeps narrowed his eyes. "You thinkin' they're trouble, Preacher?"

Preacher nodded. "That I do. I could smell it on them plain as that sweat stink. I may be wrong, but I could almost swear I saw the towheaded one with that bunch what attacked the freight wagons."

Although up well before dawn, Preacher noted that the unwashed pair had already departed. He saw to making a pot of coffee and was soon joined by Three Sleeps. The frown on the forehead of Norris indicated that he had noted the absence of the human trash.

He gestured with his chin. "They ain't gonna be missed. Not by this mother's son."

"Like I said, it'd pay to keep them in sight, or know what they might be up to."

"You've been alone too long, Preacher. That makes a man suspicious for no reason."

"You turnin' womanish on me, Three Sleeps?"

"Nope. C'mon, I'll lend a hand with that packsaddle. After we eat we can take right off."

"Now that's a good idea."

After a plate of fatback and beans, Preacher downed the last of his coffee, used the dregs in the pot to quench the fire and scuffed dirt over it. In the saddle, they made their way eastward. The trail ended at Independence,

Missouri, but there were supposed to be good roads through the state. At least as far as Jefferson Barracks, Preacher had been told. Two hours down the Santa Fe, Preacher's keen hearing picked up what sounded like thunder.

He looked around at a clear sky and produced a puzzled frown. "D'you hear thunder, Antoine?"

"Yep, sure sounded like it, but there's not a cloud up there."

Yet, the sound persisted and grew louder. Then the creak of wood on leather springs and the jingle of harness explained it to Preacher. Laboring up behind them came a six-up of spanking bays. Foam lathered their flanks and around their collars. Seated above them the driver sawed on the reins and called to his team.

"Gee up, there. Keep it brisk or no corn for you tonight."

Clouded in dust, the stagecoach grew in Preacher's vision. They must be closer than he thought to Muddy Creek Crossing, the mountain man thought to himself. Otherwise that feller would not be runnin' them horses like that. He turned in the saddle to watch the team draw up alongside. A scowling man, armed with a Purdey percussion shotgun, eyed the three mountain men with suspicion. Preacher removed his slouch hat and gave a cordial wave. The express guard acknowledged it with a curt nod.

"Well, he ain't bein' paid to be friendly," Preacher opined to his companions.

"You got the right o' that, Preacher."

"How long's it been, Three Sleeps, that the stage lines have had to run a guard on their coaches?"

Norris scratched the top of his head. "Leastwise ten years. An' it's gettin' worse, I'm told."

Preacher pondered a moment. "It's types like those yesterday that's behind it. Law's too easy on them."

"They still have hangings, don't they?"

"Oh, yeah, Three Sleeps. Used to be a man kept the law himself. Now, with law dogs mixed up in it, if a man shoots a thief, likely he'll be the one winds up in jail."

In the Black Hills of the Unorganized Territory, a young Red Cloud refused to even listen to the emissaries of Iron Shirt. Little good it would do. Since he had not yet seen twenty winters, he would not have been listened to anyway. Oh, the elders on the council would have made a show of hearing him out, but their ears might as well be plugged with wax from a bee tree. So frustrated had he become that he jumped on his favorite pony and rode out as the council gathered to hear the message of the prophet. Red Cloud sat atop a knoll and looked down into his village.

He knew every lodge. There, the one of his friend, Runner. Over close to the big drum lived White Knife. They had grown up together, hunted, then gone off to war the best of friends. White Knife had lost a little finger to a Pawnee war club while fighting at the side of Red Cloud. Now he added his voice to those clamoring for the council to approve bringing Iron Shirt and his medicine to the Lakota.

Red Cloud spat on the ground. A great shout reached his ears. The council had decided. From the looks of it they had decided in favor of the cursed Blackfoot and his iron medicine. Drums began to throb, and from every lodge, the women brought pots and baskets of food to feast the Blackfoot men. Red Cloud's lip curled in disgust.

What hurt most was his grudging admission that the time would soon come when the Lakota would have to fight the white men, but the time was not now.

* * *

A week and a half had passed since their first disastrous attempt to cross the Great Divide Basin. Fear of the unknown and indecision had kept the abandoned wagon train stranded at the same small spring that had previously provided their scant water supply. Eve Billings opened her flour barrel, and a momentary bolt of panic shot through her. She could see the bottom in places.

Provisions had run short for everyone. Eve knew she wasn't alone in this predicament. So many people had killed or run off the sparse game in the area, the men had to ride for miles to get even a few rabbits. She crumbled yeast into the bowl and began to add water to the flour. When she looked up, there stood Charlie.

The thin film of perspiration on his bare, sun-browned shoulders and sides under the straps of his overalls made his skin glow. He fixed big, cornflower blue eyes on her face. She wondered if her worry lines had become permanent. From the looks of Charlie, they must have.

"Mom, what are we having for supper?"

"Fried bread with molasses and potato soup," she answered, painfully aware of how inadequate that sounded.

Charlie's usually smooth, childish features twisted into an expression of misery. "*Again?* That's what we had last night."

"And the night before. Be grateful we have that. And that Mr. Tate shared his rabbits with us on Sunday."

"I want meat tonight!" Charlie stubbornly insisted.

"Well, we simply don't have any."

Charlie took on a coy, wheedling expression. "I could get us some. At least some rabbits. I'm a good shot, you know that, Mom. Please, let me take my rifle and go after some rabbits. I won't go far, and I know better than to shoot in the direction of the wagons."

He had already robbed her of her two best arguments. She swore that the boy would become a lawyer, or a politician some day. Or worst yet, both. What could she say to counter his intentions, good though they might be? Carefully, she framed her sentences.

"What horse would you use? The grass is so scarce that your pony's too weak to carry you."

Bright enthusiasm lighted Charlie's face. "I can always use Jake."

"A mule? One not broken to saddle at that, Charlie. I don't think it would be safe."

"I ride his back every day we're on the trail. An' when I take the others out to graze. He knows me an' he don't mind. Really, Mom."

Eve sighed. Rabbit would taste mighty good. A deep, vertical furrow formed between Eve's brows. "If you go— and mind, I said if— you would have to stay within sight of the wagons."

"Mo-oom," Charlie enunciated with exasperation, small fists on hips. "There aren't any rabbits within sight of the wagons. I'll be all right. After all, you said I would have to be the man of the family now. Please let me prove I can do it."

What could she say? What could she do? With a suppressed sigh, Eve swallowed her mother's fears and relented. "All right. But you take your father's pocket watch with you, and you be back here in two hours exactly, or you'll never go again."

Charlie abandoned his mannish stance and leaped up to wrap arms around his mother's neck. "Oh, Mom, thank you, thank you. I'll bring us rabbits, I promise. Enough we can share."

"And wear your boots," Eve added as Charlie turned from her.

When the boy scampered off to get the watch and his rifle, powder horn and bag of balls, Eve stood staring after him. Her son complaining about small portions and the lack of real meat. His little sister with a slight

fever and runny bowels. What more could she endure?
A sudden thought came to Eve.

Could it be the water? Painfully aware that they were
far from the established trail, the specter of everyone
falling victim to some terrible sickness arose to haunt
her. Surrendering to a moment of despair, Eve began
to suspect that no one would ever come along to lead
them out of this desolation.

While Eve Billings battled with her dejection, Preacher
and his companions took their nooning at Muddy Creek
Crossing. The coach that had passed them had also
stopped there. While the hostler changed the horses,
Preacher watched the passengers descend to take their
meal in the shade.

A chubby, moon-faced Osage woman, wife of the stage
agent, and her gaggle of youngsters, stair-stepped from
about thirteen to seven, brought out heaped platters of
fried chicken, bowls of baked squash and beans, stewed
onions swimming in butter and cold, boiled potatoes.
All this bounty came from a large, well-tended kitchen
garden that Preacher saw behind the ramshackle stage
station. For the hefty sum of ten cents each, Preacher
and the mountain men also sat down to the feast.

For that purpose, the relay station had trestle tables
set out under a large, gnarled old cottonwood. A young
woman passenger took note of Preacher's handsome features. Pursing her lips, she fixed her violet eyes on his
profile and batted long lashes flirtatiously.

Antoine nudged Preacher in the ribs. "You got an ad-
mirer, I see."

"Huh? Who'd that be?"

"Over to your left. There's a purty young thing givin'
you the eye."

Preacher cut his eyes quickly to the left and caught a

flutter of long, black lashes. The woman brought a fan up to cover her face and uttered a brief titter. Preacher looked away. For several minutes he dedicated his attention to a chicken leg. Three Sleeps kicked him on the shin. Preacher jumped as a result.

"She's at it again. Givin' you the big ol' come-on eye. A right toothsome lass, you ask me."

"Then you flirt with her," Preacher grumbled.

Three Sleeps Norris sniggered "Wouldn't mind at all."

Suddenly the older woman with the flirtatious one caught her at it. This ample-bosomed dowager took an abundant pinch of forearm and hissed loud enough to be heard by Preacher and his friends.

"Agatha, for shame. I'll thank you to conduct yourself like a lady."

"But he's sooo handsome."

Her visage turned to stone, the elder companion took another pinch, this time of cheek. "You disappoint me, Agatha Sinclaire. That frontier trash isn't fit to shine your shoes. If you cannot behave in a refined manner, I'll see that you return to the coach." That said, she turned her acid tongue on Preacher. "And you, you unwashed barbarian, I'll thank you to keep your lustful eyes off my ward. It's your kind that have sullied this beautiful country. Those uncouth louts with you are no better. Have they no shame? It's scandalous the way they smirk and waggle their heads. Why . . ."

Her invective slid off Preacher like water ran off a duck. When the older woman finally ran down, Preacher removed his floppy hat and scratched his head, as though looking for lice. He ran his tongue around the inside of his mouth and came to his boots.

"Well, now, ma'am. I allow as how the girl is a toothsome bit, right enough, but me an' my friends have im-

portant business at Jefferson Barracks and I can't take
the time to dally."

With a squawk of indignation, the dowager abandoned
her meal, grabbed the wrist of her charge and hauled
the two of them off to the coach. Seated at another table,
the same two scruffy ragbags from the previous day took
in all that transpired. They exchanged meaningful
glances and rose to silently slip away.

Preacher took note of that and stored it for later. He
stared long after their rapidly retreating backs. They,
too, were headed east. He and the other mountain men
finished their food and started off for the Lost Springs
Station. Something told Preacher it would be a long afternoon. One he might live to regret.

A grinning Charlie Billings returned to the wagon
train with four plump rabbits strung over the neck of
Jake. His slender-barreled .36-caliber squirrel rifle lay
across his thighs. For all her elation over the fresh meat,
Eve still noticed with irritation that Charlie had ignored
his boots. He had also fastened a length of rope around
his waist and slipped the shoulder straps of his overalls,
so that he rode bare-chested as a wild Indian.

"Charles Ryan Billings, you put up the bib of those
overalls right this minute. You're a scandalous sight. You
look like a heathen red savage." Part of her irritation
came from the memory of the four reports she had heard
distantly from beyond a hill.

She had bitten her lip at hearing each shot. Worried
that Charlie had injured himself, that he lay bleeding
and near death, she could hardly contain herself, remain
at the wagon and knead her bread dough. Now he shows
up, looking like a brown-skinned imp of Satan, grinning
and showing off his hunting skill. Abruptly her irritation
fled and an ocean of love swelled up in her chest.

"Look what I've got, Mom! It was easy."

It took all her will not to run forward and embrace him, and she failed to keep from blurting her thoughts. "My wonderful boy. We'll share them with the Tates and the Warners."

Charlie produced a pout. "I thought we'd smoke 'em and have meat for all week."

Eve put her hands on her hips and glowered at her son. "We have been gifted by others, now we can return their generosity. I'll fix you a hind leg and a chunk of loin."

"All right," Charlie agreed. He reined Jake to the right and rode to the Tate wagon.

Eve nearly called him back; he had done nothing about adjusting his clothing. "I swear, that boy would go buck-naked if he could get away with it," she said aloud to herself.

"Why, Mommy?" Anna asked from the spot of shade under the wagon.

Startled, Eve turned to her. "Because he has your father's orneriness, sweetie. Now, do you feel strong enough to help make dough balls with me for the fried bread?"

"Yes, Mommy, but my tummy hurts some."

"Oh, Anna, Anna," Eve spoke through a tight throat as tears welled in her eyes.

SIX

Preacher and his mountain man friends decided to spend the night in the dormitory-style hotel east of the stage station at Lost Springs. The Spanish had named the location during the Coronado expedition in the sixteenth century. The climate had been entirely different three hundred years earlier. The springs they had located and marked with tall stakes and flags had disappeared on their return from a fateful encounter with the Pawnee. They had called them The Lost Springs. Preacher explained the reason behind his suggestion to stay over a sit-down meal in the tavern.

"We're gettin' into country where people get suspicious of fellers campin' under the stars. Makes 'em edgy. So we might as well start gettin' used to a roof overhead."

"Sounds reasonable," Antoine Revier agreed. "Say, the feller who owns this place has got himself one powerful good cook. Who would have ever thought someone way out here could do a proper soufflé?" He smacked his lips in appreciation. His spoon paused over the gold-brown dome of the fancy corn pudding, which chose that moment to collapse.

Three Sleeps sniggered and Preacher pointed at the soufflé disaster with his chin. "It supposed to do that?"

Defensively, Antoine dug into the dish. "It's the thought that counts. My pappy. Now there's a man who could cook a perfect soufflé."

Preacher raised his brow. "That's right, your pap was a Frenchie, a *voyageur.*"

"*Mais oui.* He was also a great cook. A chef. A master in the kitchen."

Three Sleeps Norris waggled his head. "Cookin's women's work."

Antoine bristled. "Not so! The world's greatest cooks are men. Why, back in the days of knights and noble ladies, women were not even permitted to serve the food, let alone cook it. My friends, you are entirely too limited in worldly experience. Now, leave me to my soufflé in peace."

Three Sleeps sounded wounded. "It's part ourn, too."

Nose rising in the air, Antoine passed judgment on that. "You haven't the taste to appreciate it."

"Even if it is flat?" Preacher inquired.

Antoine relented, at least a little. "Awh, dig in, Preacher, it's ruined anyway."

After their evening meal, Preacher and his companions staked out floor-level, straw-stuffed mattresses and then went in search of distraction. Antoine and Three Sleeps found the bar, where a curious fellow worked fast and skillfully at charcoal sketches of some of the patrons. They watched in fascination while the features of a stolid Osage seated at one table emerged on the stretched canvas. Antoine nodded toward the Indian and his likeness.

"Right clever. D'you mind if I ask what yer doin' that for, mister?"

The artist looked up from his work. "I am preparing my canvases to do the subjects in oil."

Three Sleeps gaped at him, unbelieving. "You're gonna boil all these fellers in oil?"

Chuckling, the artist disabused him of that idea. "Far from it, my friend. I am going to paint them."

That set Three Sleeps back a bit. "Oh, oh, yes. You're an . . . an artist?"

"Just so. Would you like me to do you and your friend here in oil?"

"How long'd it take?"

The artist took a second to consider that. "An evening to do the sketch. Two, three days to finish the portrait. Then you could take it with you."

"Hmmm. Sorry, we got to keep movin' east. Be gone at first light tomorrow.

"That's a shame. Perhaps another time. My name is Catlin. If we meet again, I hope you have the time for me to paint you."

For Preacher distraction turned out to be a gaming table. Five men sat around the green baize circle when he approached.

"Evenin', gents. I answer to Preacher. Oh, no," he hastened to add when one man produced a black scowl. "I'm not going to give you a sermon on the evils of gamblin'. Matter of fact, if there's room, I'd be obliged for an invite to join the game."

Abandoning his scowl, the pudgy, soft-handed man produced a welcoming smile. "The name's Jessup. I own this place. These gentlemen are noble followers of the bullwhacker calling. Sit right down, Preacher. Your money is as good as any man's."

Jessup had his hair slicked down and smelled of bay rum. He had small, close-set eyes that missed meanness due to a warm, friendly twinkle. He and the others completed the hand while Preacher dumped a stack of gold pieces on the table. Jessup passed the deck to the man on his right, who nodded to Preacher.

"Among the teamsters, I'm known as Long Tom. What's yer pleasure?"

Preacher did not lack in card-playing etiquette. "You name it, Tom." Introductions went around the table, and

Preacher met Billy Green, Hank Lupton and Frank Spence.

Long Tom shuffled and announced, "Five-card stud."

Preacher played tight and smart. He folded after the third card. Jessup stayed to the bitter end with a bluff, Preacher noted. The next dealer called for five-card draw. Preacher was dealt a pair of queens, a ten, eight and deuce. He stayed and drew two cards. That gave him two pair. Jessup ran another bluff, raising the bet every time. Hank Lupton folded the first time Jessup did that. Billy Green's hand hovered over his stack of coins before he saw the final raise. Again Jessup lost. Preacher had the winning hand.

It soon became apparent to Preacher that Jessup should keep to his trade of tavern-keeper. He proved to be a terrible gambler. In one complete round at the table, he'd failed to take a single pot.

When it came Preacher's turn to deal again, he leaned forward and prefaced his call of game with an explanation. "There's a game I learned off a river boat captain up on the Platte one time. It's called seven-card stud. Played jist like five-card, but with three down cards, stead of one. Makes for an excitin' game."

He dealt it, watching Jessup closely. The man had a terrible hand, not even a pair or good face cards showing after two up cards. Why didn't he fold? He was truly awful. Someone real good could come along and clean him out, Preacher speculated. No matter, Jessup kept calling the bets. After the third card, he had a possible flush. A straight flush at that, Preacher noted. The bets, raises and cards went around. Preacher blinked.

Jessup had bettered his hand. This time he raised the bet. The final card went around, down. Only four players remained. Preacher had folded on his third card. Billy Green held the high hand in up cards. He bet a five-dollar gold piece. Jessup doubled it. When the pot was right, Jessup turned over his cards to reveal the straight flush.

Looking much relieved, he raked in the pot. Play resumed with Jessup dealing. He played badly over the next two hours. Preacher made it a habit never to count his stack of gold until the game ended. He did not like the idea of playing to scared money. This night proved his habit unnecessary. When he left the game, his poke bulged considerably more than when he had entered.

"Thank you, gents, for a right entertaining evening. Now I need some shut-eye before the sun catches me by surprise. Good night."

"Have a nightcap, Preacher. On me," Jessup offered.

"Thank ye kindly, but no thanks. I do need my sleep."

Makepeace Baxter had been badly misnamed by his doting parents. As a child, he had made war on small animals, tormenting them until they died. He loved to pull one wing off of several flies and watch them crawl around in circles until they dropped over from starvation. Another favorite was to pull the legs from frogs and toss them in a water trough to drown. His absolute favorite was to catch a cat on the tines of a pitchfork and watch as it writhe to a horrible death.

When he entered his teens, his tastes had become more refined. He tortured children smaller than himself, and threatened to kill them if they told. Once, at the age of fourteen, he went too far. A child died and he ran away from home, to live the next three months in terror of being caught and accused. Makepeace never went back. Over the ensuing years, he had found his niche among the lowest of the low, in the ranks of criminals.

He robbed, and often maimed, drunks for what money they might have. Lately, in this forsaken part of Indian Territory, he had taken up with the pair who sided him

tonight. Now a hulking eighteen, he crouched in the
sagebrush at the edge of the clearing on the southeast
side of the creek created by the lost springs, which
flowed sweetly from clefts in the rocks which formed a
portion of the bank. With him were his best friends. His
only friends, truth to be told. Youthful louts actually, who
could stomach his sadistic ways. Lights had been lowered
in the hotel portion of the stage station and the only
sign of life came from the tavern.

Makepeace literally slobbered with anticipation. A
bright, tall rectangle bloomed when the door to the tavern
opened and out came that salty mountain man. "Him.
He's the one," Makepeace Baxter whispered to Nate
Glover and Wally Slaughter. "He won big in that game."

Preacher turned in the direction of the hotel and was
striding toward the entrance when the three pieces of
human debris made their move. They rushed at him,
visions of gold discs filling their undoubtedly deficient
brains. This would be easy. Their target looked completely unsuspecting. Makepeace Baxter growled like a
dog when he leaped at the man in buckskins. He had
not even made contact when he ran into a fistful of
knuckles and learned that their victim had not been as
unsuspecting as they would have liked him to be.

Makepeace landed on his butt. He dimly saw the man
he attacked raise a leg. Pain exploded as Preacher kicked
him square in the chest.

"Lookin' to bushwhack me, boy?" Preacher hissed, his
face close to the pain-wracked one of his attacker. That
was when Nate and Wally joined in, grabbing hold of
Preacher by both arms.

An instant later they went flying as Preacher flung his
arms wide. They fared somewhat better than Makepeace.
Preacher slammed a fist into the side of the lout's head,
which made his ear ring. By then Nate had regained his
balance and gone for the mountain man again. Preacher

met him with a grin on his face, dodged a wild left and put a looping right into the pudding face of the twenty-year-old thug. Nate came to a sudden stop. His arms sagged and Preacher gave frightful punishment to his ribs. When the man from the High Lonesome decided his opponent had been softened up enough, he went back to work on the face.

Blood spurted from Hate's broken nose. His lips stung as Preacher mashed them into his teeth, loosening two in the process. Nate tried to raise his arms to cover his head only to have his ribs explode in exquisite agony. He flailed wildly at Preacher to no avail. Preacher finished him with a sharp uppercut that clapped Nate's mouth shut with a loud ring. Nate sighed softly and settled in the dust. By then, Wally Slaughter had screwed up his courage and come at the wildcat they had cornered. Preacher let him approach, then sidestepped and whacked Wally in the side with his forearm. Next, Preacher grabbed the youthful bandit by the hair, which was long, blond and greasy, and yanked backward.

Wally's feet went out from under him and he went down hard. A screech of pain came when his tailbone fractured. Whimpering, he crawled aimlessly around on the ground like one of Makepeace's flies. Preacher paused and looked around himself, well pleased. That's when Makepeace Baxter got back in the fray. He came at Preacher with a knife. Moonlight gave the edge a wicked, blue glint.

Preacher had his own Greenriver in hand in an instant. The knife fighters squared off. Makepeace lashed out, a testing gesture. Preacher ignored it and began to circle.

"C'mon, stand still an' fight like a man."

"I am, you little bastard. You ever been in a knife fight before?"

"N-no."

"What's your name?"

"Why you wanna know?"

"So I have it right on your gravestone."

"It's Baxter. Makepeace Baxter, an' you're the one who's gonna die."

Preacher chuckled. "I reckon you'd best make some of that peace with the Almighty, 'cause you're gonna meet him real soon."

Makepeace could no longer contain himself. He launched forward. He swung his knife, now a blur, in front of him, left-right, right-left. Preacher backstepped and circled in the other direction. Makepeace followed him, his breathing harsh gasps, born of desperation as much as exertion. Preacher's moccasin landed on a loose pebble and caused him to stumble. At once, Makepeace rushed his opponent. He made a powerful slash and sensed the contact his blade made.

Preacher grunted and took a backstep, then plunged his Greenriver to the hilt in the chest of Makepeace. An expression of utter surprise formed on the suddenly pale face of the boy. He dropped his knife and closed his hands, gently as a lover, around Preacher's, which held the haft of the Greenriver.

Baxter's attempt to speak brought forth a river of blood. Then he gained enough of an opening. "You killed me."

"You didn't leave me much choice."

"Who . . . who are you?"

"They call me Preacher."

A mournful groan escaped the bloodied lips of Makepeace Baxter. "Oh, Jesus. I . . . I been done in by the best."

"That you have," Preacher told him without false modesty. He turned the blade slightly to break it free and pulled it from the dying youth's chest. Makepeace fell to the ground.

Preacher watched the young thug's dying throes, then

turned away. He felt a lightness at his waist and reached down. During the brief fight, Makepeace had slashed open his money pouch. Half his winnings lay scattered in the dusty station yard.

"Damn, oh, damn, now I'll have to crawl around and pick it up like a beggar." Tomorrow, he speculated fervently, just had to be better.

SEVEN

Eve Billings tried once more to reason with the hard-headed men of their wagon train. "We must move on. Several children have taken a fever from some unknown source and even more are likely to."

"Fever's fever. We don't have to know what caused it." Gus Beecher stated stolidly.

"If we knew what caused it, we could avoid it. I suspect the water is tainted somehow. I have been boiling all of mine before giving any to my children. Little Anna is improving rapidly. No more stomach pain and the fever is lower."

Beecher remained adamant. "I say we should stay where we are. No one knows what's out there."

"Yeah," Enos Throcker inserted. "Look what happened when we tried. We got plum lost."

Eve was ready for that. "Send out scouts."

Throcker shook his head stubbornly. "They'll never find their way back."

Determined, Eve pressed her point. "There are several older boys and young men who are levelheaded enough. They can tell north from south and read sign. They could mark the trail for us in piles of stones."

Gus Beecher rejected her suggestion. "Wouldn't do. What if we wandered off between the piles of rocks?"

Eve thought that over a moment. Somewhere she had read something that might work. What was it and who had done it? It came to her after a long pause in which the men began to hope they had silenced her.

"There is a way. Do any of you know the story of the Llano Estocado? The Staked Plains down in Texas?" She received no answer and went on. "When the Spanish explorers first went there, they found a vast desert. Not a tree to guide one, no way to lay out a trail for others to follow. The leader had an idea. He had soldiers ride back to the last stand of tall, young saplings. They cut poles from them, hundreds of them, oh, maybe fifteen feet high. To these they attached big flags. The leader had one set up at the edge of the rolling area of sand and rocks. Then they started off, taking the other poles with them.

"When they reached a spot nearly out of sight of the first pole, they erected another. Then they moved on and put up more flags." Eve paused, to make certain the men followed her. "Each staff was numbered, so if they wandered, and came upon one, they would know where they were and which way to go. And it worked exactly like the leader said it would. They crossed that barren, waterless wasteland and went on to found Santa Fe."

Enos Throcker was not buying any of that. "When'd they do that?"

Eve had her answer ready. "Almost three hundred years ago."

Throcker snorted in derision. "There, you see? Old-fashioned ideas like that won't get us anywhere."

Unable to abide such stupidity, Eve let go. She stomped her tiny, booted foot. "That's plain crazy. If we sent out the older boys and some young men, with arms to protect themselves and a wagonload of poles and flags, they could mark the trail the same way. Even come back if they needed more, or if they ran into trouble. After a couple of days head start, the train can load up on water and any game we can get, and follow the markers."

Silence answered her. Eve looked around, her features set in grim determination. "What about you, young Honeycutt? Do you think it would work?"

The adenoidal sixteen-year-old cut his eyes to his father, who shook his head in the negative. Then David Honeycutt took a deep breath and made his bold first venture at independence. "Yeah— yeah, I do. And it would be a great adventure." He turned to a cluster of his peers for support. "What do you think, fellahs?"

"It'll work, Davey, I know it will," a defiant Eb Throcker encouraged. His father took a menacing step in his direction. "Leave it be, Paw. We ain't gettin' anywhere just sittin' here eatin' up our supplies."

It quickly got out of Eve's hands. With the prospect of something, anything, to do besides sit around, the young men clamored to go. The decision made, those who would take the risks decided to set off that afternoon to find and cut a wagonload of lodge-pole pines. Meanwhile, their mothers and sisters would fashion flags from any bright material they had at hand. They would start off within two days, taking the wagon and three saddle mounts.

Hunkered down in a tall stand of wild mulberry, the spikey-haired lout who had dogged the mountain men along the Santa Fe Trail stared out at the deeply rutted roadway. Any time now, Amos Scraggs reckoned, the excitement growing. He itched. He twitched. Uneasily he cut his eyes left and right. His ace-boon runnin' pard, Miguel Lopez, sheltered behind a fallen tree to the right. Five others were closer in by the road.

Strung out on both sides of the trail were the surviving dozen of the gang that had attacked the freight wagon train. They had been paid well to locate and kill the mountain man known as Preacher. They had attacked the wagons out of greed, but their specific charge had been to

see that Preacher, and anyone with him, never lived to
reach the Missouri side of the river of the same name.

Now their chance had come. Only the three mountain
men had broken up their raid before, Amos Scraggs recalled. Could it be they could do it again? He stiffened
when he heard the distant thud of hooves. Four horses,
he figured it to be. It had to be them. Amos saw the one
called preacher come into view first. He lined up his
sights, as he tried to quell the quiver in his hand. Slowly
he squeezed off a round.

A loud crack shattered the pastoral calm of the morning. Big mistake! the mind of Amos Scraggs shouted at
him as in the next instant the mountain men exploded
into a deadly fury.

Bright sun no longer slanted into Preacher's eyes when
he reined in. Shadows had grown so short they had become pools around the bases of the objects that made
them. He estimated their morning's travel had brought
them close to Diamond Springs Crossing. Another four
days should see them in Missouri. He had traveled the
Santa Fe Trail three times before and felt confident with
that assessment. He turned to share that with his friends
when a shot blasted to silence the warbling of the mead-
owlarks. Preacher put heels to the flanks of Tarnation
as he slid his Hawken from its scabbard. The words that
left his mouth had nothing to do with their destination.

"By dang, we're bein' ambushed!"

Three Sleeps Norris grumbled agreement. "I figgered
that out for myself. I see some of 'em over there." He
fired as he spoke, sent a ball in among the high stand of
wild mulberry, and went for his powder horn. Preacher
loosed a round. A scream answered. To his right, Antoine
emptied his Hawken into the screaming face of a pasty-

skinned outlaw who broke from cover, confident that their numbers and surprise would carry the day.

He died without knowing the flaw in his judgment. Antoine quickly drew one of his single-barreled pistols from the saddle holsters and chopped a hole through the underbrush with a double-shotted load. His second pistol brought a groan and an enemy ball discharged skyward. Quickly Antoine holstered the empty weapon and drew one of two double-barreled pistols from the wide, red sash around his hard, flat middle. He cut his eyes to his companions and saw Preacher unlimber one of his wicked Walker Colts.

Three fast shots downed two more of the ambushers. Preacher looked at Antoine and nodded. They worked well together, the gesture seemed to say. With a roar, a squat, ugly thug stormed at Three Sleeps Norris, who had a cap fail to fire. Preacher wheeled around in the saddle and put a .44 ball into the jaw hinge of the attacker. He staggered three steps closer, enough so that Three Sleeps dropped him with a butt stroke to the top of his head.

"Obliged, Preacher."

"My pleasure."

By then they had ridden in among those who had laid the ambush. Preacher struck one down with the barrel of his Colt, then shot another who sprang upward to fire wildly. The bullet cracked by Preacher's cheek and struck a resin-slicked pine a foot away. A shower of amber moisture slapped the back of Preacher's neck. He'd play billy hell getting that out of his hair, he thought crankily, while he exchanged Colts.

Stunned by the incredible firepower of the mountain men, the border trash fell back as their intended victims kept coming. In rapid order, their number had diminished to a mere seven. Yet, they still outnumbered the men they had come to kill by two to one. Preacher and Antoine quickly reduced that advantage by two.

Antoine pulled a sad face as he advised Preacher. *"Par hasard,* I have shot myself dry, my friend."

By chance, eh? Preacher thought. "You got a war hawk ain'tcha?"

Antoine brightened and brought forth a wicked-looking iron-bladed tomahawk. The thug in front of him paled and threw a wild shot. The ball made a red line along Antoine's ribs, but failed to prevent him from splitting the skull of the hapless bandit. Preacher heeled Tarnation to one side, and fired one of his remaining three loads.

Mouth puckered in a soundless howl, the ruffian who took that .44 ball bent double and toppled to one side. A second later, Preacher held his fire as a fear-stamped face popped out of the underbrush. He was not surprised to recognize the straw-haired rascal who had been dogging their trail since Cottonwood Crossing.

"Don't shoot. I give up. I'm hurt bad," wailed the young outlaw.

Another disreputable creature crawled into the open. His usually coppery complexion had turned a sickly gray-green. Thin wisps of mustache were matted around his face by sweat. He dragged a bloody leg with a bullet-shattered thighbone. *"Yo también.* Don't kill us, *por favor."*

Preacher and his friends surrounded the defeated pair. Preacher chuckled softly. "Now ain't this something?" He leaned low in his saddle. "Haven't we met someplace before?"

Groaning, the towhead with the spiky hair licked dry lips. "You know damn well we have. You gonna stop this bleedin'?"

Preacher examined the wound in the side of the ruffian without moving from his horse. "We might, if we get some straight answers. Like, to start, do you have a name?"

Anger flared a moment. "Of course, everyone has a name. Mine's Amos Scraggs. This is my pard, Miguel Lopez. But, we don't know nothin' about nothin'."

Preacher pursed his lips. "Now I believe that."

"You do?" a surprised thug blurted.

"Yep. Back some years we had us what we called the University of the Rockies in the High Lonesome. I learned me a lot of grammar there. What you did was use a double negative; 'don't know nothing' you said. Well, what rules we've got for English says a double negative is a positive. In other words, you small piece of buffalo dung, you know a whole lot we'd like to hear from you."

"What if we don't tell you?"

"We leave you here to bleed to death."

"You'd never do a thing like . . ." Then Amos Scraggs read the deadly message in Preacher's steely eyes. "What do you want to know?"

"This jist another fling for you? Like that freighter train?"

"N-no. We— we were sent to see that you never reached Missouri."

"Who's we? That include that scruffy lot you rode with?"

Scraggs' eyes strayed from Preacher's face. He forced a tone of indignation into his voice. "No. We weren't no part of them," he lied. "Ask Miguel. That bunch was pure trash. Miguel an' me joined up for that raid on the freight wagons only to make more money."

Miguel, who believed incorrectly that the artery in his thigh had been severed, and he was about to die, sought to absolve himself before he met his Maker. He motioned to Preacher. The mountain man dismounted and squatted down beside the Mexican bandit.

"What is it?" he asked.

Heat flared in Amos. "Don't tell him nothin'!"

Miguel whispered urgently, his eyes alight with the fear

of death. "I will tell you the truth, Señor Preacher. The whole gang had been paid well to keel you."

"Who paid you?"

"Three men. They are called Gross, Praeger and Reiker."

"You done good, Miguel. I'm sure the Almighty will take that into account."

"*Por favor,* please, I want a priest. I want to make my confession."

"We'll see if we can find you one. First off, we've got to bind up that wound and fix your partner."

Sergeant Stalking Elk of the Osage Tribal Police rode up to the Diamond Creek Crossing relay station. That young Ryan boy had come like a whirlwind. Had two prisoners and a whole passel of bodies to take care of. Stalking Elk wondered how Finn Ryan and his boys, both under fourteen, could have stood off so many as made up the pile of corpses outside the tavern door. He supposed he would find out soon.

Three tall, lean men in buckskin stepped out into the dooryard. The one in the middle, with a square jaw and a far-off look in his eyes, introduced himself as Preacher and named his friends. Stalking Elk nodded toward the bodies.

"Do you want to tell me about it?"

"Don't mind if I do." He went on to describe the ambush, eliminating only the purpose. Then he added, "There's two inside who need medical treatment, if any's available."

Stalking Elk pulled a wry expression. "Our medicine man is all that's near."

"That'll have to do. I've been put back on the rosy side of health more than once by a medicine man. If these two don't cotton to it, tell 'em they can walk to the nearest white doctor."

Stalking Elk studied the toes of his moccasins for a moment. "From what you tell me, they're due for a hanging under white law."

"That they are."

"White man's law does not apply out here. We don't have courts or hangmen. When an Osage kills another of his tribe, he is beaten and turned out of the camp. That is most likely what will happen to this pair."

Preacher puckered his lips and worried his tongue around his mouth a while. He didn't like the idea of exile. "It'd be a shame if they died of their wounds, then."

Sergeant Stalking Elk cut his eyes to the pile of corpses once more. Thoroughly impressed with the fighting prowess of the mountain men, he offered up a bit of embarrassing news. "I read a book once about the legendary mountain man called Preacher. Never thought I would meet him in person."

Preacher blushed hotly. "Aw, shucks, them things is pure fancy. I've never done half the things they put in there. It's jist stuff and nonsense."

"We will see to your living pair. I don't suppose they will go adventuring again. Mr. Ryan can bury the dead. There is money from your government for such needs."

Preacher extended his hand. "Thank you, stalking Elk. We'll stay and lend a hand."

"May I ask where you are bound for?"

Keeping a straight face, Preacher saved himself from a lie by only a light exaggeration. "We're set on seein' Independence, then go on to Jefferson Barracks."

"Safe journey, then."

Takes Rain and Gray Eagle looked downslope at the laboring of the draft animals. A mixed train of mules

and oxen trudged through the roiling red-brown dust of
a sage-choked basin near the banks of the Yellowstone
River. Soon they would stop to take food, Takes Rain
knew. That is when the Blackfoot would take something
else. A cold smile lifted the corners of his mouth. Before
long his Bison Eaters society would test the power of the
medicine given by Iron Shirt.

"Wagons . . . Whoooooa-UP!" came faintly on the
light breeze that blew from the direction of the train
toward the Blackfoot warriors waiting to strike.

Those words had no exact meaning to Takes Rain. He
only knew that it was what they said when the leader
wanted the wagons to stop. Obedient to them, the rolling
lodges began to slow and swing into a half circle. Women
dismounted and their birdlike chatter lifted on the wind.
Time to strike. Takes Rain cut his eyes to Gray Eagle
and nodded. Both men came to their moccasins and released their ponies. Swiftly they mounted. Thirty other
warriors did the same. Takes Rain raised the new rifle
he had been given by the followers of Iron Shirt and
waved it over his head.

"*Ki-yi-yi-yi!*" he keened to sound the attack.

Startled white faces looked up at them. Then the warriors hidden around the wagons, in the thick covering
of sagebrush, opened fire with bows and arrows. Rifles
cracked also. Three men went down, one gagging and
clutching at the arrow that stuck out from his throat,
front and rear. A woman shrieked and dropped the pot
of beans she had saved from breakfast. A red stain spread
on her ample bosom around the gruesome exit wound
a .56-caliber ball had made.

Shouting their war cries, and profane insults, thirty
Blackfoot warriors thundered down the slope to flow
through their comrades and bring more death and destruction. Several oxen went slack in their harness and
sagged to their knees. A mule erupted in agony, its rump

pierced by two arrows. Stunned by the suddenness of the attack, the immigrants finally began to react.

Several men grabbed up rifles and returned fire. Their bullets seemed to avoid all the mounted Indians. Another volley had as little effect. Five men died before they could reload. Children screamed and ran in panic. Whooping warriors rode in among them, oblivious to the crack and moan of white men's bullets. The Blackfoot bent low and scooped small boys and girls off their feet, then whirled away from the scene of battle.

Seizing a flaming brand from a cookfire, Gray Eagle hurled it into the rear of a wagon. Screams of terror came from within. The flames quickly licked up. A woman with graying hair and two barely nubile girls tumbled out. The woman died from a lance thrust, the girls were dragged aside to provide later amusement for the aroused warriors. Unable to reload in the swirl of battle, Takes Rain slung his fine new rifle over one shoulder by a rawhide thong and drew his tomahawk.

Horror filled the face of the white man who watched the grinning warrior with the war axe descend on him. Blackness quickly replaced the sight of the savage as the keen edge of the 'hawk blade sheered through the pilgrim's forehead and mangled his brain. Then a man with a shotgun found one howling savage within range and gave out a load of 00 buckshot. Five of the nine .32-caliber pellets pulped the chest of one Blackfoot, after shattering his hair-pipe bone war vest.

Dismayed, the warriors nearest him looked on in disbelief while he slumped dead over the neck of his horse. This wasn't supposed to happen, Takes Rain thought, his stomach churning. Maybe the medicine was not good against the many-balls guns. Sensing the loss of faith among his companions, Takes Rain signaled for the braves to follow him as he streaked away.

They took the young women and small children with

them. Only two adults had survived the attack. They stood in numbed despair as flames licked at four wagons. Slowly they looked around at the scene of slaughter. From over the rise they heard the shrieks and wails of the young women and girls as the savages used them in cruel and lustful ways. Helpless to do anything about it, the man and woman could only hug each other and weep.

The torment went on for a long time. At last the Blackfoot had been drained of their urgent sap and split the skulls of their abused captives. Then they rode off with the children. Silence slowly returned to the banks of the Yellowstone River.

EIGHT

At an isolated trading post on the North Platte River, Praeger and his partners received a message from Washington City. Instructions written on the outside had told the proprietor to hold it until called for. Praeger, whose aggressive qualities and dominance had propelled him without dissent into leadership, split the wax seal, and opened the thick, three-fold paper. He read it quickly and then raised his mottled-blue eyes, the slight cast in the right one disconcerting as always, and smiled.

"It is short and sweet, gentlemen. We are informed that arrangements have been completed for stage two. Those involved will be on their way within . . ." He consulted a calendar on the wall beside the bar. "A week from now."

Morton Gross rubbed pudgy hands together. "Wonderful. How long will it take them to get out here?"

Praeger considered that. "I would imagine six weeks to two months. Unless they take the mail packet or some other steam-powered riverboat."

Gross worked his thick, rubbery lips in and out. "And our little . . . ah . . . impediment?"

"You mean Preacher? By now I assume he has been taken care of. Come, this calls for a celebration. Barman, do you have any champagne?"

Mouth a black O in his thick, ebony beard, the bartender blinked in disbelief. "Any what? I ain't seed no champagne since I moved out here." He pronounced the

word champ-ag-nee. "Never saw none before that neither."

"Do you have a good rye?" Praeger asked suspiciously.

"I got a small barrel from the Cumberland Gap country."

"That will do quite well." To the others, Praeger said,
"We have to get Iron Shirt to move faster on enlisting
the Cheyenne. They are the key to the whole thing."

Across the Missouri now and drawing nearer to Jefferson Barracks each hour, Preacher felt downright uneasy.
He spared no effort putting his discomfort into words.

"It's too crowded around here. Why, there's actually
more than one house per' mile. Not fittin' nor healthy
for folks to live all shoved up against one another like
that."

Intrigued, Three Sleeps chimed in. "What do you consider comfortable living space, Preacher?"

Preacher did not even hesitate. "I reckon one per ten
or twenty miles. That be the absolute limit I can tolerate.
Among white folk, that is," he elaborated.

"Don't keep them from being ornery," Three Sleeps
observed as he indicated a group of armed men who sat
astride the high road. The bulk of their horses blocked
the advance of the mountain men.

A big, ugly brute, with orange-red hair and matching
beard, in the middle of the ragged formation, raised a
hand and pointed one thick finger imperiously at
Preacher. "What you fellers' business?" he demanded.

Preacher gave it a moment's thought and decided what
he had told Sergeant Stalking Elk would serve in this
case equally well. "Why, friend, we're on our way to . . .
ah . . . Independence."

Thunder clouds writhed in the scowl produced by
their interrogator. "It be back the way you came. So,

you'd best turn around an' light a shuck out of here.
There ain't no room for frontier riffraff the likes of you
three among civilized folk here in Missouri."

Preacher had heard all he needed to. He worked his
mouth a bit and produced a cud of Redman Premium
Braid. "Well, then," he observed as he spat the wad of
tobacco at the hooves of the delegation's horses, "we'll
just have to make room."

In a flash the fight was on. Preacher leaped like a panther from the back of Tarnation. His powerful arms
looped around the leader of the welcoming party and
dragged the bigger man from the saddle. With a lithe
twist, Preacher turned them in midair so that the carrot-
topped brute landed on his back, with Preacher atop him.

Wind knocked from his lungs in a loud grunt, the
unfriendly lout went cross-eyed while Preacher sawed the
lapels of his hairy cowhide vest across his throat.

"Gah . . . gah . . . yer chokin' me."

Preacher smiled down at him, his expression convey-
ing that he was fully aware of that. "Now, we might not
be the most sartorially splendid fellers you've ever seen,
that I'll allow. But you an' yer friends are no prize win-
ners yerselves. I'd appreciate it if you could find it in
your heart to be more cordial in your greeting."

While this exchange went on, Three Sleeps Norris let
out a whoop and sprang toward the pair nearest to him.
His point of aim was a space between them, which he
swiftly filled by a quick reach and grab. Then Three
Sleeps swung his arms inward and filled the opening
with their noggins, which made a loud *clunk!* as they
met in midair. On the opposite side of Preacher, two of
the local, lowbrow social arbiters had decided on the use
of deadly force.

Their hands barely touched the stocks of their rifles
when they heard the double click of hammers. They
looked up, startled to see the twin muzzles of a double-

barreled pistol pointed levelly at them. Antoine Revier
gave them a wide, knowing smile.

With a roar, the huge man under Preacher heaved
upright and freed himself. He drove a fist into the face
of his opponent, which caused stars to explode in
Preacher's left eye. Preacher let the force of the blow
carry him up and over. He hit on heels and shoulders
and bounded upright.

By then the brute who had dislodged him came at him
with ham fists. Preacher dodged backward, only to come
up against one of the pair Three Sleeps had dealt with.
The groggy man stirred and then reached out with both
hands to cling tightly to Preacher's ankles.

"Get him, Red," he urged.

"Thanks, Barney." Red came after Preacher with punishing punches to the mountain man's face.

Preacher's lips stung and swelled. His tongue explored
and felt several loosened teeth. His left eye was almost
closed. Then Red shifted weight to put a finish to the
interloper. Preacher seized his chance.

He put his shoulders and hips behind each smashing
blow he drove into Red's chest and gut. Although padded by fat, Red felt each one, and with increasing intensity. His arms drooped slightly. Enough so that Preacher
could go to work on his face. Red's lips split and his
nose became a rose blossom before the bully could draw
a refreshing breath. Knifelike pains filled his chest.

Preacher sucked in air and spoke lightly to his friends.
"I'd appreciate it if one of you would unwind this snake
from my legs."

Three Sleeps sprang to the task. He hauled the slighter
built Barney away from Preacher's legs and spun him.
His moccasin collided with the seat of Barney's trousers
and propelled the leech back down the road in the direction of home. Stumbling, Barney recovered quickly
and turned on Three Sleeps.

Norris set himself for the rush. When it came, he side-stepped and smacked Barney on the side of the head. Staggered, Barney turned in the wrong direction. Preacher popped him in the mouth and sent him on around to Three Sleeps.

Laughing now, Norris pegged Barney on the left hinge of his jaw and the Missourian went rubber-legged. He collided with the flank of his horse when he went to the ground. Red roared again and reached for Preacher, while Three Sleeps walked over to one of the mounted men and yanked him from the saddle.

"Reckon I can put this away," Antoine speculated aloud.

He released the hammers and did just that. Then he dismounted and hauled the other thug from his horse. Knuckles met flesh and a new brawl was on. By then, Red had brought himself upright and planted a fist between Preacher's shoulder blades. It staggered the mountain man, who turned as he jolted forward.

"Some fellers never learn," he grumbled as he blocked a punch and answered with a short right.

It gradually dawned on Preacher that fists would simply not do it with this brute. When Red bore in again, Preacher flexed his legs, cocked the right one and slammed the heel of his moccasin into Red's exposed belly. Eyes bulging, Red did a pratfall that jarred his teeth. Preacher turned slightly and kicked Red in the side of his head. Bells and birdies went off inside Red's skull. His eyes rolled up and he fell backward, arms widespread. His body stirred up puffs of dust, and he let out a soft snore.

"Welcome to Missouri," Preacher panted and the trio of mountain men chuckled sardonically. Then, "Think they've had enough?" Preacher asked his companions.

"Just about," advised Antoine as he drove a hard left

to the jaw of the last standing Missourian. His target flopped onto the ground and lay still. "Now they have."

It worked for them like it did for the Spanish on the Llano Estocado. Eve Billings thrilled at the sight of the fifteen foot shafts, their colorful cloth pennants fluttering in the hot breeze that blew across the sandy soil of the Great Basin. From the ridge where her wagon rested, she could see a line of them leading back to their starting place and on into the distance beyond. Progress had been slow at first.

They'd barely made seven miles a day the first three days because the neophyte scouts frequently dashed back with alarms that proved unfounded. Such a misgiving had stopped them at the saddle of this ridge not half an hour ago. Davey Honeycutt had galloped a lathered horse back, his eyes as enlarged as his mount's.

"Injuns!" he had shouted. "Injuns not five miles ahead."

From the color of his face one would suspect they were the ghosts of Indians. A party of armed men rode forward to investigate. Eve could see them returning now, small, black specks against the blasted earth. Beside her, Charlie stirred on the seat and shifted his rifle.

"They're not wavin' a red flag, Mom." Charlie sounded disappointed that the agreed-upon signal to warn them of hostiles was not fluttering above the riders.

"We can thank the Lord for that," his mother responded.

"Aw, Mom, I want to shoot an Injun."

Shocked, Eve almost slapped the boy's face. "No you don't, Charles Ryan Billings. You don't want to shoot any human. Hunting for food is a necessity, killing someone is a horrid crime."

"Even if they are tryin' to kill you?"

That left Eve speechless for a long moment. "You're just a boy, Charlie. Leave those sorts of things to grown men."

Some of the less alarmist among the travelers started their wagons out toward the approaching men. There would have been shots, after all, had there been Indians. Overall, Eve remained highly pleased at their progress. Even better, the game which had been absent on their first attempt now seemed to have come back in abundance. Anna was growing stronger every hour, and Charlie had become quite an expert shot, adding to his credit deer and antelope as well as rabbits. She put the Bridesburg Arsenal rifle aside and turned to Charlie.

"Put your rifle up, Charlie. We're heading out."

"Can I take Star out and hunt a little?"

"No need today, son. Remember those plump rabbits Damion Brewster brought us?"

Charlie did not sound enthused over that. Damion, an acne-riddled youth with a crush on his mother, was a pain in the butt. "Oh, yeah, those."

Charlie replaced his rifle in the wagon bed and scampered out to his usual place, astride Jake. His bare heels bounced with the churning rhythm of the stolid animal. Once again Eve surveyed her world and found herself entirely at peace. Then she looked up from the rumps of her team to see a solitary Indian sitting on top of a close-by mound.

Sudden cold clutched at her heart. Could he be the forerunner of the Indians the Honeycutt boy thought he had seen? If not, where had he come from? She tensed and reached for the rifle at her feet when the Indian slowly began to raise his lance. Extended to full arm's length, the Indian moved his lance from side to side.

Fearing that to be the signal for an attack, Eve filled her lungs for a cry of alarm, only to realize that it was only a friendly wave, backed up by a broad smile.

* * *

At Jefferson Barracks at last, Preacher found the situation and the troops even sorrier than he expected. The Dragoons turned out to be raw and green, barely aware of what was expected of them. While Preacher and his companions walked their horses through the gate, sergeants bellowed at the hapless soldiers, their faces scarlet with their fury.

"No, damnit, Mallory! For the love of Jazus, how many times do I have to tell ya? Ye mount so yer facing the same direction the horse is, ye do."

Mallory made the mistake of whining. "I don't know why I get so mixed up, Sergeant Muldoon. Honest I don't. Maybe I ain't a horse person."

Battalion Sergeant Major Terrance Muldoon threw down the riding crop he carried and strode to Mallory's side. He shoved his face to within an inch of Mallory's and bellowed. "It's Sergeant Major, ye dimwit. It is. Ye'll go get yer knapsack. Ye'll fill it with rocks, ye will. An' ye'll report back here to me on the double."

"I know what's gonna happen then, Sergeant Major," Mallory recited, his stupid face alight. "I'm gonna run around this big ol' field here."

"Parade Ground goddamnit! Parade Ground."

Mallory looked puzzled. "Ain't seed no parades go by since we been here."

"Yer a sorry son of a . . . Aw, what the hell. It's no use, you're no use. Sure an' sometimes I think I'm of no use, I do. Get that knapsack."

"Yah, sure, Sergeant Major."

Preacher approached the infuriated noncom. "Excuse me, Sergeant Major, could you tell me where I can find Colonel Danvers?"

BSM Terrance Muldoon turned to Preacher with a sour expression. "In Saint Louis."

"May I ask what he is doing there?"

"Who be ye?"

"They call me Preacher, this be Three Sleeps Norris an' Antoine Revier. We are reporting in as guides for this battalion through the Injun country."

Fists on hips, feet wide apart in a belligerent stance, Muldoon introduced himself. "Battalion Sergeant Major Muldoon. An' fer yer information, the good colonel and those young gentlemen officers of his wanted a last fling among the ladies an' the sparklin' wine before makin' their great sacrifice fer God and country."

"They left you in charge?"

"No, Mr. Preacher. We've got us one officer with his brains in his head, not in his pants, we do. Captain Edward Dreiling is commanding at present, he is. Ye can find him at battalion headquarters. Across the parade ground there, it is."

"Thank you, Sergeant Major." Preacher turned to leave as Mallory returned.

The knapsack bounced viciously against his shoulders and back as he began to run. The black visor of his flat-topped bill-cap slid slowly down his forehead until it obscured his eyes. Preacher stared at him as though seeing a creature from another planet. Then he began to laugh. At his side, an amused Three Sleeps questioned BSM Muldoon.

"Does it do any good?"

"Does it now? Not with that one, sure an' it doesn't. There's some's fine lads, smart and quick to learn. But that one has to take off a boot to count to eleven, he does. I fear what will become of him out there." He gestured to the west.

Preacher and the other mountain men walked to the headquarters building. Inside, an orderly told them that Captain Dreiling could be found on the firing range on the far side of the cantonment. Preacher got exact directions and led the way to the sound of erratic firing.

Seated on a canvas-backed camp stool, an officer observed while sweating, swearing sergeants conducted firing exercises. The captain wore the split-tail, regulation blue uniform coat with thick, shaggy, brass epaulets at the shoulder points, matching insignia of rank— three horizontal strips — -on the high, tight collar. His trousers, with the gold stripe down the seams, covered the high tops of his black boots. His shako style hat, of black, patent leather, complete with horsehair plume that drooped over the front, sat squarely on a round, blond head.

Somehow he managed to seem cool and comfortable, while the NCOs and enlisted men showed wide rings at their armpits and long wet smears down their backs. Their appearances made even Preacher feel uncomfortable. Captain Dreiling had no difficulty in recognizing the newcomers. He rose and extended a hand.

"You must be our guides. And, I would say that you are Preacher." He unerringly picked the right man.

"That I am. You'd be Captain Dreiling?"

At six foot even, the broad shoulders, full chest and narrow hips gave Dreiling a handsome cut by anyone's standards. He answered Preacher with alacrity. "Yes. However, on informal occasions, you may call me Edward."

Preacher prefaced his remarks with a softening smile. "An' you can call me Preacher. I don't mean to pry into Army business, Captain, but may I ask why you did not join your associates in the pleasures of Saint Louis?"

For an instant, Preacher thought the expression of contempt that darkened Captain Dreiling's face was intended for him. "Bloody damned children, you ask me. Most of these rabble cannot yet tell right from left foot, let alone conduct themselves as soldiers, and the ones with the responsibility to hammer them into shape go off skirt-chasing."

To emphasize his point, a Hall Model 43 rifled carbine discharged loudly in their direction. The ball from the breech-loading weapon cracked past close enough for Preacher to feel the wind. Immediately a sergeant burst forth in a flurry of profanity.

"You goddamned idiot! You'll get the effing lash for that. I said to clear all weapons before leaving the line." A fist lashed out and knocked the offender sprawling. The sergeant kicked him in the ribs twice.

"Excuse me," said Dreiling politely before turning to the sergeant. "Enough of that, Sergeant Peters. Extra duty for Emmons and four punishment tours should suffice. No one was injured."

Suddenly rigid in the position of attention, Sergeant Peters saluted smartly. "Yes, sir. Very good, sir. It will be done as ordered. Now, you worthless reprobate, keep that muzzle downrange at all times, you hear."

A fair-minded man, as well as conscientious, Preacher thought to himself. The rest of the day's tour of the battalion established some strong opinions in Preacher. At the stable area, soldiers tried rear vault and running side mounts, most falling in the dirt over and over. Sergeants screamed and cursed. Those who could ride, Preacher soon learned, could not hit a bull in the ass with a bass fiddle, let alone score on a target from the prone position with their weapons.

Which left him with a rather dim view of Colonel Arlington Danvers, the battalion commander. If the other officers, save Captain Dreiling, are as ill-concerned about the readiness of their men, they could all be in for a hell of a time out in the High Lonesome. Instinct told him to seek out the Battalion staff in St. Louis at once. Logic told him to wait here, lend a hand where he could and hope for the best when the errant officers returned. Whatever came of this, Preacher promised himself, he would sure as hell never take a job with the Army again.

NINE

Lieutenant Colonel Arlington Danvers and his officers returned to Jefferson Barracks five days later. To the expert eyes of Preacher and his mountain-man friends, they all looked powerfully hungover and sadly dissipated, an all-around surly lot. By the lights of the mountain men, based on the harshness of the noncoms and the appearance and deportment of Lieutenant Colonel Danvers, the colonel was a martinet and thorough popinjay. This opinion was reinforced when they reported to Danvers in a borrowed office, intended for some of the permanent staff. The colonel looked up and his lip curled with contempt and disgust.

"You're a scruffy-looking lot, I must say. Do you ever take baths? You'll have to in this Army."

"Pardon me, Colonel," blurted Preacher. "But we ain't in 'this Army.' We're just hired to guide you to where you want to go in the Big Empty."

Nattily dressed in a freshly pressed uniform, Danvers looked Preacher up and down. Preacher had a classic shiner, all purple, yellow and blue. He had a cut on his chin, and a red mark on one cheek. Danvers worked his mouth as though he wanted to rid himself of some foul-tasting object.

"You have obviously all recently been in some sort of drunken brawl. From now on, until the completion of your employment, you will all refrain from spirits— liquor of any sort— and you will clean up your clothing and present a well-washed appearance at all times. Your hair is to be cut to regulation length, and all facial hair is forbidden.

"You are to ride out before dawn each morning, scout the territory ahead and send back reports." Danvers' arrogant tone continued while he ticked off each point on long slender fingers. "You will not fraternize with the officers, noncommissioned officers or the enlisted men of my command. You will negotiate safe passage for us with any savages you encounter. You are to make certain that the path we take is wide enough to accommodate mounted troops— four abreast, with our field piece at the center of the column— and wagons, two wide to the rear."

Preacher bristled. He'd heard all of the "You will" and "You are" that he could swallow without getting a sore stomach. He raised a hand to cut off the tirade.

"Now whoa up there a second, Colonel. Exactly who are to be the guides for this expedition?"

Danvers blinked. "Why, you three, of course."

"Well, then, don't the colonel think that the men in charge should have some say in how the soldier-boys will march?"

Lieutenant Colonel Danvers countered at once. "Regulations cover that quite nicely, I believe."

Fire fanned in Preacher's eyes. "Ain't no regulations out there in the High Lonesome. An' as for the trail, dependin' on which way you intend to go, there ain't no real trail at all. We just have to find the best way through, over or around the rocks, rivers, gorges and hills as we can. And do it without breaking every wheel or upsettin' any loads.

"Now, marchin' four abreast might be well an' good on a wide street or grassy meadow, but not out there. There's cactus with thorns long and sharp enough to pierce a horse's hoof to the cannon bone. There's prai-

rie-dog holes jist waitin' to bust a leg." Preacher paused
for a breath, which he took, swallowed deeply and went
on. "Then you have bison who'll stampede at any loud
sound, and rattlesnakes that can fell a horse as easy as a
man. Not to mention Injuns by the thousands. Nope, two
men to a file, an' they alternately walk and ride their
mounts. Another thing. No horn tooting or drum bang-
ing. That's the surest way to attract some unpleasant Injuns. Those fancy sabers yer so fond of has got to be
padded and tied down so they don't rattle, an' all tack
and loose gear also. An Injun can hear the noise they
make a mile away."

Filled with equal parts of bluster and indignation,
Danvers protested hotly. "We absolutely must have trum-
pet calls and drums to convey orders. Typical civilian
ignorance," he summed up.

Preacher cocked an eyebrow. "Ever hear of arm signals? The Injuns have used 'em for ages and get along
jist dandy."

Danvers continued his resistance. "And field music is
essential for morale."

"I wonder how serious you are about getting there and
getting your fort built before you take on the hostiles?
If you have your soldier-boys practice arm signals while
we're still in friendly country, they'll know them when
they need 'em. Me, I say it's the smart thing to do."

"They are Dragoons, Mr. Preacher. Dragoons."

No matter what Preacher proposed, Lieutenant Colonel Danvers balked at adopting. At last, Preacher had
reached his limit. "Here's my final word on this, Colonel. We're gonna do it my way, or I quit the job and
hand the money back to the government."

Realizing that this assignment was his last hope of providing for his future, Danvers knew he had no choice.
He had been passed over for promotion too many times,
so his career would soon be at an end. If this did not go

the way he had been told it would, the years ahead would be bleak indeed. Mustering his will power he suppressed his outrage and caved in.

"Very well, it will be as you say."

With a single drum marking time, the column moved out early the next morning. To Preacher's surprise, the troops had improved greatly. They sat their horses straight and tall, all of them required to be no less than five foot ten to six foot two in height. Not a one fell off his horse. Not even simpleminded Mallory mounted backward.

On the highroad outside the barracks ground they rode four abreast. For all their smart appearance, Preacher sensed something odd. He rode in a relaxed slouch with Three Sleeps and Antoine some two hundred yards ahead of the battalion commander and his staff and flag bearers. Cardinals warbled and woodpeckers kept up a steady *rat-a-tat* on hollow trees. Preacher glanced constantly behind them, his gaze resting long on the files of men and horses. At last, he decided to confide in Three Sleeps.

"D'you feel it, too? I got me a strong sensation that something is mighty wrong."

Three Sleeps Norris showed indifference. "I don't follow you."

"I don't know exactly how, but these greenhorn soldier-boys— er, excuse me— Dragoons have done messed up the works somethin' powerful."

"We'll find our eventual." Three Sleeps stifled a yawn, then swatted at a huge horsefly that had lined up an enticing spot on the neck of his horse.

Preacher cut his eyes to the column again. "I certain sure hope it's soon enough."

* * *

"Sure, an' what do you mean they were left behind, Hadley?!" roared BSM Muldoon.

Preacher and his companions turned to see what caused the outburst. Slanted backward from the glowering, red face of the Battalion Sergeant Major, who leaned over him, the Quartermaster Sergeant, Hadley, gulped hard before answering. "That's what happened, Sergeant Major. Four of my teamsters reported to sick call this morning and there was no one to drive the wagons."

"An', why wasn't I told of this?"

"Y-You were. I reported four men confined in the infirmary."

BSM Muldoon poked a thick finger into Hadley's chest to emphasize each word. "But . . . you . . . didn't . . . tell . . . me . . . four . . . wagons . . . didn't . . . have . . . drivers!"

Sergeant Hadley looked like he was about to be sick all over his shiny boots. "I . . . I thought you'd figure that out for yourself, Sergeant Major."

"Yer flirt in' with insubordination, Hadley, b'God ye are. An', Lord love us, we'll have to send men back to recover them." He spun on one heel. "You there: Collins, Masters, Pickerel and Sawyer. Can you drive a wagon?"

"Yes, Sergeant Major!" they chorused.

"Then mount up and ride like hell back to the barracks. Ye'll find four of our supply wagons there. Bring them up with the column right quickly, lads."

"What about evening chow, Sergeant Major?" Corporal Collins asked.

"Take food enough with ye for two or three meals."

Sergeant Hadley tugged urgently at Muldoon's sleeve. "Bu-but they're not teamsters."

"Sure an' I don't give a damn if they're old-maid schoolteachers. We need those supplies."

Preacher turned away in disgust. "Here we are; haven't made fifteen miles the first day and we have lost half of the supplies. At this rate, we'll make the North Platte come December."

Far from the foothills of the Ozark Mountains in Missouri, at a large, well-tended trading post on the North Platte River, Quinton Praeger sat at a table with his co-conspirators and their chief henchman, Blake Soures. All four men lapsed into silence when a large platter of roasted bison hump arrived at their table.

They ate heartily, pleasurably chewing slabs of the layered meat and fat along with boiled turnips and onions, squash and chili peppers, all washed down with tankards of beer. Not until the last morsel disappeared did Praeger bring up business.

"Everything is going according to schedule. The money is starting to roll in from back East. The Dragoons are to have left Jefferson Barracks yesterday." He paused and wiped greasy lips with a soiled napkin. "We should have us a tidy little Indian war before too long."

Always a blunt, direct man, Blake Soures spoke his mind. "Exactly what is behind this plan to stir up the Indians? That is, after all, a dangerous thing to do."

Morton Gross looked amused. "How is that, Mr. Soures?"

"A feller can be their friend and ally one day, an' the next they'll lift his hair. They're . . . changeable, moody."

"The idea is to get rid of them once and for all," Praeger explained patiently. "And the best way to do that is to get an Indian war started. We can count on the Indians doing their part through Iron Shirt. He has tremendous influence among the Blackfoot, and now with the Cheyenne. His power grows daily."

Soures frowned. "That's the part I don't like, what I'm tryin' to warn you about. I've got seventeen good men ridin' with me. Then there's you three. Twenty-two guns don't amount to a fart in a windstorm if Iron Shirt decides he don't need us anymore."

Aaron Reiker gave Blake Soures a condescending smirk. "I think you are overestimating his capacity for duplicity. We provide him with rifles and ammunition, and we brought him out of obscurity and made him famous. No, friend Soures, we can trust Iron Shirt."

"But why get rid of the Injuns at all? That's what I want to know."

Morton Gross answered, his voice sugary, as though talking to a dolt. "The East is getting crowded. The land these Indians occupy will be valuable in any westward expansion. Certain high-placed interests in Washington City have a desire to lay claim to that ground. At least, once the savages have been eliminated."

Soures produced an expression of concern. "But, ain't it Injuns' land?"

Praeger turned a condescending gaze on their chief gunman. "Our friends in Washington City are paying exceedingly well to see that it no longer is. Well enough to assuage any conscience."

Soures frowned. "What's that mean, ass—assuage?"

"To pacify, Mr. Soures, to calm."

None of the conspirators mentioned the presence of gold in the mountains of Montana. Instead, they directed him to an assignment as backup to the men sent to stop Preacher.

"There is only one impediment, one man who might be able to prevent an all out war of extermination," Praeger pressed on. "His name is Preacher, and he is known and respected by both sides. Only, if all went well, he should be out of the picture by now. If he is not, it will be your job to remove him."

* * *

True to Preacher's prediction, a whole lot was wrong with the expedition. Trouble began before the troops got out of Missouri. After the four supply wagons joined the column, they made better time. A lot of good that did them.

BSM Muldoon came to Preacher one evening in camp. A harried-looking Dragoon had just ridden in on a lathered horse. He must have galloped the animal for a good ways. What he revealed, sent Muldoon to seek help from the mountain men.

Now Muldoon stood contemplating the three rugged guides, his bristly red hair and florid complexion making a torch of his head. "Gentlemen, I come to you with a . . . wee problem, it is. Now mind, I could send some of me sergeants to deal with this. But then it would become an official matter, it would."

Preacher laughed softly at this circumlocution. "Spit it out, man."

"The thing is, it is, that some of the lads have taken it to mind to slip off from our encampment and indulge themselves in some spirituous waters." Muldoon's perpetually rosy nose gave testament to his own fondness for such diverstions. "In the process, so's to speak, they have got themselves afoul of some of the local citizens." He paused and cleared his throat, as though the words bore thorns. "The fact of the matter is, there's one hell of a fine brawl goin' on between some eight Dragoons and some sawyers from a nearby mill, that's what."

"And you would appreciate some small gesture of aid from the three of us?" Preacher got to the point.

"Sure an' it would avoid the messiness of a court-martial and the need for punishment."

Preacher gave him a hard eye. "We'd not be taking sides. We'll bust anyone who gets in our way."

"It's skinnin' yer knuckles on all comers, is it?" Muldoon clapped his hands together in approval. "Then, so be it. I'll be accompanyin' ye buckos. Though not in an official capacity. Thing is, we don't need any floggin's before we get beyond civilization. That's how I see it."

" 'Floggings'?" Preacher echoed.

"Aye. That's the usual for such infractions. Six of yer best, laid on with a will."

A thunderous frown creased Preacher's brow. "By damn, I'll not be party to any of that."

"So it's the four of us, is it?"

Preacher gave a curt nod. "Right, Muldoon. We'll head out now."

Screams, curses, and the crash of furniture could be heard from two hundred yards off when Preacher and the cleanup squad reached the tavern. They trotted up to the tie rail outside and looped reins over the crossbar. Preacher looked up at a particularly loud, tinkling crash and saw a man fly bodily out through a window. He grunted and cut his eyes to take in the others.

"Looks like we have a job of work on our hands."

Three Sleeps nodded enthusiastically. "Yer not lyin' there, Preacher."

With determination, the four men stalked to the door. It flew open in their faces and two men, wrapped in a mutual bear hug stumbled out. Being nearest, Preacher reached out and grabbed both miscreants by the hair and slammed their heads together. They went down like heart-shot elk. BSM Muldoon bent and separated the Dragoon from the lumberman and dragged him to the hitch rack. The three mountain men entered the establishment.

It had been a nicely appointed place, Preacher noted, before the fight began. Now splintered tables and chairs floated like driftwood in a tidal pool of beer which had come from a ruptured hogshead. There had once been a mirror behind the bar. It lay in diamond spears of brightness amid overturned bottles and small casks. One of the ceiling supports had been snapped in two, the roof sagged dangerously above it. Showing even worse signs of wear, eight men remained on their feet, flinging fists with wild abandon.

One of those went down as the mountain men gained the doorway. Preacher stepped through and took the knuckles of a huge sawyer at the under edge of his right eye.

"Aw, hell, now it's the other one," he grumbled.

Then he set his feet and pile-drivered a steady rain of punches to the sturdy frame of the sandy-haired man who had hit him. It seemed all too easy to Preacher. The man went down and was out at the first pummeling Preacher gave him. Three Sleeps and Antoine waded in behind him and the three started picking Dragoons off their opponents and hauling them toward the door.

"Take yer damn hands off me," one snarled.

Three Sleeps released the complaining soldier and raised both open hands, in a gesture of surrender. "All right, all right." Then he swiftly closed his right hand into a fist and popped the Dragoon flush in the mouth.

With all the rolling muscle of his powerful shoulders behind it, the blow decisively felled the private. His boot heels bounced off the rough boards of the floor. Three Sleeps grabbed him by the collar and dragged him out into the dooryard. Then, with a grin, he turned about and went back for more.

"By Jaazas, those mountain fellers sure love a fight. They must be Irish," Muldoon said to the unconscious Dragoon. Then he added the young soldier to the stack growing by the tie rail.

Preacher hurled another protesting Dragoon out the door and Muldoon saw the spitting, cursing lout stumble toward him, then quickly corrected that with a hard left to the jaw.

A furious bellow came from the mill workers inside the tavern. "You let us at those soldier-boys. We'll tear them limb from limb."

Preacher's voice sounded. "Calm down. We're takin' 'em all back where they belong."

His words were followed by the loud click of a hammer being cocked and the sharp report of a single-barreled pistol.

TEN

Following instinct and training, the remaining Dragoons dropped to the floor the instant the shot went off. Preacher and his companions did not. Antoine reached down and felt a hot, burning gouge along his ribs that oozed blood. That made both sides. Damn, he'd be sorer than a fresh-gelded hound dog for more than a month. He reached for one of his double-barreled pistols, but Preacher beat him to the draw.

A big Walker Colt appeared in Preacher's hand and the hammer dropped on a percussion cap. The fat ball sped across the short distance and pinwheeled the belligerent sawyer in the breastbone. "Yer lucky to be alive, Antoine. He was a lousy shot."

None of the Missouri lumbermen had ever seen a revolving pistol before. They stared at it in wonder. One, who had gone for the butt of a small pocket pistol, let go of it with all the speed of a cat making contact with a cookstove. Preacher cocked the weapon and put a menacing look on his face.

"Unless any of you is eager to argue with my friend, Mr. Walker here, I'd advise you forget all about tearing anyone limb from limb."

"You kilt Tucker Blake," accused one of the less intimidated mill workers.

"Didn't know his name. That don't matter. What matters is, your Mr. Blake drew first. What's more, he shot a friend of mine. I don't take kindly to that. Though I will say I'm sorry your friend is dead."

Unmollified, the talker challenged. "You won't get away with this. We'll get the sheriff on you."

"It was self-defense, any fool can see that."

Three Sleeps Norris stepped up and touched Preacher on the arm. "Not any Missouri fool, Preacher," he said tightly. "I suggest we send for the sheriff ourselves and let him hear both sides of the story."

Preacher eyed the mouthy sawyer. "How far off is your sheriff?"

"He's right here," came a hard voice from the doorway. "I'd put that smoke-pole up if I was you."

The man who entered the tavern was a size with Preacher, though he carried authority and power with him enough to make him ten feet tall. "Bill Parker." He introduced himself as he gave the corpse a casual glance. "What happened here?"

All of the lumber company men began to speak at once. The one who had challenged Preacher overrode his friends. "This stranger came through the door, bold as brass, and shot down Tucker Blake in cold blood."

"Yeah, that's right. That's what he did, all right." A chorus of agreement.

Shrewd enough not to be deceived by men whose thick noggins he had thumped more than once, Sheriff Parker pursed his lips, eyed the scene again and then spoke. "If that's the case, George, what accounts for the pistol in Tucker's hand?"

Stunned at having his version disputed, and by a fellow Missourian at that, George gaped a moment before he could find new words to butter his lie. "He . . . uh . . . one of his friends put it there. Ain't that right, boys?"

Sheriff Parker turned and eyed Three Sleeps and Antoine. "Was that before or after this feller got his ribs skinned?" He whirled back to face the sawmill men. "My maw didn't raise any stupid sons. What do you take me for? That's Tucker's pistol, I've had to take it off him enough times when he got drunked up. I was on my way here when I heard the shots. Kylie Burks came by to tell me there was a big fight goin' betwixt you boys and some soldiers. I'd have been in here sooner if I hadn't stopped to have a word with the sergeant out there."

"That's Sergeant Major, if ye please, Sheriff. Battalion Sergeant Major Muldoon," said that worthy from the doorway. "Now, if ye don't mind I'll be takin' my lads and our brave frontier guides back to our camp."

Sheriff Bill Parker made a mock bow. "Go right ahead, Sergeant Major Muldoon." Then, to Antoine, "I'd get that patched up right quick. Might fester."

Antoine cocked an eyebrow. "Thank you for good advice, Sheriff."

Outside, Muldoon surveyed the subdued but conscious, and the unconscious Dragoons. "Thank the Virgin an' all the saints, their horses are right at hand. Be a thankless task rousin' them all to walk that far."

"We'll lend a hand getting them across their mounts," Preacher offered.

"That won't be necessary. There's enough of them with their wits about them to do that."

Not to be denied the last word, mouthy George stood in the doorway and shouted to them. "If I was any of you, I'd get me as far and as fast out of Missouri as I could. We've got friends."

No sooner had the errant Dragoons been returned to the camp near Sedalia than Lieutenant Colonel Danvers summoned the necessary members for a drumhead court-martial. Having been assured that he had acquired a second shiner and more sore ribs for the purpose of avoiding this very event, Preacher had his curiosity piqued. He went along to witness. Naturally, his companions accompanied him.

Preacher could not believe the abrupt nature of the proceeding. All eight of the disobedient Dragoons were hauled before a lantern-lighted barrel head, over which Danvers presided. He read off a list of charges, including desertion, absent without leave, public drunkenness and inciting to riot. He did not ask how the accused pleaded.

"Now, as regards Corporal Evers, and Privates Fields, Smith and O'Banyon, the charges of desertion and absent without leave are dismissed. On the counts of public drunkenness and inciting to riot, the above-named soldiers are fined two-thirds of a month's pay for three months. Now, Privates Babcock, Upton, Venner and Killeen, you are sentenced to be stretched upon a wagon wheel and given six strokes of the lash."

"Are ye not givin' them a chance to plead their case, Colonel, sor?" BSM Muldoon burst out, unable to bridle his umbrage.

"Contain yourself, Sergeant Major," Danvers said in an aside.

"But, Colonel, sor . . . it's . . ."

Lieutenant Colonel Danvers snapped at him in black humor. "Would you like to join them at the grate?"

Captain Dreiling leaned close to Lieutenant Colonel Danvers and whispered in his ear. "Regulations, Colonel. You are always saying that. And in this case, regulations will not allow you to flog the Battalion Sergeant Major without a full general court-martial."

Lieutenant Colonel Danvers swelled and seemed ready to burst, then sighed until deflated. "Yes . . . yes, you are right, as usual, Captain. Much to my regret, I might add. He should never have gone after those fools." Then back in his judicial role, "Sentence to be carried out at once."

Although outraged by the barbarity of the punishment, Preacher remained to watch it carried out. Afterward, he fetched a jug from a parfleche on his packhorse and, regulations be damned, got riproaring drunk along with his friends and BSM Muldoon.

Two wagons had broken down that day. Eve Billings was beginning to have second thoughts. After the past three days of soul-searching, she had made up her mind to go to Isaac Warner, who had been elected captain for their attempt at crossing the basin. She put aside the last of the dishes from supper and walked reluctantly to his wagon. Eve had hardly begun when Warner interrupted her.

"I have an idea what it is you want to say. And I want some of the other men to be here to hear it." He gave a wave of one arm to Damion Brewster to summon him from his family cookfire a third of the way around the circle of wagons. When the youth arrived, Warner gave him curt orders.

In short time, Renard Labette and Hiram Tate ambled up. They were immediately joined by Gus Beecher and Cecil Brewster. Tate gave a polite nod to Eve and asked, "What's up, Isaac?"

"The Widow Billings here has something she wants to tell us. Now, go ahead, don't be shy," he prodded Eve.

Cheeks crimson and hot from his patronizing manner, Eve glanced at each man in turn. "You know about the breakdowns. Not only those today, the others. They are taking a heavy toll."

Warner jutted his chin defiantly. "Yep. Said that was what would happen. Go on."

"Also, game and water are growing scarce again. I feel . . . it seems to me the time has come to examine our decision to try making a crossing."

"What you're gettin' at is?" prompted Warner.

Eve wanted to shout. Out of pure spite this pompous man was forcing her to say every bitter word. Nervously she cleared her throat. "Those of us who favored the attempt had no idea how strenuous it would be. It is perhaps time to consider the possibility of turning around and following the stakes to the edge of the basin and then going beyond to fresh water and plentiful game." There, she had said it and they could smirk all they wanted.

To her utter frustration the same men who had stubbornly insisted upon that course of action from the outset now objected to the idea with perfectly straight faces.

"I say it's the wrong thing to do," Isaac Warner snapped.

"Yes. We've come this far, there can't be much more like this," Gus Beecher added with a taunting smirk.

Eve's torment and humiliation lasted a long time, while the men wrangled over what should be done. Her patience at last exhausted by their circular reasoning, Eve slipped away. Dredging up new hope, she went to seek out the wives. The first was Hattie Honeycutt, to whom Eve recited what she had pointed out to the men.

"We have to make them see reason," she summed up to Mrs. Honeycutt. "There has to be a way."

"But we're mere women. Our menfolk have total sway over us."

An idea forming, Eve countered quickly. "Not in all things."

"Name me one," came the challenge.

Eve leaned forward and whispered in Hattie Honeycutt's ear.

Eyes wide and mouth in an O of astonishment, the portly woman sputtered a while before regaining her tongue. "That would never work. Why, they would just . . . just . . ."

"No they wouldn't, not if we all stuck to it. And not if we slept with a loaded gun at hand."

"My word. It's such a strange idea."

Eve went from wife to wife, explaining their womanly rebellion. Whenever she was told it could not possibly work, she smiled enigmatically and dropped the final gem of her argument.

"It has worked before. It happened back in ancient times. There was this woman named Lysistrata . . ."

After that it became easy. One by one the women approached their husbands and whispered in their ears.

"You'll what?" bellowed Isaac Warner. His wife told him again.

Several other men repeated Isaac's shocked response on being informed, only to be assured that their wives meant what they said. Visibly shaken, by nooning the next day, they began to admit that maybe that pushy woman, the Widow Billings, might be right for once. If they did return to the foothills, they would have graze for the livestock, fresh water and a chance to hunt for their food.

Independence, which they had skirted on the way to Jefferson Barracks, teemed with people. Droves of wagons appeared to be bound for destinations at every point of the compass. Men, women and a surprising number of children swarmed the streets, bustled in and out of stores and shops. Few of them took time to stop and stare at the column of Dragoons who rode their mounts at a walk down the main street to the distant docks. Only the night before had Preacher learned that he and his companions were in for a rare treat.

Lieutenant Colonel Danvers had summoned Preacher to his tent, yet he would not directly meet the eyes of the mountain man. "Due to the delays," Danvers began, clearing his throat frequently, his embarrassment clear in his posture, "I have decided that we shall negotiate this portion of our journey by riverboat. It will cut a month off our travel time."

Hiding his surprise and pleasure, Preacher spoke sincerely. "That's mighty smart thinkin', Colonel. I'd never have come up with it myself, what with bein' used to crossin' the mountains by horse or shanks' mare."

"No . . . no, I suppose not. Advise your assistants and be prepared to board tomorrow when we reach Independence."

Now they did just that. Two by two, the Dragoon horses went aboard a livestock barge, to be towed by the rearmost of six steam packets requisitioned by Lieutenant Colonel Danvers. They had been paid for by voucher drawn on the Department of the Army. Danvers, who oversaw the operation from beside Preacher, turned to the mountain man.

"Due to your positions as scouts, you hold ranks equivalent to a captain's and to lieutenants'. Therefore you will be billeted aboard the lead vessel with myself and the other officers." His expression told how little he liked that.

Preacher beamed with insincerity. "That's plum considerate of you, Colonel."

Danvers's expression became pinched. "It is not out of consideration, believe me. It's— "

Preacher stifled a guffaw. "Yeah, I know. It's *regulations.*"

"Well put," Danvers replied tightly.

"It'll be a pleasure for all, I'm sure," Preacher concluded as he turned away.

Steam Packet *Prairie Spirit* shrilled a lively blast on its tall, brass whistle and pulled away from the dock in Independence at three-thirty that afternoon. On board were the battalion commander, his staff, the captains commanding the four squadrons and the three scouts. Also one company of Dragoons. The blunt prow nudged into the Missouri River's brown water and began to struggle to overcome the current to make way upsteam. The

huge side-mounted paddle wheels thrashed the water
and sent off a fine mist of spray. Rainbows formed in a
nimbus around each churning wheel.

More steam-whistle blasts and then everything began
to settle down. The fifteen civilian passengers left the
rail and went to their staterooms to open trunks and
prepare clothing for dinner. Several of the men made
their way to the Gentlemen's Salon. Preacher and his
companions located their accommodations and dumped
their belongings in the corners.

Preacher confided in his friends. "I don't know if I'm
gonna like this. Outside of the time it will save, of course."

"Why is that, Preacher?" Antoine inquired.

Preacher studied his moccasin toes. Embarrassment
pinked his cheeks. "I've never felt entirely comfortable
on the water. Nothin' I can put a finger on, but it jist
don't seem . . . natural. Water's for fishes and beaver."

"What about small boys?" asked Three Sleeps. "Didn't
you like to swim when you were young?"

Preacher looked up at them. "Tell you the truth, I was
over twelve an' livin' with the Cheyenne before I learned
how to swim right proper like. Up to then, I jist paddled
around like a spaniel after ducks. An' not likin' it much,
either." He sighed. "It's funny. I put money in Mr. Fulton's steamboat works, an' this is only the third time I
ever rid one of the contraptions."

Antoine turned an anxious face to Preacher. "I have
heard that the boilers blow up sometimes."

Preacher nodded, which did little to allay Antoine's
worry. "That they do. Usual it's because the stokers over-
fill the fireboxes or the metal is old."

"How does one tell if the metal is old?"

"Antoine, my friend, I don't know. I jist have to hope
the captain and the engineer have some idea."

* * *

They changed into cloth suits and boots and took dinner at seven o'clock, an hour before the sun went down. That only served to amplify Preacher's uneasiness. The truth that Preacher would not admit to was that prolonged travel over water made his stomach queasy. Although he did not suffer dizziness and nausea, it did make him develop gas. Preacher soon found himself out on the foredeck, a hand gently pressing his belly.

He was still there, the rumbles somewhat subsided, when a conversation among three fellow travelers advised him that there were card games in the Gentlemen's Salon. Despite his precarious internal state, the lure of the pasteboards drew him like a dead critter attracted flies.

After sitting in for an hour, Preacher's situation made it understandable to a reasonable person that he grew increasingly edgy when an oily fellow with a remarkable deck of cards made deep dents in his "government money," paid in advance for services rendered.

Beauregard Calhoon, still slim and dapper, with a thin, pencil line of a mustache and manicured fingernails, gave a shark's grin as he raked in yet another pot. He laid a particularly offensive sneer on Preacher, who had lost steadily. Preacher allowed as how he must keep an eye on Calhoon and discover the source of his unusual luck.

"Y'all seem to be havin' a terrible run of luck," the fashionably overdressed Calhoon observed to those at the table. "I learned to court the lady at a tender age an' I never fail to pay her homage."

Preacher's words had a coating of ice. " 'Pears to me that her favors have been phe-nom-inal."

Calhoon gave Preacher a fishy eye. After three more hands, two of which were won by Calhoon, Preacher deliberately discarded an ace of clubs during the next, which he discreetly creased with a thumbnail. Sure enough, Calhoon won again. His full house of aces and tens contained the ace of clubs.

Before Calhoon could pick up the hand with which he had won, Preacher came to his boots, leaned across the table and clamped a hard hand over Calhoon's wrist. His composure broken, despite his oily, black hair neatly parted in the middle and his fancy, shiny boots, the gambler could only splutter.

"See here, there's nothing to be gained by this sort of conduct. Release me, my man."

"I ain't yer man, nor any other's. I find it right interesting you won that hand with the ace of clubs. Special since I discarded that same card in the draw."

"You can't prove that," Calhoon gulped.

"Oh, yes, I can. You see, gents," he addressed the entire table. "I took the trouble to crease that card with a thumbnail before I dropped it on the table. By that time I had got myself the idee that this particular deck had a special set of marks Calhoon, here, can read."

Preacher squeezed tighter as Calhoon began to squirm. It caused the voice of the tinhorn gambler to rise two octaves. "I must protest. You'll not find a crease on that card, suh."

Preacher shook his head. "Nope, I don't reckon I will. But, I am willin' to bet I'll find the crimped one up your sleeve, or in a vest pocket. Somewhere anyway. You saw what I was gettin' rid of an' couldn't resist the urge to put another one into your hand to improve it."

"Are you calling me a cheat, suh?"

Preacher's eyes bored deeply into those of Calhoon, while his free hand delved into the sleeve of the fancy suit Calhoon wore. Deftly he produced the card in question. "That's exactly what I'm sayin'."

"Then, I demand immediate satisfaction." With these words, Beauregard Calhoon thrust his left hand under the wing of his coat and came out with a small, .36-caliber, double-barreled pocket pistol.

ELEVEN

Preacher responded with the speed of a puma. His open hand, still holding the evidence, flashed across his body. Preacher's shoulder rolled when he made powerful, backhand contact with the exposed cheek of Calhoon. The impact could have been a thunderclap. Beauregard Calhoon shot back from the table, spun slightly and reeled drunkenly toward the bar. At the last moment, before he made violent impact, he remembered the pistol in his hand.

Fighting to control the movement of his body, Beauregard swung the small .28-caliber, four-shot, revolving-barrel pistol to bear on Preacher. One hammer fell on a cap. A thin stream of smoke spurted from the nipple an instant before detonation of the small powder charge. Several gentlemen gasped as the little ball made a loud *thock!* when it struck the wide, thick, bull bison-hide belt Preacher wore around his middle. Immediately Beauregard rotated the barrels and fired again. And hit Preacher again.

Concussion from the two slugs bulged Preacher's eyes and stabbing pain doubled him over. Air shot from his open mouth. For a long, spellbound moment, no one moved. Then Preacher straightened shakily, erased the agony-drawn lines from his face, and extended his right arm. The hand at the end held a Walker Colt, its hammer full back and ready to drop. This gun Preacher

pointed steadily at the center of Calhoon's chest. He
fought for air and, at last, spoke in sepulchral tones.

"You done played yer last hand."

Stunned by the incredible staying power of his target,
Beauregard Calhoon only then recovered enough of his
wits to turn, cock and aim the third barrel. This time,
Preacher beat him to the mark.

Flame lanced from the muzzle of the .44 Colt, as it
bucked and snorted in Preacher's hand. The round, two-
hundred-grain ball sped across the small distance to the
center of the exposed chest and smashed bone and tissue
with destructive force. Flattened slightly now, it
ploughed a wide furrow through the aorta, only slightly
off center, and into back loin muscle, before blasting
one of Beauregard's vertebrae into fragments.

Reflex jerked the trigger of the pistol in Calhoon's
hand. The woefully underpowered ball shattered the
glass chimney of a wall-mounted lamp and rang musically off the inside of its brass shade. Gleaming shards
tinkled to the deck in the silence that followed. A thick
layer of powder smoke undulated in the space between
Preacher and the dead cheat. Slowly, Preacher reached
down and plucked one of the little balls from the thick
leather of his belt. A worried player hurried up to him.

"Neither one got all the way through," Preacher informed him. "But I'm gonna be sore as hell for a week.
Awful bruise, you can bet."

Awed, the well-dressed man spoke for everyone in the
salon. "You've been saved by a miracle."

Preacher shook his head. "Nope. Buffalo-hide belt.
That little popgun didn't have a chance."

Another of the men who had been at the table spoke
from where he crouched beside Beauregard. "He's
dead."

"I didn't aim to only tickle him some."

A cluster of onlookers at the doorway gave room for

the first officer to enter, buttoning his jacket as he crossed the room. "Someone tell me what happened?" he commanded. "Oh, and put away that revolver."

Preacher complied while the man at his side made explanation. "I'm Norton Babbott, Babbott Bobbin Company. This gentleman caught a cheat in our game. The scoundrel pulled a gun on him. Shot him twice. The rest you can see for yourself."

"I know this man," the first officer declared. "It's Beauregard Calhoon. We've had complaints about him before." He paused, cut his eyes to Preacher. "You're a brave man to have faced him down . . . or a fool."

Preacher winced and unconsciously touched his aching middle lightly. "Right now I feel more the fool."

"It happened as Mr. Babbott said?"

Preacher shrugged. "More or less."

"How did you manage to detect him cheating?"

"I spend as much time watching the players as I do the cards in a game. Calhoon had a marked deck and he used hold-out cards, too."

Turning to look at Calhoon, the first officer spoke over his shoulder to Preacher. "I'll explain to the captain. He may want to speak with you. You're not planning to disembark soon, are you?"

"Nope. Not until I get these baby soldiers to the upper North Platte."

"And your name, sir?"

"I'm the one they call Preacher."

Eyebrows rose. "So that's why you're standing and he's not. Yes, I see, now. Very well, Preacher, from here on, it's merely a formality."

Far up the North Platte River, after an uneventful passage, the squadron of Dragoons disembarked. While the long, tedious process of unloading the horses, wagons and equipment progressed, Preacher consulted with the captain and river pilot. The latter showed Preacher a map of the river's course. With a stubby finger he pointed out their present location. Preacher nodded with satisfaction.

"This is where we are now. It's not much of a town, called North Platte. End of the line this time of year. I reckon you'll be heading northwest, through the small settlement of Scottsbluff. Nice folks there. Last trip, we brought them five ton of flour in barrels. You can re-supply there without any problem."

Preacher studied the sparse details on the map. "Don't see why you can't get on up there. The map shows the river runnin' all the way into the Wyoming country."

"Too shallow. Why, by August, most of the river west of here will be dried up into a series of mudholes connected by a foot-wide trickle. No, sir, this will be our last run this far. Next trip will be no farther than the town of Grand Island. There's two hundred folk livin' there now. Makes for profitable hauling when the river's up."

Preacher matched the map's representations to images in his mind. They would still have close to two weeks travel to reach the part of the Bighorn Mountains Danvers had selected for his fort. He thanked the river men for their assistance and strode off onto the dock.

A small warehouse fronted the river at North Platte. In its tiny office, Preacher approached the factor. A portly, bald-headed man with an open, friendly face and jolly manner, the manager greeted Preacher affably.

"You came with the soldiers?" he inquired.

"That I did. Anything goin' on in these parts that I should know about?"

"Nothin' much. Except that the Pawnee have been kicking up their heels a mite."

"Do tell. Never could abide nor trust a Pawnee. Go on, if you please."

"They've made periodic attacks on the trail. Burned

a small settlement west of here. Scared hell. outta the folks in Scottsbluff. Matter of fact, they did a good bit of scarin' around here."

"When's the last time they hit?"

In an unconscious gesture left over from when there was something to scratch, the factor rubbed fingertips on his bald pate. "About a week ago. Least, that's the last we've heard of here in North Platte."

Preacher split his darkly tanned face with a grin. "That sounds good. Don't imagine they'd be eager to take on a squadron of Dragoons."

"I wouldn't say so. You be settin' up a fort around here by any chance?"

"Nope. We're headed way northwest."

"What? The whole frontier is on the verge of a massive uprising and those idiots in Washington City send troops clear the hell and gone into where?"

Preacher answered him, his voice somber. "Northeast corner of the Wyoming country. Someone's got a wild idea that a fort out in the middle of nowhere, supported by nothing, will scare the breechcloths off the Injuns."

"You ask me, mister, a person has to be certified to have no brains at all to qualify to be a politician. I mean them all, an' I can say that 'cause I'm neither Whig nor Democrat."

Preacher clapped a big hand on the factor's shoulder, and winced at the pain in his bruised belly. "I have to agree with you there, friend. What else can you tell me?"

"There's talk flyin' around about some hotshot medicine man amongst the Blackfoot talkin' a holy war against us whites. Though I doubt you need to be told that. Part of the reason they're puttin' that fort out there, ain't it?" He gave Preacher a conspiratorial wink.

Preacher replied in kind and added, "Government secrets. Ask our illustrious squadron leader, he'll tell you it's to show the flag to the Sioux and Cheyenne. Whatever that means."

They jawed over other matters for a while and then Preacher departed to rejoin the column of Dragoons. He found them on the edge of the tiny village of North Platte. As usual, Lieutenant Colonel Danvers was in a foul mood.

"I have heard that the Pawnee are raiding in this area."

Preacher cocked his head to one side. "I hear the same, Colonel. We'll likely find evidence of their prowlin' before long."

"Such as what?"

Studying the officer closely, Preacher drawled an answer. "Oh, broke arrows, burned buildings and wagons, bones. The usual Injun leavings."

"Would they attack us, do you think?"

Preacher raised an eyebrow. "Not unless they've plum taken leave of their senses. We're too many and we have that little cannon."

Not entirely convinced, Danvers took on a belligerent posture. "I'll remind you of that in the event the need arises. For now, head out and scout ahead of our line of march." Danvers emphasized his order with a crisp snap of his riding crop.

"I'm sure you will," Preacher muttered, stung by the implied lack of confidence.

"What's that?" snapped Danvers.

"I said, I'll get the long view from the top of that hill." With that he wheeled Tarnation and sprinted off, leaving the colonel with an open mouth.

"Forty miles a day on beans and hay," turned out to be more than a boast Preacher soon discovered. The first day on the trail, the Dragoon squadron made twenty-five of that. Even burdened down with eight huge freight wag-

ons and a field piece, the column covered fifteen miles by midday. They also found the first sign of Pawnee raids.

A well-established trail paralleled the North Platte River, which some were already beginning to call the Oregon Trail. It being wide enough at this point, Preacher relaxed his double-file formation rule and let the troops move along four abreast. In a hidden defile, which kept them from sight on the rolling prairie, Preacher and Three Sleeps came upon the blackened remains of three wagons, along with the bones of the owners.

"Look over here, Preacher," Three Sleeps called to his friend. "Arrow shafts. Most broken, some with the feathers burned. They've had the heads removed."

"Thrifty folks, those Pawnee," opined Preacher.

He studied the ground a while, found little clear and easy to interpret due to time passed. He estimated the attack to have happened at least a week ago. With that established, Preacher remounted and rode back to report to Lieutenant Colonel Danvers.

The colonel heard of the attack with mounting fury. "We have a treaty with the Pawnee," he exploded. "It has been in force for twenty years. Their chiefs should have stopped this outrage."

Patiently Preacher explained. "Among the Injuns, the chiefs have no absolute power. They ain't rulers, Colonel. They lead, give advice, represent the tribe or band with others. An' yes, make treaties. But the folks they represent don't have to obey them or hold to any agreement made in their name by the chiefs."

"Why . . . why, that's preposterous. What sort of leadership does that represent? The Army would get nothing at all done if the troops were not required to do as I order them."

"There might be somethin' good in that," Preacher observed in a muttered aside.

"What did you say?" demanded Danvers.

"I said, there's more to it than that. Most likely the chiefs who signed that treaty are dead now or replaced by someone else the folks are more willing to follow. And so, the people are free to decide whether or not to continue to honor the treaty."

"But they can't do that!"

Preacher could no longer stifle the guffaw that climbed his throat in a rush. "Oh, but they can and do, Colonel. They have always followed their way— it's their law, for want of a better word."

Colonel Danvers made it clear that he was unimpressed and definitely not amused. He addressed Preacher with dismissive authority. "We'll push on. The scene of this massacre would be too depressing a place to camp."

Hump Jaspar had survived the fury of the mountain men by the simple expedient of running like the devil was after him when the ambush failed. He had headed north, robbing folks occasionally to build up a stake. When he reached the North Platte, after running three horses to the ground under him, he took passage on a riverboat for as far as it would take him. Then he started out West on horseback.

Jaspar stopped in his quest only long enough to inquire at trading posts about Praeger and his partners. He had to find them. No matter that the news he brought would probably send them up like July Fourth rockets, he knew he might receive some benefit from it.

Hump had never heard of the old tradition of kings killing the bearers of bad news. So, when he found Branson Naylor, one of his friends who had joined the gang run by Blake Soures, at a trading post far up the Platte, he learned that Praeger could be found in a Blackfoot camp not far from the Bighorn Mountains and rode there with all speed. Only to face the fury of Quinton Praeger.

"*You* got away? Only you? How many men did you say sided with Preacher?"

"Two." The smallness of his voice startled Hump Jaspar.

"Impossible! Three men killed twenty-five?"

"Yeah. But it was in two fights."

Sarcasm enveloped Praeger's words. "Only two fights? Only two? Why in hell did it take more than one to finish off three men?"

"The first fight wasn't against Preacher."

"Then kindly tell me about its purpose?"

"We . . . ah . . . we decided to rob this train of freight wagons."

Quinton Praeger went white. "In the name of all that's holy, what in hell possessed you to do that?"

"We . . . thought we'd make some quick money."

Praeger could not suppress the shudder that came from a foretaste of doom. "I see. Yes, I really do. But you said you fought Preacher there?"

"Yes, sir. He and these two fellers came along and broke up our attack on the wagons. Only at the time we did not know it was him."

Eyebrows arched, Praeger ran a finger along the knife scar on his left cheek. His voice purred with feigned reasonableness "That explains it all. And the next time you met, he finished off all the rest, right?"

Hump Jaspar forced an expression of wide-eyed innocence. "Yes, sir. All except me."

"Thank you, Mr. Jaspar. Now that everything is in a shambles around my feet, I feel constrained to correct the one error Preacher made."

Puzzled, Hump Jaspar asked a fateful question. "Uh, what's that, Mr. Praeger?"

Praeger drew a compact .60-caliber, Miquelet Spanish pistol from under his coat and cocked the hammer.

"Killing you," he replied a moment before he squeezed the trigger and shot Jaspar through the heart.

Praeger was still furious when he reached the council lodge. Iron Shirt showed his usual irritation at being summoned forth. He stood with arms folded over his chest, face black and in a glower.

"I was discussing important matters. What is it you want? We hear soldiers are coming. Is this true?"

"Yes. They are all a part of the plan. Right now I must speak with you and the war chiefs. It is an important issue."

"We will meet with you when we are ready."

Anger flared again in Praeger's chest. "Listen to me. I made you what you are. I gave you that iron shirt. I made up the ritual you use. Without me, you are nothing. When I want a meeting you will see that it happens. Is that clear?"

Iron Shirt's lips curled in contempt. "White man, you are a flea trying to bite a bull bison. When we are ready to listen, we will send for you." He turned on the heel of one moccasin and stomped back inside the lodge.

White, shaking with rage now, Quinton Praeger fought back a hot burst of profanity. Slowly he realized that his time with Iron Shirt had come near the end. Every day, every hour, had to be balanced with utmost care. Starting with regaining the dependency of Iron Shirt, he acknowledged. So, he smiled and waited.

Three hours went by before a young warrior came to summon him to the council. When he entered and went through the formalities, Praeger quickly explained the situation with Preacher. He concluded with a suggestion that when Preacher arrived with the squadron of Dragoons, the Blackfoot kill him themselves. To their credit,

Quinton admitted, the war chiefs listened politely and with interest. Then they began to respond.

To his surprise, Praeger soon began to understand that the ferocious Blackfoot did not seem the least eager to face the living legend. When the last speaker's words had been translated for him, Praeger could not contain his profound exasperation.

"But we can't let him interfere with your war to drive out all whites," he blurted.

Two Moons rocked forward and came to his moccasins. "Why is it," he asked, "that you and the other two white men are so anxious to stir up war between our two peoples?"

Praeger worried that question a while, then made an oily, evasive answer. "I have learned your ways and have come to love and respect them. I wish to live as one of you after the whites are gone from this land."

Two Moons, as did the other chiefs, carefully kept his features neutral, in order not to reveal that they did not believe a single word of what they had heard. If it is true that ignorance is bliss, Quinton Praeger left the council lodge a misinformed but happy man.

TWELVE

Lieutenant Colonel Danvers had even less reason to be happy the next day. Antoine Revier came fogging back to the column at a quarter past ten with news that electrified the battalion commander and his officers.

"Colonel, we cut sign of a Pawnee war party about three miles ahead."

Danvers blinked and took a backhand swipe across his forehead. "Preposterous. We are at peace with the Pawnee." The last thing he wanted was to have a hostile force at his back when they settled in to build a fort.

Antoine gave him a mischievous eye. "Maybe this bunch don't know that. Preacher recommends that the tro— ah-Dragoons be mounted 'til this is worked out."

"We shall proceed afoot," Danvers decided aloud, ignoring the good advice. "Please inform Mr. Preacher that I wish him to extend his scouting activities over a much wider area."

With that dismissal, Antoine rode back to the point. The colonel waited until he had ridden out of hearing, then turned to call over his shoulder. "Captain Dreiling, flankers out, if you please."

"Yes, sir. Lieutenant Brice, take Sergeant Holcomb and twenty men to form flankers."

"Yes, sir. Holcomb, divide the platoon. You take the right flank, I'll take the left."

"Right, sir. First and Third Squads, follow me."

Lieutenant Brice wasted no time. "Second and Fourth, you're with me. Platoon . . . prepare to mount. . . . Mount."

With a flurry of dust from two hundred hooves, the flankers moved out smartly. Danvers watched them go in grim-lipped silence. He did not want to stir up trouble with the Pawnee. His orders were explicit. They were to proceed to the Bighorn Mountains, avoiding hostile engagements, and establish a cantonment area sufficient to house a regiment when completed. He had other orders as well, which he preferred not to think of. Sighing, he took up his reins, raised his arms and signaled for the column to advance. The Dragoons remained on foot twenty minutes later when the Pawnee raised up, seemingly out of the ground, and attacked the column.

Blind Wolf looked to the west, down the shallow slope of the rolling prairie. How foolish these white men. To go afoot when they had perfectly healthy horses to ride. More so for doing it in this country where death awaited them at every turn. This would be easy. Once his hidden warriors had them halted and confused, he and the rest of his brave Pawnee would sweep down on them at a gallop and ride the length of the column, killing many. He squinted to see the lead soldiers start up the next swell. He raised his feather-decorated rifle and gave the shrill call of a hunting eagle.

Responding to the signal to attack, Pawnee warriors came out from under their dirt-covered blankets and quickly sent a flight of arrows into the unsuspecting whites. Here and there a rifle cracked. Other braves, risking certain death, rushed forward to flail with their blankets and bison robes to frighten the horses of the white men. Even at his distance of a quarter mile, Blind Wolf saw several mounts' forehooves pawing the air.

Two even broke free of their owners' hold and bolted
away from the noise— war whoops, shots— and the
ghostly song of arrows. Any time now, he thought. Some
of the soldiers had recovered and began to fire at the
attackers. Blind Wolf knew he could wait no longer.

Raising his rifle again, he looked left and right, then
brought it down smartly. At once he and twenty-five
mounted warriors streaked forward. Swiftly, they closed
on the wagons at the rear of the column.

An arrow made its uncanny moan past the ear of Lieutenant Colonel Danvers. Another thudded into the valise
cover behind the cantle of his Grimsley saddle. A third
bounced off the pommel of his adjutant's saddle. Instinct drove Danvers to take cover behind the stout fore-
quarters and neck of his horse. This gave him a clear
view of his holster, with its sheepskin cover.

To his credit, the Dragoon commander was the first
to get off a shot. He threw back the tube of sheepskin
and drew one large, unwieldy .44 Dragoon pistol and
fired two fast rounds, one of which entered the screaming mouth of a Pawnee warrior who rushed at the horses
with a flopping blanket.

Off went the left rear quarter of the brave's head as
the flattened ball, now approximately .60-caliber in size,
burned through brain and blew away bone and scalp. A
Model 43 Hall, breech-loading carbine went off close by
and Danvers flinched involuntarily. The hot wind of ex-
panding gases from the foreshortened rifle brushed his
cheek. Another flight of arrows seethed through the air.

One found a home in the forearm of Private Sawyer,
who screamed as the point pierced the skin of his inner
arm and protruded toward the forestock of his Hall. Corporal Collins, who'd gone back for the wagons left behind, came quickly to Sawyer's side, Danvers noted.

Deftly, the NCO broke off the shaft of the projectile and pulled the remainder through the wound. He quickly had Sawyer bound with a light blue neck scarf he had pulled from the open collar of his uniform jacket. Seemingly unfazed, Sawyer calmly reloaded his weapon, seated a percussion cap on the nipple and took aim on another screaming savage. Sergeant Simmons and the other lead NCOs bellowed commands to restore order among the milling, confused troops.

Gradually more of the Dragoons unlimbered their weapons and returned fire. For a moment, the Pawnee rush faltered. Then the thunder of pounding hooves attracted the attention of everyone to the rear of the column.

Gunfire crackled out as another swarm of hostiles raced along the eight freight wagons, rifles blazing. Unable to reload on the run, the Pawnee slung their rifles over their shoulders and resorted to more conventional weapons. Now the teamsters and their swampers plied their firearms. At a rate of fire three times that of muzzle-loaders—three per minute—the breech-loading carbines poured a steady stream of lead in the direction of the Pawnee attackers. In a short time, the scene became obscured to the Dragoons and their enemy alike.

Blind Wolf had seriously underestimated the firepower of these flashily dressed soldiers. He had never encountered a breech-loading weapon before, had no idea of the speed with which they could be loaded and fired repeatedly. When the moan and crackle of balls thickened, and the reports of the short rifles grew to a deafening volume, he gave the signal for his warriors to pull back.

"We have hurt them We will come again," Blind Wolf told his son, Tall Raven, a boy of sixteen winters, who rode at his side.

Fired with the excitement of his first raid as a warrior, Tall Raven showed his disappointment. "Why not now, Father?"

"They are too many. They have shoot-fast guns we know nothing about. But, see, two of them are down, never to rise again. I count two hands of those who have felt the sharp teeth of the Pawnee. Soon again they will be off guard. It is then we will hit them."

Lieutenant Colonel Arlington Danvers rode the length of the column, inspected the damage and spent a minute with each of the wounded. Upset over the losses and the speed and surprise of the attack, he wore a deep frown. Beyond him, the flankers appeared over the swells to north and south while the Pawnee streamed away to the east. Danvers watched with mounting anger as the security details drew closer.

When Lieutenant Brice reported, the colonel icily cut him off in mid-recitation. "Explain yourself, mister. Why did you not get here in time to strike the hostiles from the rear?"

Brice stiffened. "No excuse, sir. But, for the record, we were pretty well spread out, screening for hostiles, sir, and it took some while to regroup and return, sir."

Realizing the correctness of this explanation, though loath to admit it, Danvers delayed his response. "Quite right, Lieutenant Brice. We will maintain flankers, only this time, they are to remain within visual contact of one another, and work in teams of two."

"Yes, sir. We'll go out at once, sir."

"Keep a sharp eye. Those savages caught us quite by surprise the first time," he grudgingly added.

"You expect them to come again?"

"Oh, yes, Lieutenant. Indians never give up with a single attack."

Brice and his platoon of flankers rode off to their assigned areas. A moment later, Preacher and Three Sleeps Norris cantered over the rise ahead of the column and located Lieutenant Colonel Danvers.

"We heard the ruckus, Colonel. Thought we'd best come see what went on."

"We were attacked by hostiles. Pawnee, I believe."

Preacher bent and retrieved an arrow. "That's what this says. Pawnee markin's right enough. They're fierce devils. Can't figger why they broke off so soon."

Danvers produced a satisfied smirk, recalling the surprised and confused expressions of the enemy. "I imagine they had never encountered breech-loading weapons before. We put out a volume of fire nearly triple that of older arms. I have flankers out. I think we can expect a return call from the Indians."

"Oh, yes, that you certain can. You want us to stay back with you, Colonel?"

Danvers considered it. "The warriors seemed to rise up out of the ground. Total surprise for us. I think it best if you do stay with the column, work out to the edges. Maybe you can detect another such shock tactic."

Preacher had more bad news. "One thing sure, Colonel, they won't play the same trick twice. The Pawnee have a whole bag full."

Blind Wolf bided his time for the second attack. The soldiers had made another five miles before the mounted Pawnee rushed over the lip of a ravine to the left of their route. Driving hard, they rushed down on the flank of the column. From his vantage point, Blind Wolf watched with satisfaction as the soldiers once again reacted slowly.

Faint shouts in the white man's language, which Blind Wolf understood only poorly under the best conditions, came to his ears. The soldiers wheeled left and lifted short rifles from where they hung on the saddles. A faint smile lifted his full lips and flickered momentarily. Then he raised his arm and waved it left and right.

A flight of arrows soared upward from beyond the edge of a high creek bank to the right of the mass of soldiers. Before they landed, the left flank disappeared behind a wall of smoke. A moment later, another volley crashed across the prairie. Blind Wolf's lips compressed and his eyes narrowed. He had expected this. Yet, he ached for each of his brave men who fell in the withering fire.

Short of the soldiers by only three pony lengths, the Pawnee reined in, those with rifles fired, then they wheeled and galloped away. Another flight of arrows went aloft from the creek bank. Orders shouted in a thin, high voice, turned half the mounted troops in that direction. Two heart-stoppingly fast volleys ripped into the verge and chewed chunks out of the bank. Rifle in hand, Blind Wolf extended his arm and pumped it up and down.

Again his mounted warriors charged. Their ponies pounded down on the stationary ranks. Shrill whoops came from strong, young throats. The short rifles crashed again. Several braves flew from their saddles. Inexorably, the opposing forces grew closer together.

Then three buckskin-clad, white demons cut diagonally across the advancing warriors. Their gunfire rippled across the waving grass, the aim incredibly accurate. First one, then a second of Blind Wolf's leaders slipped from the backs of their ponies. In a flash, the surprisingly disciplined charge of the Pawnee warriors dissolved into a confused, milling mass.

With hardly any pause, the soldiers changed the shape of their defense. Alternating groups turned their horses left or right and began to move toward their attackers at a walk. In five heartbeat intervals, the walk became a trot, then a canter, then a gallop. With a raw roar from parched throats, the Dragoons charged.

* * *

By sheer volume of fire, the Dragoons stopped the Pawnee in their tracks. Then, while the men reloaded, Preacher and his companions dashed between the contesting forces, firing with their multiple-shot weapons. Preacher downed a leader, then wounded another. Antoine Revier killed a second subchief. That did it. The leaderless warriors turned, scattered. Cursing the showoff stunt of the mountain men, Lieutenant Colonel Danvers suddenly realized that it gave him the opportunity he sought. Now he could bring a decisive end to this. He stood full in the stirrups and issued commands in his high-pitched voice.

"By alternate companies, form as skirmishers, left and right. Draw pistols. Prepare to charge. Trumpeter, sound the charge!" As the crisp, tingling notes sounded, Danvers drew his saber. *"Chaaaaarge!"*

Haunches flexed, the big Dragoon horses bounded forward. Clods of turf flew in the air around them. Snorting and grunting, they increased their pace increased with each step. Quickly the Dragoons closed on their enemy. Suddenly, frightened faces turned toward them. Isolated islands of resistance formed here and there. The big, broad-shouldered soldiers in the two-tone blue uniforms grew huge in the eyes of the Pawnee. At extreme pistol range, the chilling order came.

"Take aim . . . fire! Take aim . . . fire! Take aim . . . fire!" On they thundered. "Fire at will!"

At that point, the flankers returned and struck the enemy in the rear. Quickly the huge, six-shot Dragoon pistols turned the tide. The Pawnee held fast for a moment, then broke in wild disarray, to be swept from the field. Within minutes, the battle ended. Silence settled over the field, save for the groans of the wounded. Abruptly, Preacher stormed up to Danvers.

Seeming furious, he lashed out verbally. "I thought I said no damn trumpets." Then he grinned broadly. "But it sure was a sweet, purty sight."

Danvers relaxed his usual brittle, disapproving attitude toward Preacher. "Yes, it is. A full-out, Dragoon charge is awe-inspiring." Then he frowned. "I see only one advantage coming out of this fierce, protracted fighting. It has blooded these green troops." He had not finished with that.

"This skirmish could have been, should have been, avoided. I want a plan drawn up that will insure we are not delayed by such actions. Those savages are supposed to be on friendly terms. What can we expect when we encounter real hostiles?"

It had been intended to be rhetorical, but Preacher took delight in answering. "More'n likely you'll git yer hair lifted."

Despite himself, Danvers cut his eyes to Preacher and acknowledged the remark, which made it more to the point. "That is not amusing. Any more delays like this will make us seriously overdue on our arrival in the high country."

Preacher considered the colonel's upset over the raid to be excessive. Yet, he bided his time for the present. What would come, would come.

Early in the afternoon, the forsaken wagon train arrived in what was seen as a safe haven tucked into a fold of the northeast slope of the Medicine Bow Mountains, a lush, gentle valley spread along a buttress of the foothills. The clear water of the Platte River ran in front of their hidden vale. Their tired eyes explored the bounty and found it good.

Isaac Warner halted his wagon at the entrance and repeated his instruction to all who came by. "Go on in, find a likely space and settle in. We'll organize a hunting party soon as everybody is unhitched."

Each family quickly staked out areas of the belly-high grass for their draft animals and saddle stock to graze on. The women set about preparing firepits and rigging lines to air out long-confined clothing and blankets.

With her chores completed, Eve Billings ambled over to the site selected by the Honeycutts. Eve spoke her innermost thoughts to Hattie as she approached. "What a pure delight, all the water we want."

"And pure, too," Hattie added with a shake of her gray-streaked auburn hair. She had started the trek with uniformly coppery tresses.

"There will be plenty of game. And the chance for our livestock to fatten up for a long haul." She saw the older woman strain to move a boulder that she wanted elsewhere. "Here, let me help you with that."

They worked together for the better part of an hour. Eve soon noticed that neighborliness had once more come to life all over the encampment. Gone was the bickering and petty spite of the trail. It took far less time than usual to establish comfortable living areas. With the work out of the way, and the animals at graze, everyone seemed to decide at once that the time had come to wash away the dust and grit of the sun-blasted Basin.

While the adults and older youths decorously washed themselves in the shallows of the North Platte River, Eve watched as Charlie joined the other boys under fourteen and, along with the others, gleefully threw off his clothes and leaped into the chill water of the river. Eve could only cluck her tongue and shake her head. Not a streak of modesty in the lot of them. How like his father as a boy Charlie is, she thought.

Sudden tears sprang to her eyes at thinking of the man she had loved so dearly and who had died in her arms. She lowered her head to conceal her private grief from the others. Slowly her suppressed sobs, changed from gulps to sighs, and at last into long, slow, deep breaths. Eve looked up to see a sparkling, naked Charlie leap from a slippery boulder into the water in an awkward dive. A worried mother's words escaped her before she could cut them off.

"Charlie! Look out!"

A deep rumble of thunder came from the northwest to drown out her appeal. Swiftly, the temperature dropped fifteen degrees. The children ran shouting from the water to hurriedly wipe themselves down and dress. Eve chuckled softly. At least there was something that would get Charlie into clothes without an argument. If only Howard could see him now, she thought with fierce pride. This time, fond, loving tears filled her eyes.

She glanced up to see a blurry figure on horseback across the river. Curious, and wary, Eve wiped away mistiness to discover the same Indian she had seen nearly a week before. Behind him were foothills and huge columns of boiling black clouds. Again he raised his lance in a salute and smiled at her. Mystified, Eve stood, the hem of her dress dripping, and watched him until he turned and slowly rode away.

THIRTEEN

Celestial keglers made strike after strike ahead of the route of march. From north to south, the horizon had turned a boiling black. Skeletal fingers, edged in orange, lanced through the obsidian stew. With a swiftness known only to denizens of the West, the towering, anvil-headed cumulonimbus arched out to engulf the whole dome of the sky.

Preacher had been watching the approach of the storm. He prudently exchanged his hunting shirt for one of faded green flannel and his fringed buckskin jacket for an oiled-skin *capote*. His floppy felt went into his saddle-bag along with his skins. A spanking new, stiff-brimmed one took its place. Preacher used a fist to punch the crown into a faint resemblance of its original shape.

While he industriously made these alterations in his clothing, the thunder rumbled, increasingly louder. To his dismay, when he looked back at the column, the Dragoons appeared to ride along in blissful ignorance.

"Them fellers is gonna get a first-class soakin'," he confided to Three Sleeps.

Norris nodded. "I reckon so. They've got them those fancy India-rubber *capotes* they use for ground sheets. I wonder why nobody's given the order to break them out?"

Preacher's face twisted into an expression of sudden enlightenment. "Now, that's the entire trouble with the

Army. Somebody's always got to tell you what to do. They yell and cuss at a body until he forgets how to think for hisself, an' then they don't let them anyway."

Three Sleeps removed his coonskin cap and scratched at a thick thatch of silver-blond hair. "I *think* I understand what you jist said, but I ain't gonna answer any questions on it."

Preacher started to make a wounded reply when the light breeze that had been in their faces dropped to dead still. That held for several heartbeats; then a strong, cold blast rushed at them out of the east. At once, the temperature plummeted ten degrees and continued to fall.

Preacher tightened the chin strap of his hat; the brim fluttered wildly. "B'God, here she comes."

A tremendous peal of thunder came right on the heels of a searing, white tongue of lightning that slammed into a pile of boulders a hundred yards from the trail. The ground shook with the violence of it. Despite the powerful gust of wind, the air tingled with the scent of ozone.

Insubstantial shouts came from the column. Preacher looked down to see the Dragoons halted, dismounting now, and digging into the cylindrical valises behind their saddles. From them, the troops hurriedly took their water-proof ponchos and donned them.

"That seems to have got their attention," he said dryly.

Widely spaced, huge, fat drops made silver streaks in the air. Another blinding flash and boom. The thunder erupted directly overhead and continued to grind and growl across the sky. Echoes of its passage bounced from the sun-baked ground. More rain fell, thicker now, with the main downpour close behind. It arrived with a seething hiss and swept like a giant's broom across the ridge where Preacher and his friends sat their mounts.

Tarnation made wall-eyes and twitched his ears. His hide followed suit when the heavenly cannonade fired another battery of forked electricity at six wide-spaced places in rapid succession. Down below, Preacher saw the Dragoons had a lot of trouble with their horses. Having dismounted, they could barely control the animals in the fierce teeth of the storm.

"Those boys are gonna lose some horses," opined Antoine Revier.

Preacher nodded agreement. "I reckon they will." Another near miss by a sizzling bolt put Preacher in motion. "Let's quit playin' target for that stuff."

Halfway down the grade toward the column, the rattle and drumbeat of swiftly approaching hail reached the ears of Preacher. He drubbed heels into Tarnation's ribs and streaked for a low, spreading plain tree that stood in valiant isolation in the shelter of a gully. He reached it only seconds behind his companions.

Shredded leaves fell in green confetti around them, while out in the open, the Dragoons did not fare so well. Two horses, painfully pelted with fist-sized ice stones, squealed and reared. Rain-slicked, the reins slipped through the hands of the Dragoons who held them. At once, the frightened, hurting animals bolted.

In spite of orders to the contrary, their hapless riders ran after them. In no time, the Dragoons and their mounts disappeared over a low swell. Preacher spat on a fallen leaf.

"There goes a couple of damn fools."

"You got the right of it, Preacher," Antoine Revier agreed.

"Any bets as to who'll have to go after them?" Three Sleeps Norris put in.

Preacher grimaced. "None at all. Soon's this downpour ends, we'd best be making tracks."

* * *

For all its violence, the storm had been a welcome sight
for the unfortunate members of the wagon train. Eve Billings had hurried back in time to gather in the bedding
and clothes she had out to air. The rain, when it came,
was warm and inviting. At the insistence of her children,
Eve relented and erected a screen of spare wagon-top canvas. Within its confines, Charlie and Anna cavorted, bare
as the day they had been born. The only protest the youngsters made was when Eve produced a bar of soap.

"Mind you do your ears, Charlie Billings," she admonished.

Smiling and humming an old tune, she sat out the tempest in the shelter of the wagon box. Blue-lipped and shivering, Charlie and Anna had held out to the last drop,
then had oohed and aahed over a rainbow that formed on
the northern end of the storm's back. At last, they climbed,
dripping, over the tailgate. Eve toweled them dry.

"Ow, Mom, that hurts," Charlie complained of the
stiff, prickly cloth.

"Yeah, that hurth," Anna lisped.

Another sacrifice of the trail. Eve had been able to
wash clothes in the water of streams they had passed,
many of which were rich in lime and iron particles. Her
supply of bluing had long since run out, and she regret-
ted the stiffness her efforts put into the items she had
washed. She would have given anything to capture barrels of that marvelously soft rain water.

Now that the tempest had rolled away to the east, the
leaves of beech and oak, and pine needles, dropped, as
if doing a slow dance, into puddles that had formed on
the long-dry ground. The pioneers began to stir in their
wagons. Eve reflected on her mystery Indian as she laid
a fire from dry wood that she'd sheltered from the elements in a net sling under the floor of the Conestoga.

Obviously he was not hostile, she told herself. Why
was it he only appeared to her? She had mentioned him

after the first sighting, but none of the men had admitted to seeing the lone figure. Gus Beecher had even snidely suggested that she was seeing things. Maybe she was, her mind mocked.

Dismissing that, she knelt by the pyramid of sticks and pulled a tuft of oily wood tinder from the brass box. She struck sparks from flint and steel and gently blew an orange spot in the kindling into lively flames. Careful not to burn her fingers, she shoved the lintwood in under a mound of shavings. They reluctantly ignited and sent larger, hotter tendrils of fire among the larger pieces of wood. She looked up as Charlie approached. He was dressed as usual, shirtless, in his one-piece overalls, bare toes squishing in the mud.

"Mom, I want to go with the hunters. I'll get us something good."

"I'm sorry, but no. It's not safe. Some of the men can't . . ." Eve cut herself off short. She had admonished herself not to criticize the men in the group after Charlie had repeated her scathing evaluation of their abilities weeks ago. It did little good this time, as Charlie provided her opinion of their marksmanship.

"Hit the broad side of a barn."

Mad at herself more than the boy, Eve spoke hotly. "Charles Ryan, what have I told you about speaking ill of your elders?"

"Oh, boy, am I in trouble?" His lower lip protruded in a pink, wet pout.

Eve looked down on his sweet face and could only shake her head in the negative. Then she had to turn away to keep from breaking out in gales of laughter.

After two hours of searching, Preacher had nothing to show for it but some muddy hoofprints. Again he cursed the Army, and Lieutenant Colonel Danvers in particular. The muddle-headed nincompoop had insisted that at least some of the guides remain with the column. His idea of some turned out to be all save Preacher. Well, Mrs. Houghton's little boy Arthur had not turned out dense.

Preacher figured it was Danvers's idea to get him killed by the Pawnee, which likely had happened to the idiots he attempted to track. He sighed heavily and urged Tarnation forward. While the miles ticked off, he grumbled about the stupidity of officer-type soldiers or gnawed on a strip of jerky which he had softened between saddle and blanket.

With only three hours of daylight left, he at last found the missing men right enough. A big cloud of bluebottle flies led him the last fifty yards to a dry wash that cut like a knife slash across the prairie. They made quite a sight, one that wrenched even as experienced a stomach as Preacher's.

They had been stripped, staked out, mutilated, killed and scalped. Though not necessarily in that order, Preacher noted. One had been slit from sternum to groin, and had his private parts stuffed in his mouth. The other had been cut deeply from crotch to ankle of both legs and armpits to wrists. It had been done slowly, Preacher reckoned from the contorted condition of the unfortunate fellow's muscles.

Cautiously, Preacher looked around the scene. His keen eyes took in everything. First, he noted that there was no sign of their uniforms, weapons or gear. There was plenty of sign of Pawnee warriors. Oddly enough, one of the dead men's horses placidly chomped grass at the bottom of the ravine. It had been stripped of all equipage.

"Damn an' double damn," Preacher swore aloud.

Moving with care, he walked to Tarnation's side. There Preacher fetched a short length of rope from a latigo tie and fashioned a crude hackamore. He approached the Dragoon mount with patience. When the creature's bulging eye first registered his presence, Preacher began to coo to it and speak softly.

"There now. There, nobody's gonna hurt you. Good boy. Stand still, ya hear?"

Step by mindful step, Preacher's moccasined feet took him up to the heaving flank of the horse. He touched the animal lightly, ran his hand along the curve of its back to the neck. Another pace forward, a second. Murmuring platitudes, he raised the makeshift halter. Then, with a deft movement, Preacher slipped it over the muzzle.

Only a slight jump came from the creature. Preacher patted his arched neck firmly and blew gently in a cocked ear. Then he carefully led the beast away from the patch of grass.

"Come on, boy, you've got an unpleasant task to do."

After adding a lead rope to the hackamore and fixing that to a ground anchor, Preacher cut free the dead Dragoons. He wrapped them in his ground sloth and an old blanket and slung them over the back of the captured horse. A nervous twitching rewarded his efforts. With a grunt of acceptance of a bad job done the best he could, he mounted Tarnation and took up the lead. Mindful of the bodies he brought, he put the noses of the horses in the direction of the column. He did not relish making a report to Danvers on what happened.

Preacher had predicted the result accurately. Lieutenant Colonel Danvers stomped back and forth in his tent, cursed and railed, then concluded his tirade with a wholly uncalled-for accusation.

"Why did you not get to them sooner?"

Preacher cocked his head to one side. "I don't put up

with that kind of talk from you or anybody. What did you expect me to do? I counted sign of fully sixteen Pawnee warriors around them bodies. I ain't fool enough to ride in among 'em and pass the time o' day, or bargain for the release of those idiots what ran after their mounts in hostile country. Besides, I don't think it would have done much good. They looked to have been dead since shortly after the storm passed by. Now, *Colonel*, I'll accept your apology, or I'll demand satisfaction right here an' now."

Surprise painted Danvers's face. "Duel with you? Why, you're not even a *gentleman*."

Preacher looked astonished. "I didn't intend on no duel. Death's a serious matter." He turned abruptly and started for the front flap of the tent.

"Then what did you have in that primitive brain of yours?"

"I jist figgered to tom-turkey stomp the shit out of you, Colonel. But I've cooled off some. We'll forget it . . . for now. Good night, Colonel."

"Wait!" Danvers started after Preacher. "What are we going to do to stop these treaty violations?"

Preacher stared coldly and levelly at the colonel. "These incidents will continue unless the Pawnees learn not to mess with us. The best way to do that is to raid their villages, burn their lodges and supplies, run off their ponies, kill a few warriors."

"That's madness, man!" Danvers went on to protest vehemently. "There is a treaty. These are not the Indians we came out here to fight."

Preacher's amused expression turned to one of intense curiosity. "What Injuns are you supposed to fight? The way I understand it, we didn't come out here to fight any Injuns. Jist to 'show the flag,' " he tossed the pet phrase of Arlington Danvers back in his face.

Danvers paled, cognizant that his mouth had overstepped his reasoning. "Yes . . . yes, you're right about that. The fort is to enforce the peace, not incite war. Yet, I must maintain that nothing can be gained from pushing a dispute on the Pawnee."

Preacher grinned and gave the colonel a wink. "I can think of something. It will provide excellent trainin' for yer baby Dragoons, that it will."

Grudgingly, Danvers saw the sense in that. Reluctantly he agreed to allow Preacher and one other guide to observe any Pawnee camps or villages in close proximity to their route of march.

Over the next two nights, Preacher and Antoine Revier scouted as many Pawnee villages. Preacher had reasoned correctly that such a large number of warriors could not come from a small raiding band on the warpath. It took him only to the second night to find what he sought. He would make a third foray to verify what he had learned.

Preacher squatted behind a stunted, wind-twisted bristle-cone pine and looked down into a village. Flickering firelight turned the scene a Dantesque orange. His ears soon picked up the spine-chilling throb of drums and the eerie, wailing of the Scalp Dance, a song he'd painfully learned long ago and had lived to remember. From the gyrating shadows projected onto lodge covers, he estimated that at least six of the marauders lived in this community. At the time, he did not realize he had missed the count by ten.

After half an hour of careful study, Preacher slipped away into the night to rendezvous with Antoine. The first thing the French-Delaware mountain man said was: "You saw it, too?"

"Yep. The Scalp Dance."

"I counted eleven of 'em got the hoop with the scalps on it passed to them."

"You did? I marked it as six. My eyes must be goin' bad. Or I left too soon."

"May have. From the other side I could see real clear. Made my blood run cold."

"We'll check that other village tomorrow night, then tell the good colonel where to hit."

"I'm for that."

Together, they turned their mounts to the south and started for the trail of the Dragoon column. On the way, Preacher began to formulate a plan of attack.

After the third night's visit, Preacher completed his strategy on the ride to the Dragoon camp. He explained it to Lieutenant Colonel Danvers and to his utter surprise, the constantly critical officer agreed entirely. He did make a couple of changes and offered a suggestion.

"Standard Dragoon tactics call for keeping one element of one's force in reserve. In this case, I think they should be deployed. They can act as a screen, at some distance, to see none of the hostiles escape us."

"You're sure gonna make life hard for those Injun folk. I reckon we can work it out right smart."

Shortly before dawn the next day, the Dragoons eased into position to attack the slumbering Pawnee village. When all was in readiness, Danvers gave the signal. Howling like banshees, the Dragoons stormed in among the lodges. Some of these they set afire. Others they pulled down. Rearing horses trampled firepits and cooking pots. Yapping dogs bristled in challenge, only to be shot down by Dragoons. Preacher took his own course to enter the encampment.

Shocked, he felt a tangible chill along his spine when he saw the horse herd had disappeared. Sudden premonition caused Preacher to try to shout a warning. The

first words had barely left his mouth when disaster
struck.

Suddenly the tables turned on the Dragoons. Howling
Pawnee warriors attacked them from outside the village.
Whooping war cries and screaming insults, they charged
into the bewildered soldiers.

FOURTEEN

Panic struck the green troops on the outer edges when the Indians appeared so suddenly. It rippled inward to those still occupied with trashing the village. Entire companies milled about in confusion. Who was it shooting at them? There weren't any Indians. Those furthest removed from the Pawnee menace had no idea of the terrible death that threatened them.

Preacher put heels to the ribs of his stallion and drove a wedge through some Dragoons paralyzed by fear. "Spread out an' get them weapons workin', damnit! There's Injuns right over there." He pointed the way and his calm, purposeful demeanor broke the spell.

First by ones and twos, the Dragoons opened space between one another and brought their Hall carbines into action. An arrow hissed past Preacher's ear and he jinked his head to the side automatically. A Walker Colt filled his right hand, and he fired almost point-blank into the chest of a Pawnee warrior. With a final shriek, the brave rolled backward off the rump of his pony.

Preacher sought another target, to find himself face-to-face with Three Sleeps Norris. "Muldoon is over on the other side, tryin' to organize some sort of defense."

Preacher assimilated the information and nodded. "Antoine is right over there. I'll send him to Muldoon. You an' him can keep us in touch."

* * *

BSM Terrance Muldoon found himself alone in the command structure. Two young lieutenants had gone down in the first bevy of arrows to descend on the unsuspecting troops. Both officers took only wounds, but one was serious. No sign of Captain Dreiling, the most reliable and steadiest of the company commanders. None of the others had been on this side of the village. After the initial shock of the swift, swirling assault, Muldoon shouldered his mount into that of one Dragoon after another and shouted loudly enough to break their glazes of shock.

"Get that damn rifle to workin', soldier!"

"Bu-But the Indians," one had blathered back at him.

"Sure an' they ain't bulletproof, ye idiot."

By the time he had bullied enough of the wild-eyed troopers into a passable defensive formation, with every other man dismounted, the Pawnee had disappeared into the tall grass to prepare for a second rush. When the seed clusters at the tops of the stalks began to weave in snake-like patterns, Muldoon spoke low and reassuringly to the men he commanded.

"Easy now. Let 'em come to us. Be ready, stand fast, lads. Standing men kneel. Prepare to fire by volley. Hold yer fire. Take aim . . . Kneeling rank . . . fire!"

Lighted by the muzzle flash of fifteen carbines, the predawn murk turned to orange sunrise. "Reload. Mounted rank . . . take aim . . . fire!"

Again the sun rose in the south for the Pawnee. "Reload. Kneeling rank, take aim . . . fire! Reload. Steady, lads, steady. Mounted rank, take aim . . . fire! Reload. Kneeling rank, take aim . . . fire!"

Seemingly oblivious to the hail of balls that snapped through the air in their direction, the warriors came on. At each volley, ten to twelve Pawnee fell in the grass, killed, stunned or wounded by the Dragoons. After the third volley, the distance between them and the soldiers had narrowed enough that the Dragoons did not have time to reload their carbines.

Muldoon judged the situation well. His voice rang calm and clear over the defenders. "Replace carbines. Draw pistols . . . Fire at will."

A wave of staccato reports rippled along the file of Dragoons. The sheer volume of fire sent dread through the swarm of warriors. In disarray, they thrashed their way back into the concealing grass.

"Keep it up, bies, that grass can't stop a bullet," Muldoon cheered on his rag-tag band of soldiers.

"Muldoon's checked them on the north," Antoine Revier reported to Preacher after he rode up in a fog of dust.

Preacher gestured to the empty plain that stretched from the village to a deep gully. "They ain't showin' themselves so free and easy over here. I found a couple of the company commanders. They got their troops outta their daze and blasted hell outta the Pawnee a short while back." He beckoned to Three Sleeps. "Git yerself over to Muldoon, take some of this surplus of officers we've got here with you. Tell him I expect the next charge will come at this side any time now. I'm gettin' tired of runnin' this show for the Army. Time to let the one's supposed to do it." He paused and looked around, a puzzled frown creasing his powder-grimed brow.

"Speakin' of which, where in daylights is Colonel Danvers?"

"Don't see him anywhere," Antoine remarked.

Then Preacher replayed the first moments of pandemonium when the Pawnee attacked. He pursed his lips and slapped a thigh with an open palm. "As I recollect, when the hostiles fu'st hit us, Danvers disappeared into one of the tipis still standin'. Funny thing, I ain't see him since."

Antoine was full of helpful suggestions. "Let's go see if we can find him."

"We will, soon's I figger out which one he went to."

Preacher and Antoine drew blanks on the first two lodges. At the entrance flap of the third, Preacher found a private standing post as though on garrison guard duty. He poked his head inside and found Lieutenant Colonel Arlington Danvers.

Seated on a camp stool that Preacher sometimes thought must have grown out of his ass, Danvers directed his officers by way of messengers. One of the latter saluted smartly and stepped hurriedly in Preacher's direction. Taken aback by the unreality of what he witnessed, Preacher stared in disgust. At last he found control of his vocal cords and stomped into the lodge, Antoine right behind. Danvers's high-pitched voice elevated more in complaint.

"I don't understand why we have not heard from the north side of the village. Has Captain Dreiling taken leave of his senses?"

Preacher stepped in front of the colonel then and spoke with an obvious effort to control his loathing. "Might I suggest, Colonel, that if you were out there, where the fighting is goin' on, you could learn firsthand what is going on and why. You might even be able to personally direct your subordinates, which would free up all these messenger-boys to take part in the battle."

Danvers tried to wither Preacher with his most contemptuous stare. "That's what company commanders and platoon leaders are for," he told Preacher coldly. "Company commanders are supposed to observe, supervise and direct."

That he failed to intimidate became immediately obvious. Preacher turned partway from the prim, icy-eyed colonel, then swung back, fists balled and eyes turned to steel. "My point is, Colonel, that you sure as hell can't see much cringing inside a tipi like a yeller-bellied cur."

He stomped to the entrance to the lodge and was bending to exit when a shrill roar came from Danvers, only to be drowned out by war cries and explosions of Hall carbines from outside. Preacher made for the fight at once.

Warriors from the other villages had to be in on this, Preacher reasoned correctly. Even if all sixteen of the braves involved in the torture and killing of the Dragoons lived in this camp, there simply weren't enough lodges to account for the number of Pawnee who surrounded the troops. A man usually figured three warriors to a lodge. By count of tipis, this village should account for some fifty-four warriors.

Hell, Preacher thought, that many had already been killed or knocked out of action. And, he recalled, the other two villages had been larger by half than this one. Ruefully he acknowledged that the sneaky Pawnee had gotten one up on him again. Time to worry about that later. Preacher took aim and shot a lance-wielding warrior off his pony. Quickly he reloaded his Hawken. There had to be a better way of ending this, he told himself.

During the next assault, an idea came to Preacher. When the lull that followed the charge extended far longer than the previous ones, he decided to put it to use. To do so, he sought out Antoine Revier. He found Antoine standing in the shade cast by a lodge, loading his pistols.

"Antoine, ol' friend, I think we're overdue in bringin' an end to this mess. Get that long-range Frenchie rifle of yours an' let's go out an' change the odds."

Antoine turned a beaming countenance on Preacher.

"I think I know what you have in mind. We should have done this sooner."

"They hadn't settled down enough. I'd say they was gettin' some grub right about now. Should work perfect."

Ten minutes later, Preacher and Antoine Revier slipped out of the besieged village and headed due east. A mile from the circles of lodges, they turned north, skirted the Pawnee flank and worked their way to within half a mile of the enemy. Both mountain men spent a tense fifteen minutes in concentrated study of the hostiles through long, brass telescopes. Satisfied that they had identified the proper individuals, they moved in a bit closer.

Being long-range sporting arms, both Preacher's Le Mat and Antoine's Alouette had been fitted with simple, unsophisticated telescopic sights. At ranges up to six-hundred yards, they could reasonably be expected to hit a man-sized target with every shot, and cause a fatal wound three out of five times. At least, in the hands of these expert marksmen that was possible. They used Y-shaped metal barrel rests that came with the weapons, carried in the stock, behind hinged butt-plates. After easing their way into suitable prone positions on a gentle upslope, they settled in and sought their targets.

Preacher found one first, took careful aim and pressed the set trigger. Then his finger curled around the firing trigger, and he fined his sight picture. A gentle squeeze and the .36-caliber rifle fired. At that range, he had the weapon clear of the stand and the old cap off the nipple before the head of a tall, wiry Pawnee with a face split by black and white war paint, snapped backward slightly and a geyser of gore spurted from the back of his crown.

Preacher had the powder charge rammed home by the time the other Pawnee reacted to the startling sight. Muffled by distance, the report of his Le Mat did not reach them until nearly two seconds after the ball that killed

one war leader. A stiff crosswind had disbursed the powder smoke. Confused as to how and from where this
blow had come, the Indians milled about, providing Antoine a target as easy as Preacher's had been.

His man went down rubber-legged a moment before
Preacher fired again. A third war leader died. "I reckon
one more each and we'd best get out of here," he advised
Antoine after the latter had fired his second shot.

"Mais oui. Or we will leave our hair with the Pawnee."

Their guns reloaded, they sought out fresh marks and
fired simultaneously. Another pair of war leaders
clutched their chests and keeled over, their hearts
pierced by deadly metal. Quickly, Preacher and Antoine
folded up their gear and crawled off through the tall
grass to where they had left their mounts on the far side
of the low swell.

Six most important men killed in less than three minutes
did it for the Pawnee. Muttering darkly about bad medicine, they abandoned the fight and rode off toward the
other nearby villages. Even the inexperienced Dragoons
knew that the battle had ended long before Preacher and
Antoine rode into the battered encampment.

Iron Shirt stood before the assembled councils of the
Northern Cheyenne. Many had journeyed far to hear the
message of the Blackfoot messiah. Not all, though, were
captivated by his promise to drive out the whites and
bring back the old days. Some, including Cloud Blanket,
privately believed, like the Crow, that some means must
be found to live alongside the whites in peace. Cloud
Blanket had heard appeals such as Iron Shirt's before.

They had failed to impress him then, and still did. He
winced as Iron Shirt reached the part about how his
secret medicine would make ordinary red men proof
against the white man's bullets.

"Not a man shall die of white bullets after joining in the ritual of the Iron Shield Society. Some of you may have heard of how some warriors died from the white man's many-balls gun. Recently the Spirit who guides us revealed to me what needs to be done to make my medicine proof against even these."

What nonsense, thought Cloud Blanket. At close range, a shotgun— yes, he knew the proper name for it— could bring terrible destruction. An old friend among the whites, Preacher, had once told him that it was the awful shock to the body from being hit so many times at once that killed. Unless, the mountain man had added, a man took a load in the heart or got his head blown off. Iron Shirt had reached the climax of his boastful speech, the exhortation to join.

"I want ten double-hands of brave Cheyenne warriors to step forward and become brothers in the Iron Shield Society. All is in readiness for the ritual. Those who do not join us are asked to leave now."

It heartened Cloud Blanket to see so many turn away. Yet, some eighty stood as though enchanted by the words of Iron Shirt. This would be a bad thing for the Cheyenne, Cloud Blanket admitted to himself. He turned to an old friend, Four Bears.

"I am thinking of moving my band toward the Black Hills. Iron Shirt is like a stick of green wood in a fire. It spits and pops and throws sparks in the air. But sparks are not a blaze . . . unless they land in your sleeping robes."

Four Bears nodded thoughtfully. "You are right. I will ask my people to do the same."

Back on the march again, the Dragoons seemed more confident and at ease, though somewhat subdued. Five of them had been killed; more than thirty took wounds.

Most bore only minor injuries, and wore their white swatches of courage with noticeable pride. The six serious cases rode in wagons, under the care of Major Claire Couglin, the company surgeon. Troubled by the condition of his charges, Major Couglin left the wagon in which he tended three of them, and on his dapple-gray mare rode to the head of the cavalcade.

"Colonel, I am greatly concerned for the recovery of the seriously wounded men. I urge you to slow our pace. At this rate of march, the wagons are doing more harm than the Pawnee did."

Danvers snorted. "Nonsense, Doctor. We need to put as much distance between us and the Pawnee as we can, in order to avoid any more such . . . incidents."

The balding Major Couglin raised his eyebrows in astonishment. "I'd hardly call a pitched battle an 'incident,' Colonel."

Danvers gave him a hard, level stare. "Officially, that is what it has to be. Otherwise, we might be charged with violating the treaty."

Couglin scratched his chin. "Preacher has given me to understand that it is highly unlikely we will have a repeat of hostilities."

Snorting, Danvers glared in disdain. "Preacher? What does he know about it, *Major* Couglin?"

In a quiet voice, the doctor added his clincher. "He's lived out here for thirty years."

It had little effect on Danvers. "I regret to inform you that we cannot slow the pace, Major Couglin."

The major bristled. "Need I remind you that in matters of the health and well-being of the troops, I have authority to supersede your decisions?"

Fire flamed in the eyes of Danvers. "Your objection is noted— and rejected. In the presence of hostiles, my decisions alone are binding."

Defeated, Couglin tried one final appeal. "At least, let

me have a suitable escort so that the wagons can proceed at a rate consistent with the best interests of the wounded."

Lieutenant Colonel Danvers relented. "Very well. You may have two platoons. This discussion is concluded."

From a short distance away, Three Sleeps Norris had overheard the entire exchange. He muttered to himself his heartfelt opinion of Lieutenant Colonel Arlington Danvers: "Heartless, miserable son of a bitch." Had he heard it, Norris knew, Preacher would have agreed.

FIFTEEN

Blooding the troops had side benefits born of their increased confidence. Preacher soon noted that the Dragoons' smart deportment made the old saw about forty miles a day solid reality. On one fine afternoon, he found the Medicine Bow Mountains on his left. He had seen their matte-black ramparts over the previous three days. Now sure enough they had gained the red-orange pinnacles covered with tall stands of lodge-pole pine, juniper and fir so dense that had the Black Hills of Lakota country not been seen first by white men, these would have borne that name. What Preacher did not expect was to come upon a mounted white man, who appeared suddenly out of one of the deep folds on the northeast face of the Medicine Bows.

A cry of surprise reached Preacher's ears a fraction of a second before the stranger energetically waved his arms in a show of peaceful intent. He spurred his horse and came on fast. Preacher urged Tarnation toward the approaching rider. Face alight with hope and relief, the newcomer reined up in a shower of turf.

"Mister, am I glad to see you. Thank the good Lord you've come at last. How many in your party?"

Preacher blinked and studied the man in an attempt to determine if he was addle-pated. "There's nigh onto two hundred."

That startled the stranger. "Lordy . . . lordy, that's the biggest wagon train I've ever heard of."

"Not a train. I'm guide for a squadron of Dragoons. Folks call me Preacher."

Face glowing with joy, Isaac Warner introduced himself, then added, "You have no idea how grateful we are to see you. Many of our people have given up hope."

Preacher rubbed his chin. "Maybe I should ask how many there are of you folk?"

"We number seventy-three souls, Mr. Preacher. Two of those are in danger of departing if we can't get medicine."

"It's jist plain Preacher, no mister about it. An' we've a surgeon along, so your sick can get help."

Warner raised his eyes to the sky. "Praise God, Preacher. Now we have a chance."

"That'll depend more upon Colonel Danvers than on me, I'm sorry to tell you, Mr. Warner."

Warner looked perplexed. "Surely he is a compassionate man. He'd not leave children stranded in this wilderness?"

Preacher pulled a long face. "Oh, it's entirely possible, Mr. Warner. To put the best light on it, he could be said not to have much use for what he calls 'civilians,' present company included."

"He's a harsh man?"

That had been amply proven with the flogging of the four Dragoons, to Preacher's way of thinking. "That's about the right of it."

"Wh-what sort of man can he be?"

"I'd say you would most likely say he resembled the north end of a southbound jackass."

That left Warner without a reply. After a moment, he broke the strained silence. "I had better show you to our encampment. Everyone will be so excited."

Preacher pulled a droll face. "Oh, I've no doubt of that. Even Colonel Danvers."

On the ride into the lush valley, Isaac Warner explained to Preacher how they had come to be abandoned in such an, as the pilgrim saw it, unforgiving land. When the perfidies of their guides and captain had been revealed, he concluded with a plaintive remark.

"So, we're not sure where we are, or how to get where we were going."

"Where might that be, Mr. Warner?"

"Why, the Northwest Territory, of course, to Oregon."

Preacher sighed regretfully. "You're about two hundred miles too far north for the Northwest Trace."

Warner frowned. "What's that?"

Preacher called on all his patience. "The trail you should have been on. The one folks are takin' to callin' the Oregon Trail."

"We're that far off?"

"Yep. And intentional, I'd judge. It's an old game. Lead a party out into nowhere, rob them and leave them for the coyotes and buzzards. I'm surprised they didn't take your livestock as well."

Warner shrugged. "I suppose we were too many, too well armed. They snuck away in the dead of night."

Preacher turned philosophical. "No accountin' for some folks." A moment later, the sheer volume of cheering, waving and hugging that greeted him left the mountain man utterly speechless.

"Absolutely not!" High as his voice might be, Lieutenant Colonel Danvers still managed a bellow. "Civilians," he spat out the word like an epithet.

"Complaining, dragging their feet, whining, they'll hold us back, make us a month late reaching our goal."

Preacher tried calming words. "Come, now, Colonel. We're only five to seven days from where you want to build that fine fort of yours. Even if they cut our daily advance in half, that's only two weeks."

Danvers slammed a small fist on the table. "I say leave them to their fate. They were fools enough to come out here without proper guidance, they should get what they deserve."

Chillingly, Preacher heard his own words thrown back in his face. He'd said the same thing at Bent's Fort. Coming out of the mouth of Arlington Danvers they sounded dirty and mean. That served to make him more determined.

His eyes narrowed as he pressed his argument. "Am I correct in believing that part of your purpose in being out here is to protect settlers moving through?"

Danvers paused before he fired off another hot retort. "Yes, yes, we have that assignment. It is secondary to keeping the tribes at peace."

Preacher cocked a brow. "Wouldn't it serve your purpose better to protect this partic'lar group of settlers? If you leave them here an' there's a massacre, the howl that's sure to go up back East will light a fire that'll singe your fingers way out here."

The colonel could not deny the truth in that. With a visible exertion of will, he toned down his demeanor. "Perhaps you are right, Mr. Preacher. Like it or not, I don't suppose I have any choice. Say, I thought you had short shrift for these immigrants?"

Shrewd ol' pup, Preacher thought silently. "Now, that's true. I've had me more'n one belly full of pilgrims. Damn fools the most of them. But that was then, and this is now. An' we got them on our hands. It's up to you an' me to do the best for them we can."

Danvers threw his hands in the air and walked away. Outflanked and defeated, he didn't want to admit it. Preacher spent no time gloating over his victory. Instead, he went directly to Isaac Warner. With Warner, he found a young woman. A particularly good-looking young woman.

"Preacher, this is Eve Billings. She and her two children have a wagon in our train."

Remembering his parlor manners, Preacher removed his hat and extended a hand. "Pleased to meet you, ma'am."

"Please, it is Eve. I came to find out what the colonel has decided."

Preacher found himself liking what he told her. "We're gonna escort you as far as we're goin'. When the fort is built, you can winter there and go south toward the Oregon Trace next spring, join another train."

In a gesture that harkened back to childhood, Eve clapped her palms together and did a couple of dance steps. "Oh, that's just wonderful. You're a . . . ah . . . minister?"

"No, that's jist what they call me in the High Lonesome." Preacher seemed uncomfortable to his friends. Three Sleeps sniggered.

"This calls for a celebration. I'm going to cook a regular feast for you and your fellow guides, Preacher. My son got us a deer today. You'll meet Charlie and Anna and . . ." Eve realized she was chattering and cut it off abruptly. "You'll be there? Good. An hour before sundown."

While his companions whooped and slapped each other on the back, Preacher stripped to the buff and entered the water of the Platte to wash away his accumulated grime. Following his ablutions, he dried, donned fresh, clean buckskins, tied back his hair with a strip of tanned rabbit hide, the fur still in place, and slid into his fancy pair of beaded and quilled moccasins. Three Sleeps and Antoine howled with laughter. They found his preparations uproarious.

Preacher did not share their mirth. "You two could stand a good douchin' off, ya know," he grumbled.

"Me? Three Sleeps gasped. "Why, I smell sweet as a May flower."

"Road apple's more like it," grumped Preacher.

Eve Billings greeted them warmly, an apron around her slender waist, a big spoon in her hand. "We have venison stew, and I made pot pies from the kidneys and sweetbreads. You must take some along for your nooning tomorrow. Ah, here are the children," she gushed, then gulped back her flow of words and proceeded at a slower pace. "Preacher, Mr. Norris, Mr. Revier, this is Charlie. He turned ten two months ago. This is Anna. She's eight. Children, these are our guides, who are going to find a way out of here for us."

"I hope they're better than Mr. Beecher."

"Charles Billings, you watch that mouth of yours," his scandalized mother cautioned.

Preacher squatted to put himself on Charlie's level. "Don't you think it'ud make a body cross-eyed, watchin' his own mouth? Without a lookin' glass, that is."

Charlie had a giggle fit, and Eve surrendered in the presence of these carefree men who obviously knew this country so well. By the time she served up supper, with the help of Anna, Preacher and Charlie were fast friends. Eve exerted constant efforts to curb her babbling. To his companions, it soon became obvious that Eve had eyes for Preacher. She batted them at him throughout the meal. While totally oblivious to this, the object of her attentions enjoyed himself thoroughly.

* * *

During the next day's nooning, Lieutenant Colonel Danvers summoned Preacher back from point. "I trust you are aware we are making only half the speed today we did in the past two weeks," he said.

"Yep. That's what I said before. Half the pace will take us two weeks to make the Bighorn Mountains."

Danvers had a dire prediction. "It will get worse, mark me on that. With these wagons hanging on our backs, we will have all the problems and delays of any of their kind."

Preacher considered a moment. Ten miles a day would be disastrous for the pilgrims, too. Not to count the effect on the morale of the troops. Too many good-looking gals among the civilians. But not enough to go around.

"I can go to them and force more speed, but not a whole lot. And I think I can avoid a slowdown to ten miles a day. There are ways to trim time off all sorts of things."

"I certainly hope so," Danvers snapped.

Preacher went to where the immigrants cooked and ate at some distance from the soldiers. Several looked askance at him. Puzzled, he found a stump near the center of the circle of wagons. He jumped up on it and raised an arm to draw attention.

"Gather around, folks. There's some strips of stringy meat we've got to chaw on." When those who had finished their meal and those who had not started the cleanup had formed a semicircle around him, Preacher went on. "I've been told by the colonel that we're not makin' good enough time. He feels that the blame falls on you. Now, I don't take to that entirely. But there are some things you could do to speed us up."

Fully expecting it, Preacher at first absorbed the torrent of complaints and excuses that rained on him. "Our wagons will break down," Renard Labette objected.

"We can only move faster if we lighten our wagons."

"That means we'll have to abandon precious possessions," Martha Brewster blurted, near to tears.

Gus Beecher came up with what he thought to be the clincher. "It'll be too hard on our livestock. They'll start to die off."

Isaac Warner took a more personal outlook. "The soldiers will just have to move at a pace we can keep up with. It's their duty to protect us."

Preacher waited out the storm, arms across his chest. Then he jutted his jaw and laid out the alternatives. "Fact is, the soldiers do not have to do more than leave a small escort with you. They have their orders from the War Department. They have to carry them out. Colonel Danvers wants to leave you behind. He has every right to do that. If you can't keep up, if there are more delays, it will result in you being abandoned again. If that is the case, the Indians will find you. You won't be able to defend yourselves. Not even if the colonel leaves a company behind. On the other hand, if you exercise some imagination you will be able to keep up."

Fists on hips, Gus Beecher spat truculently. "Says you."

"Yes, says I. You have two choices; adapt and keep up, or be left behind."

Beecher wasn't ready to leave it alone. "Somethin' tells me we were better off before you came along. Might know you'd side with the Army."

Suddenly Eve Billings appeared beside Preacher. "Listen to him. He's fought hard against the colonel's determination to leave us to our fate. He must know lots of ways to help us save time."

Good girl! Preacher wanted to hug her. "That I do. For instance, buildin' fires and cooking meals at noon slows the whole column. From now on you might try cooking enough in the morning, or the night before, to provide for the noonin'. In this climate, meat cooked over a smoky fire will last several days. Biscuits will hold a week or more. If you have any cornmeal along, or dried corn that can be ground into meal, you can make mush.

"Warmed on a hot rock," he went on to explain, "it can be mighty tasty dipped in a little molasses at noon. Another thing, I see you have firewood slings under yer wagons. Send your kids along the route of march each day and have them collect deadfall. Stow it while yer rollin'. Then you don't have the hankering to stop early to gather wood. Those of you with spare draft animals, change 'em off at the noonin'."

"We still can't move as fast as the soldiers," Gus Beecher objected.

"Not unless you lighten your loads. An' I've already heard all the sad stories about grandma's treadle organ half a hundred times. For instance you, Mr. Beecher. I notice you have a whole lot of heavy iron things in your wagon."

"Of course. I'm a blacksmith."

"Thing is, it makes you lag behind the other wagons. I'd suggest you dump yer anvil and a lot of other stuff. They can be had off the ships that call on the Oregon country."

"I'll do no such thing. My life's work is in there."

Preacher planted a glower on his face and bent forward so he came eye to eye with Gus Beecher. "Mr. Beecher, you can either voluntarily lighten your load now, or you can have it done later by the soldiers at gunpoint."

Beecher turned red-purple. In a blink, he swung at Preacher's jaw. Preacher blocked the blow with steely fingers coiled around the offending wrist. He pivoted with the force of the swing and carried Beecher past him. All the while he squeezed tighter on the wrist. Beecher's hand opened and turned the same dark color as his face.

"Mind yer manners, friend. I've got no reason to give you real grief, unless you insist."

For all his great strength, the blacksmith could not

take control of the situation. Defeated in mind as well as body, when Preacher let him go, he stumbled through those gathered to listen and headed to his wagon.

"Sorry for the little interruption, folks. Like I was sayin', it's up to you. If you have any questions me an' my friends will be proud to help."

Snaking silently through the aspens, a large party of Blackfoot and Cheyenne, armed with the mystical power of Iron Shirt and aided by his modern rifles, closed on an Arapaho village. Located in the foothills of the Bridger-Teton Range, along Little Sandy Creek, the Arapaho band had long enjoyed a peaceful existence. That ended suddenly in the keening war cry of the Blackfoot leader.

Swift and deadly, the warriors swarmed in among the lodges to take women and children for slaves, horses to build their importance in their tribes. Only belatedly did the Arapaho men begin to offer resistance.

SIXTEEN

Screaming, a portly Arapaho woman ran behind a brood of frightened children. She shooed them before her like a flock of chickens. Suddenly she stumbled and lurched forward when the head and half of a lance shaft entered her back between the shoulder blades and burst out her chest in a welter of scarlet droplets. Yipping his triumph, the Blackfoot warrior who had run her down yanked his weapon free and turned to overtake another fleeing Arapaho.

"This is easier than we thought, Black Hawk," he shouted to a companion.

Black Hawk agreed. "The Arapaho have become women. They do not fight."

"They do not have these fine new rifles, Gray Otter."

Gray Otter's face clouded a moment. "Yes. That is true, but the fancy-dressed soldiers have even better weapons than we do. They load without a ramrod, and fast, too. They punished us badly three suns ago."

Black Hawk copied Gray Otter's frown. "Men died. Is the medicine of Iron Shirt not as strong as he claims?"

Gray Otter spoke what would, under other circumstances, be considered blasphemy. "I do not think his is good medicine at all. For all its power, it seems to follow the way of the dark spirits."

Black Hawk looked worried. "Do not let Iron Shirt

hear you say that. He will have you stripped of the medicine and made a target for all men."

For a moment Gray Otter could not believe what he heard. "Do you mean he would have me killed?"

Nodding thoughtfully, Black Hawk revealed something else to the new recruit. "It is possible. Iron Shirt has three white men for council. They wear our clothes, but they are white. I have seen them."

"Then what do we do, Black Hawk?"

"Fight, and watch. The Great Spirit will show us what to do when the time comes."

More screams attracted their attention, and they turned to join in the final roundup of the children. In the distance, the stolen pony herd kicked up a dense fog of dust. Flames flickered from several lodges. Moments later, a sharp, clear peal of brassy notes alerted Black Hawk and Gray Otter to an unexpected danger.

Preacher sent back word when he first heard the rifle fire. There should not be anyone out here, he reasoned. Twenty minutes later, he topped the ridge he now sat upon and looked down on what appeared to be an Arapaho village. What were they doing this far north? Never mind that for now, he decided. Another, bigger problem faced him.

Someone had attacked the Arapaho. Preacher could do nothing. He and the other two scouts could not turn the tide. A large force had swarmed into the village to kill, loot and carry off captives. In the distance he saw a large cloud of dust that had to be the pony herd. This would be a matter of waiting it out, or taking the entire battalion in to drive off the raiders.

To his credit, Lieutenant Colonel Danvers brought the column up smartly and wasted no time in bluster or examining options. "We'll deploy as skirmishers and charge. From the sound of those rifles, I'd say we have encountered some of the renegades we've been informed of."

"I reckon you're right, Colonel."

"Very well, Mr. Preacher— "

Preacher winced. "It's jist *Preacher,* Colonel."

"Yes, as I was saying, Mr. Preacher, take your fellow scouts and reconnoiter our route of approach."

"Which will be?"

"Straight down this slope and have at them."

A fleeting smile turned up the corner of Preacher's mouth. "Sounds good. The sooner the better, they're stealin' the children down there."

When it came, Preacher saw the charge to be every bit as awesome as the first time he'd witnessed it. It caught the looters and slavers by surprise and riveted many in place, their hands coiled in the braids of small girls and boys. Several died that way before the spell dissipated and the survivors raced for their ponies. A dozen courageous ones formed a rear guard while their companions removed the captives. Then they swung astride their mounts and whirled away across the prairie. For once, Preacher found Danvers ready for continued battle.

"We should go after them, chase the savages down."

"That's not all that good an idee, Colonel," drawled Preacher. "When troops split up and go in pursuit of a war party that size, there's good odds they'll be ambushed. Injuns love to run away, only to spring a trap. No, sir, if you don't want to wind up staked out like those fools who chased their horses, you'd best let the Blackfoot get away with their new slaves."

Three Crows Walking, a young Arapaho war chief, came up to the gathering of officers. He recognized the cut of the buckskin-clad trio, if not their faces. Accordingly, he addressed himself to them.

"The Blackfoot do not fight like themselves." Then,

in the best English he had, he repeated himself to make certain they understood. "The Blackfoot fight like crazy men. Not afraid of bullets, not afraid of arrows. Fight like Great Spirit watch over them. Crazy men."

Preacher nodded and cut his eyes to Danvers. "What is it you had on this Iron Shirt feller?"

"He is promising to drive out all whites, bring back the white buffalo. He is supposed to have some sort of magic that makes him bulletproof."

Not 'magic,' Colonel. Medicine. Powerful medicine," corrected Preacher. "An' I'm willin' to bet he's told his followers that if they keep to his ritual, maybe eat an' drink certain things, or don't eat or drink some others, they'll be jist like him. It's big stuff among the Injuns."

Danvers made a puzzled frown. "We've killed them, haven't we?"

"We've been fightin' Pawnee. These are Blackfoot, accordin' to . . . ah . . ."

"I am called Three Crows Walking."

Preacher nodded. "Accordin' to Three Crows Walkin'. And, accordin' to these here . . ." Preacher bent to retrieve two arrows with red paint markings. "There was some Cheyenne mixed in among 'em. This thing is spreadin', Colonel. I think you've got your first job already cut out for you."

More than you know, Lieutenant Colonel Danvers thought to himself. "Are you suggesting we interrupt our march to pursue, round up and punish these renegades?"

"Naw, Colonel. Nothin' like that. Partic'lar we got these pilgrims with us. We'll jist go along, keep a sharper eye and see what develops."

What about the behavior of these Blackfoot in the face of armed resistance? Have you ever encountered anything like that before?"

Preacher considered a moment. "Nope. Not personal.

I've heard of Injuns chargin' into the mouths of guns like that some while back. Comanche, it was, down south in Texas. They had them a war chief name of Iron Shirt, jist like this one, who wore one of those Spanish iron breastplate things."

Captain Edward Dreiling stepped up to provide the correct term. "Cuirass. It's called a cuirass."

"Whatsomever, he could stop a ball from a flintlock musket, even some of the earlier caplock rifles. Feller who stopped him, he was a Texas Ranger, shot him right betwixt the eyes. His medicine didn't work too good against that."

Captain Dreiling had a question, which the colonel should have asked. "Preacher, do you think that is the answer in this case?"

"Sure enough. If you can get these grass-green youngsters to hold steady and hit what they aim at. Now, we'd best be doin' what we can for the survivors. Most special, that includes a big pot of coffee."

"Very well. Then we will push on in the morning."

Eve Billings hastily removed her stained apron and dabbed at a smudge of flour on her nose. She rinsed her hands and walked quickly to where the guides had their small gathering, putting on her best smile and patting back a stray strand of auburn hair. When the men looked up from the coffee they shared with two fierce-looking Indians, she repressed a shudder and spoke lightly, trying not to reveal in her tone the importance the invitation held for her.

"Preacher, it would greatly please me if you would take supper with my children and myself this evening." Before he could make reply, she stumbled on. "There will be another guest. Captain Edward Dreiling has graciously accepted an invitation."

Preacher rolled that around in his head a moment. "Well now, there's a couple of things I'd like to take up with him, he bein' the only officer in that outfit with a lick of sense. I thank you for the invite, and I'll be pleased to be there. What time?"

"Oh, say an hour before sundown. I've made a dried apple pie."

"Yer a treasure, Miss Eve. I'll bring along a little jug to wet our whistles." Preacher gave her a big wink.

After she departed, Three Sleeps Norris and Antoine Revier rolled on the ground, holding their sides in merriment. "Well, lah-di-dah! Formal invites from the little lady," Norris choked the words out over laughter.

"Best look out," advised Antoine. "She's set to make you the rooster in her henyard."

For a moment, Preacher looked thunderstruck, contemplating the future *that* promised. He rejected the notion out of hand. "I don't believe that for a minute. Naw, sir, not for a minute. She's only bein' friendly."

Antoine would not let it go. "Last time, when we all went, *that* was being friendly. Mark me, Preacher, she's got her cap set for you."

Preacher remained adamant. "Not by a long shot. You wait and see. That gal's jist bein' nice."

Preacher timed his arrival at Eve's wagon to coincide with that of Captain Dreiling. Eve greeted them warmly, showed them to straight-back chairs she had dug out of her household goods and had had Charlie dust to a suitable turn. Playing the good hostess, she accepted a very watered-down whisky from Preacher. The mountain man and the Dragoon officer took theirs straight and tall.

"Are we far from where you are going?" Eve asked to make conversation.

"Only a week or so, give or take a few days," Preacher responded, distinctly uncomfortable after the ragging given him by his companions.

"I must admit, I am grown quite weary of living in a wagon. What will it be like going on to the Oregon Country?"

Edward Dreiling smiled weakly at Eve Billings. "I'm afraid I can't help you there. Army travel is quite different."

"As I have observed," Eve answered, then added to soften the snippy sound of her words, "Riding free and easy on a horse, living in a tent. It seems so . . . romantic."

"Believe me, Miss Eve, it is far from that," Dreiling felt compelled to advise her. "Even for us, accustomed to going on horseback, it took a week after leaving the steam packets to rid ourselves of saddle sores."

Eve's light laugh rang musically. "My, sir, the image that presents. Should I be scandalized?" she asked rhetorically. "No, I think not."

As the evening progressed, Eve flirted with them both outrageously. She secretly wanted to strike sparks of jealousy from Preacher. To all outward appearances, her plan failed miserably. Preacher was charming and gracious, and entertained all present with tall tales of his trapping years. When the time came to end the gathering, Charlie asked permission to accompany Preacher to his fireside.

Once the boy had the mountain man out of earshot of his mother's wagon, he crooked an index finger to draw Preacher down to his level. Preacher hunkered down. Then Charlie spoke earnestly, in a low whisper.

"You'd best look out, Preacher. My mom's tryin' to kindle the fires of romance in your heart. I know so, 'cause I heard her tellin' Mizus Honeycutt."

A low chuckle came from Preacher's throat. "Why,

shucks, son, I know that. Women have been hatchin' such schemes since the first Eve kissed a snake."

Charlie widened his eyes in shocked indignation. "But, don't you just hate it? How can you abide a woman who'd sneak about and plot behind yer back?"

"No problem at all. Truth is I sorta hanker after the affection of a pretty woman now and again. That ain't all that bad, is it?"

Hesitant, Charlie studied his toes. Given his age, his first response was predictable. "Girls ain't good for anything." He paused, considered a moment. "No . . . I guess not," he replied. "If— if you don't mind."

"How about you, son? Would you object to my bein' around your momma somewhat?"

Feet forgotten, Charlie glanced up with a bright, happy expression. "Oh, no, sir. Not at all. I'd like to have you around more."

"Well, then, don't let all of it fret you. Ol' Preacher can manage for himself right enough. Now, good night."

Early the next morning, the Dragoons prepared to move on. The wails of the mourning Arapaho women, those few who were left, trembled in the air. Tight-faced, Three Crows Walking and five braves, one slightly wounded, came to Preacher.

"If you would have us, we would come with you, help to scout. Maybe we find the ones who did this."

Preacher hid his smile behind a pensive pose, hand over his mouth. "Now, I don't know about that. You'd have to provide eats for yerselves. Army won't feed you. Won't pay you, either. But, I might find a few coppers, some silver you can rub together when this is over."

Comprehension brightened the face of Three Crows Walking. "You would pay us? White man's wampum?"

"You do a good job, I sure will."

Three Crows Walking explained to his fellow Arapaho and they all produced expressions of eager approval. With that settled, they mounted the ponies they had managed to save and fanned out ahead of the column which was forming. They rode out of sight to the northwest.

Preacher gave them half an hour, then he and his companions mounted, ready to set off. But not before Lieutenant Colonel Danvers had his say. "Mr. Preacher, I trust you have made it entirely clear to the immigrants that the same fate as befell these peaceful Arapaho will be theirs if they fail to keep up?"

Preacher could not keep his disregard for Danvers out of his expression. "They've got eyes. I didn't need to put it quite that way. They'll keep up, be sure of that."

For all his assurances, by nine o'clock in the morning, a considerable gap had developed between the Army freight wagons and the civilian train. Something about the specter of the Arapaho village must have influenced Isaac Warner. He became more aggressive in setting the pace for the cumbersome vehicles. Constantly, he urged greater speed. At times his shouts to his mules could be heard far ahead by Preacher, in the stillness of the high plains.

By the nooning, it took only ten minutes for the pilgrim train to catch up to the Dragoons. After stretching their legs and working the kinks from their backs, the civilians ate in the shade of the Conestogas and drank water to wash down the food. Warner actually had his charges ready to depart before the soldiers had completed their meal.

To Preacher's surprise and satisfaction, he calculated they had made fifteen miles. shortly after Preacher and Antoine Revier took their places ahead of the column, which had gotten under way without complaint or delay, a faint ripple of gunfire came from the rear. Preacher had a sinking sensation that it was not hunters out to bag fresh game for the evening meal. His suspicion was verified shortly when a messenger came pounding up from the head of the column.

"The Blackfoot. They've come back."

SEVENTEEN

Warriors of the Iron Shield Society raced their ponies along the high-sided wagons of the immigrants. Fired with confidence by the medicine of Iron Shirt, they abandoned any of their usual caution. It came as a total surprise to two of them when young Davey Honeycutt leveled his side by side, 10-gauge Greener and pumped thirty 00 buckshot pellets into them.

Instant fire erupted in the lungs and belly of the first Indian Davey shot. Shock-borne blackness swept over him and he slumped forward onto the neck of his churning pony. The right side of his chest and face shredded, his jaw hanging from a single hinge, the other Blackfoot flew off his mount when Davey loosed his second load.

Ahead of the Honeycutt wagon, rifles began to crackle as the well-armed Blackfoot poured a stream of lead into the stout vehicles of the immigrants. After several confused minutes, it appeared the hostiles would buy an inexpensive victory. Eve Billings had been caught up in the middle of the fighting. Huddled low behind the three-inch-thick oak sideboards of the Conestoga, she made good use of the Model 40 Bridesburg Arsenal rifle and a shotgun. Hunkered beside her, Charlie industriously reloaded and handed the weapons to his mother as she fired at the Indians.

"Faster, Charlie, there's a whole lot of them out there."

"Sure, Mom, I know that." He paused in the act of ramming a ball home in the Model 40 as a warrior leaped at the open front of their wagon.

Swiftly, Charlie snatched up his .36-caliber squirrel rifle and popped a cap on the invader. A small, black hole appeared in the left side of the Blackfoot's chest and his grip on the dashboard relaxed. Screaming, he fell under the steel-tired wheel on the right front.

"Oh, sweet Jesus, Mom, I shot him," Charlie wailed.

Eve didn't consider this the time for commiseration. "Good boy."

Control came out of the confusion as Preacher and his companions, accompanied by Captain Dreiling and some of his company, turned back and fell on the Blackfoot. The hostiles saw them coming and those in the lead on both sides of the column reined in sharply. Several fired at the soldiers, while others reared their mounts and turned about. Few cared to run the gauntlet of the settlers again, yet the prospect of clashing with the soldiers held even less appeal. Preacher quickly pointed out their apparent milling confusion and hesitation.

"We got 'em bottled up betwixt us," he shouted to Captain Dreiling.

"Looks like it. I only hope those amateurs know enough to shoot at the Indians and not us."

Preacher quickly allayed his concern. "We'll be pushin' the Blackfoot hard. Likely those pilgrims won't have time to shoot at anyone."

Within a breath's span, the mountain man and those with him clashed directly with the hesitant Blackfoot. Their faltering ceased abruptly when face-to-face with the white troopers. Unable to reload, the Blackfoot soon discovered themselves to be at a terrible disadvantage. Armed with a dozen immediate shots each from the big Dragoon pistols, the soldiers blazed into the faces of the enemy. Preacher, too, unlimbered his Walker Colt and

fired point-blank into the eagle wing-bone breastplate of
a screaming warrior.

Another came at him, screaming defiance, tomahawk
raised. Preacher turned to meet the threat.

Short Tail and three others took the brunt of the Dragoon charge on the opposite side from Preacher. Led
by Three Sleeps Norris and Antoine Revier, the soldiers
under the command of Lieutenant Brice swept along the
rear of the Army column and caught the Blackfoot by
surprise. Short Tail made to swing away, only to find his
way blocked by a grinning man in buckskin.

"Gonna run out on yer friends, eh?" Three Sleeps
asked Short Tail in incomprehensible words.

"May your mother's Entrance to the World, through
which you came, rot and fall off," Short Tail cursed back
in Blackfoot.

Three Sleeps knew only enough Blackfoot to catch the
drift of the insult. "I love you, too, you horse's patootie."
Then he shot the tomahawk wielder through the breastbone.

An expression of consternation and disbelief washed
over the warrior's face. How could this be? He is a white
man, his bullets can do no harm. A moment later Short
Tail learned that the truth ran radically contrary to his
belief.

Three Sleeps sidestepped his mount as the Blackfoot
fell dead at the side of his pony. He turned in the saddle
and triggered off the second barrel of his pistol. The
big, .60-caliber ball shattered another brave's shoulder
joint, rendered his left arm useless and sent his pony in
a frightened sideways dance ending in a frantic dash
away from the sounds and smells of battle.

Two Moons witnessed the swift, sure deaths of eight
of his warriors. Quickly the number of wounded

mounted to thirteen, with another two dead. He could not believe that this could be happening. What of Iron Shirt's medicine? Had the shaman lied to them, deceived them as to how much power his rituals, dances and dunkings in the river contained? In a tortured half minute, fanatic belief changed to repudiation. Hooting the recall signal, Two Moons rallied his warriors and led the way from the sure and certain death that prowled among them at the hands of the bluecoats and their plainsfolk allies.

Charlie Billings stood on the outside edge of the night camp, legs widespread, body bent forward and down. His stomach cramped, lurched and shot forth another spew of bitter, slimy liquid. Tears of shame and misery coursed down his face. The misery came from his appalling sorrow over having taken a human life. The shame came from his reaction to what he had done.

He had actually killed one Blackfoot, shot him right through the heart. He had wounded two others; one of them had spewed blood from his mouth as he fell away from the wagon.

God, this is awful! Whimpering like a sissy, Charlie thought desperately. How could he ever face himself, or anyone else, again? He tensed as he heard the rustle of a footfall in the leaves behind him.

"Takin' it hard, are you, son?" The warm, gentle voice of Preacher flowed over the boy who fought to hold back a sob of relief.

Misery returned in an instant. "Don't look at me."

"Why not, Charlie? D'you think you're the first and only man who's been upset by killin' someone?"

Preacher's praise— he had called Charlie a *man*— was unmarked by the boy. "Yeah, but, I'll look like a sissy to everyone, *especially you.*"

" 'Yeah, but,' "— Preacher put the words back on the boy— "do you think I didn't puke my guts out the first time I killed a man? An' I was four years older than you."

Amazement arrested Charlie's anguish for a moment, "You did? You were?"

Preacher took a slow step forward, reached down and put an arm around the boy's shoulders. Gently, he raised him to an upright position. "Yes. You might not believe it to see me now, but I went through everything you're experiencing. Trust me, it's never an easy thing. You saved your mother's life, and your sister's. You should stand tall Charlie, be proud. Yer a man now."

Charlie blinked his dark eyes. "I am? I mean . . . I am. I really am. I . . . I . . . ah . . . thank you, Preacher. I was so scared. I wanted to throw up all the time we were fighting. I wanted to run away and never hear a gun go off again."

"That's natural."

"But I . . . thought there wasn't that much difference between killing an animal or a man. That it would be easy."

Preacher patted him affectionately. "You had best thank yer God it wasn't easy for you. Those what find it like snappin' their fingers are plum crazy. They're bound to meet a bad end."

"Really?"

"Yeah. I oughtta know. I've brung more of 'em to that bad end than I care to count. Now, come on, yer maw has supper ready."

After the meal, Eve confided in Preacher. "That was the worst thing that's ever happened to us. Those . . . those Indians didn't seem to care. They kept coming, no matter how many of us shot at them."

"They believe themselves to be bulletproof. It's some

crazy, Injun medicine thing," he dismissed the fanaticism of the followers of the Blackfoot messiah.

"Please, don't misunderstand, Preacher. It's not that I fear for myself. It's only . . . only if some harm came to my children I could not bear that. I've heard the stories. H-How the savages use children in horrid practices. They have their way with girls as young as seven. Anna is eight. Some, I've been told, even use boys in the same manner."

Keyed to the intensity of her emotion, Preacher could still not refrain from being truthful. "I've never seen or heard of such-like happening to the younger children. An' it's only a few tribes practice such vile things. Mostly, the younger ones, like Charlie and Anna, are used as slaves, or to take the place of a child who has died for one reason or another. Especial if the kids show some spirit. Why, the way Charlie fought off those warriors, he'd be a prize to them Blackfoot. One of them would adopt him, certain sure, an' have him in a loincloth and moccasins, with a pony of his own, an' his hair in a braid in no time."

That prospect registered more horror on the face of Eve Billings than the possibility of abuse and eventual murder. Quickly, she put her emotions into words. "What a terrible fate! How could he possibly endure such a miserable life?"

He'd take to it like ducks to water, Preacher wanted to tell her, but refrained from doing so. "You gotta understand, men are kings amongst the Injuns, even when they're little kids. Most boys who are captured don't want to give it up when they've got the chance. They have ponies of their own, which makes for how rich a body is among the savages, and they learn to use a bow, set snares, all sorts of things civilized folk have forgotten how to do."

In a sudden shift of mood, Eve nervously tittered, then spoke. "That's not exactly reassuring, Preacher. You've described my Charlie exactly."

Preacher showed surprise; then his lips turned down. "Well, I was only tryin' to show you that somethin' else could be at hand in such an event."

"And bless you for it. It's only . . . only that I— I'm so frightened for my children."

Although he still did not fully understand, Preacher recognized her position and acted with alacrity. When tears brimmed in her eyes, he took her protectively into his arms to calm her trembling. Eve let go then. She stifled harsh sobs against his broad shoulder. Unconsciously, she pressed her body tightly against his.

Awkwardly, Preacher stroked her long, auburn hair, circled her trim waist with a strong, reassuring arm. Instead of tensing, as did so many women in the arms of a powerful man, Eve melted into his chest. Slowly her sobs diminished, grew less violent, to finally cease. She gasped for air and fought inwardly to regain composure.

Her eyes still shone from the recently shed tears when she tilted her head upward to gaze into Preacher's eyes, alight with concern. At a loss for words of appreciation, Eve rose on tiptoe and placed her lips on those of Preacher. It started out as an expression of gratitude, then quickly changed into a long, hungry kiss that sent tendrils of fire through both of them.

When it ended, both were breathless. Eve said not a word, only freed herself from Preacher's embrace and hurried into her wagon. His lips tingling, Preacher walked off to his blankets, thoroughly confused. That had been the best kiss he had shared in . . . what? Maybe ten years? Yeah, that was it. There had been that Cheyenne gal . . .

Camped alone for the first time in six months, Praeger, Gross and Reiker experienced an overpowering sense of relief and safety. They paid little attention to the splendor of the Bighorn Mountains. What commanded their concentration glowed dully in the light of a coal-oil lantern. Its main attraction centered on size. Fully as large as the third knuckle of Praeger's middle finger, the gold nugget lay on a square of black velvet that perfectly set off its splendor. Praeger reached out and caressed its smooth, warm surface. Then he nodded to the chunk of gold.

"It weighs a bit over six ounces."

Avarice glowed in the eyes of Morton Gross as he spoke. "Where did it come from?"

"The area I told you about before. It came out of the Lolo Range of the Rocky Mountains, near the Continental Divide. There are more like this, lots more," Praeger assured his partners.

A sudden rustle at the tent flap drew their attention and Quinton Praeger quickly concealed the nugget. Blake Soures, dressed in Blackfoot garb, entered. "The men are ready to ride out, Mr. Praeger."

"Where this time?"

"There's a clutch of Psalm Shouters nestled down to the east of here. Near the headwaters of the Tongue River. I figgered we ought to pay 'em a visit. We'll leave enough living behind to swear it was Blackfoot who did it."

Praeger beamed and came to his boots to shake the hand of Soures. "Excellent. Be sure that no one knows you are white men. That could be a disaster."

Brother Frankel could not sleep. He sat alone by the dying embers of the central fire in the circle of wagons. Behind him, the mules and horses of their wagon train milled about in drowsy stubbornness. None wanted to lie down and sleep. Like himself, the good brother thought.

Not a man familiar with the ways of horses, Brother

Frankel failed to note when the animals became silent at the soft whuffle and stamp of hoof from the most dominant beast. Two more laid back ears and stomped the ground in warning. Still it went unnoticed by him. Reacting as though to an invisible pressure from beyond the circle, the livestock began to move inward. They exerted increasing pressure on the single strand of rope that restrained them.

At last, Brother Frankel looked up, affected by the unrest that emanated from the usually placid creatures. A yellow-orange streak suddenly arced through the blackness of night. A shooting star, Brother Frankel thought at first. While he was in the process of eliminating that due to its closeness to the ground, three more arcs of fire fluttered through the air. Two struck a wagon's side and the canvas top burst into flame. Jerkily, Brother Frankel came to his boots. Throat churning, he fought to get out the words.

"Indians! We're under attack. God protect us."

For two long minutes nothing happened. Brother Frankel continued to cry the alarm, though with little response. Then six burning brands shot through the night and struck two wagons. Shouts of alarm came from the three burning Conestogas. From beyond the crude stockade came raw yelps— war cries— followed by a steady stream of war paint-decorated savages who flowed into the unprotected center. One, armed with a rifle, took time to aim and fire a bullet at Brother Frankel. It pierced his skin low in the belly. He went down with a shriek of incredible agony.

By then, his fellow evangelists had roused from the stupor of sleep. Yelling in fright, the men and women poured from their rolling homes to spill onto the ground. There they cowered in the dirt, quaking in absolute terror. They died that way, cut down by arrow, tomahawk or bullet. Screaming children, the younger

ones, peered out over tail gates to have their brains
dashed out by war clubs and already bloody 'hawks.

Only at one point did some resistance show. The train
captain, scouts and cook took up firearms and fought a
desperate, no-win engagement. By the light of burning
wagons they clearly saw their enemy. The attackers
looked to be Blackfoot, the experienced frontiersmen
agreed. Three of the savages died in less than a minute
after the trained men returned fire.

"Stupid goddamned fools, I told them they needed
guns out here," the captain spat out in useless anger.

"Lot of good that would do," the cook retorted.
"Chances are, they'd try to pray these heathen scum into
peacefulness." He took careful aim with a Hawken and
shot another Blackfoot off his feet.

"Ain't no prayin' gonna get us out of this," a surly
guide scoffed.

More howling Blackfoot shoved into the melee. The
horses and mules had broken free and added another
hazard to the confused struggles of the nonviolent missionaries. It did not take the invaders long to subdue the
wagon folk. The slaughter was fierce and methodical.
When it ended, the only evangelists left standing consisted of the nubile girls, those newly ripe, and those not
long in that state. Under the rough direction of one big,
burly savage, they were herded aside.

Once the livestock had been gathered and corralled
again, the raping began. The screams and wails, sobs
and moans of the young victims filled the night, bearing
witness to the unending horror of the brutalized girls.
Unnoticed, one of the guides, the cook and the captain
slipped away into the night while the raiders wallowed
in their lust. One of the rapists, who would be heard by
no one in the attacked party who would be left alive,
commented on the object of his bestial attention.

"Mighty sweet. I sure do thank you, Blake, for lettin' me be first to pleasure myself with this one."

"Think nothing of it," Soures responded. "You did a good job, you deserve a reward."

When the gang of murderous whites had expended their churning appetites, they fired all the remaining wagons, took the livestock and rode off. Blake Soures made certain that ample items of Blackfoot manufacture remained to be discovered by those who found the remains of the unfortunate missionaries.

EIGHTEEN

Lieutenant Colonel Danvers counseled with Preacher and the mountain men at noon the next day. "We are to turn northward after our mid-day meal and head for the Powder River. Our objective, as I have explained before, is where the Powder cuts through the lower foothills of the Bighorn Mountains."

One long, soft, artist's finger pointed to a spot on the crude map. "Right here. There's supposed to be an ideal bluff on which to build the fort."

Preacher knew the country well. He studied the indicated location, gave it several moments' thought, then shook his head. "Nope. I wouldn't recommend it. Trees are scarce in those parts."

"Why, I've been assured the trees grow right down onto the bluff."

"May well be true. But, after you build your fort, you'd be required to go outside every day or so for firewood. An' another thing. From what this map shows, that bluff is exposed to higher ground on all but one side. Well, one side, an' part of a second. A feller could fire right down into the fort. Won't matter much for a while. Only consider this: what happens when the Cheyenne get their hands on some of those new rifles like we took off the Blackfoot t'other day?"

Danvers raised his voice. "That is not your concern. Your job is to see we get there."

"True. Only pointin' out some things. Like for instance, unless you don't want to dig a well down sev'ral hundred feet, you'd have to take the livestock out daily to water at this little creek that feeds into the Powder, an' haul more water to have some for people."

"That's nonsense. You don't know what you're talking about. I've been given assurances from the United States Survey Office, backed up by the highest authority. They have assured me there is ample wood for lumber— and for cooking and heating— lush grass and easy access to water."

Preacher agreed readily. "Sure, so long as you don't rile the Injuns. That's Cheyenne country, an' the land of their cousins the Sioux. Now, they don't look on owning land the same way we do, but they're mighty territorial jist the same. An' I ain't even mentioned the Crow and Blackfoot."

Danvers loftily dismissed that argument. "Savages are savages. We will be prepared to take them in stride. Let it suffice that this is the location chosen at the War Department, and it is where we will build."

All through the next day, Preacher and his companions found plentiful Indian sign. It took little time to come to the obvious conclusion. They were being watched. Three Crows Walking returned to the column to report the same.

"What do we do now?" the Arapaho war chief asked.

Preacher had an answer ready. "Make real certain of every lump you see on the ground. Some of them might breathe." Three Crows nodded knowingly. "Also, I'd have my weapons at hand ever' minute. Never can tell."

"My thoughts exactly. We already keep watch on dust clouds in the sky."

Preacher reached over and clapped the Arapaho on

the upper arm. "Good man, Three Crows. With you as
our eyes out front, we don't need to worry."

For the rest of the afternoon Preacher rode along in
higher spirits, though not oblivious to the plentiful sign
of a Blackfoot presence. After camp had been made for
the night, he walked away from the bustle of soldiers
and pilgrims to find a little solitude for himself. He had
only pulled a twisted, black, dry-cured cigar from the
pocket of his buckskin shirt when he looked up and spotted three Cheyenne warriors on horseback. Silhouetted
against the ruddy ball of the setting sun, they sat at ease,
one bent forward with a hand on his bare knee.
Preacher's eyes narrowed as he studied them.

Each wore two feathers at the back of his head, the
frizzed and fox fur-trimmed tips pointed upward, a sure
sign of being on the war trail. Slight motions of the
watching Indians revealed that they both carried lances.
Preacher jerked his gaze away from the Cheyenne at the
sound of a footfall behind him. He turned cat-quick,
with a hand on the butt of a Walker Colt.

Little Charlie Billings stood there, eyes wide with
shock at the swift movement of Preacher. He swallowed
hard and rubbed a bare foot against his overalls leg. "It's
only me," he squeaked.

"Sorry, Charlie. Somethin' out there spooked me."

For the first time, the boy looked beyond Preacher.
His eyes went round and white, and his jaw clapped shut.
Before he could speak, he had to swallow hard.

"Are those Injuns Blackfoot?"

"Nope, Charlie. They's Cheyenne. An' done up for
war. No reason to keep the truth from you. Yer man
enough to handle it, an' I trust, man enough not to
spread alarm amongst the rest of you pilgrims."

Charlie nodded solemnly. "Yes, sir."

Preacher clapped the boy roughly on the shoulder,
nearly dislodging Charlie from his feet. "Good. You do

me proud." No one who observed them, except his
mountain man cronies, would have suspected how much
discomfort Preacher experienced relating to small children. "Now, Charlie, what did you come out here for?"

"Mom told me to ask you to come to supper tonight."
Charlie looked unhappy. "But now, with those Injuns
out there, I don't suppose you can."

The prospect of a good meal, and good-looking com-
panionship, pleased Preacher. "I don't see why not.
Only, if I were you, Charlie, I'd sleep with your shotgun
beside you tonight."

Dressed in white men's suits, Quinton Praeger, Morton Gross and Aaron Reiker sashayed into the most ele-
gant saloon that graced a large, prosperous trading post
on the south fork of the Powder River. All three paid
token deference to current custom with the wide,
brightly colored sashes around their middles. That the
red one worn by Praeger, the green cloth strip on Gross,
and the electric blue chosen by Reiker concealed at least
one pistol each was a given. Several roughly dressed individuals at the bar gave them cold, inhospitable stares
as they took a table to one side.

"Friendly sort, aren't they?" Morton Gross observed
fastidiously. "Two months back they fell all over us, offering to buy the drinks."

Praeger shrugged. "We were dressed like they are
then. I doubt if they recognize us, let alone remember
how hard they tried to be hired on to work with Soures."

Reiker sighed. "We had us some times then, didn't
we?"

A huge man with greasy, long, black, curly hair and a
matching mustache pushed himself away from the bar
and turned in their direction. He had thick, rubbery lips
that shone wetly and made it obvious he had been drink-

ing heavily. Waving a huge, ham hand, he encompassed the well-dressed trio.

"Hey, fancy-boys, this here's a man's bar. They call me Dandy Spencer, an' I want you to know we don't allow no prissy Eastern folk to come in and spoil the at— at-mos . . ."

"Try *atmosphere*, my good man," Praeger suggested.

Spencer's face flushed dark red. "I ain't your 'good man,' nor any other's. I'm my own man and proud of it. Talk like that could get yer head busted out here."

"Are you challenging me, Mr. Spencer?" Praeger asked, his voice suddenly cold and menacing, although the tone went unnoticed by the bully.

Dandy Spencer rose on tiptoe and began to rock back and forth. "You goddamn' right."

"Well, then, since I'm the challenged one, I have choice of weapon, time and place, right?"

A puzzled frown creased the bull head of Dandy Spencer. "That's a mighty useless way to go about it, ya ask me. Around these parts, we jist open the dance and set to clawin'. You ain't got sand for that, turn tail and light out of here."

Quinton Praeger maintained an air of amiable civility. "Oh, I can understand the faint customs of such drunken louts as yourself without explanation, Mr. Spencer. My point is that I wish to make clear the terms of our duel."

"D-Duel? What duel?"

"Why, the one you challenged me to," Praeger tossed out lightly. The whitish cast in his right eye gave him a piratical mien.

Dandy could only splutter. "I didn't challenge you to a duel. I said I wanted to rip your sissy head off."

"Good enough. Same thing. You want to fight with me, I have agreed. Thus, the choice of weapons, place and time are mine. It's only fair."

Insulted, Dandy Spencer set things straight. "Ain't never fought fair in my life."

Praeger appeared unfazed. By far the toughest of the three partners, one more than willing to kill when necessary, the cold glint in his eyes betrayed to all but the dullest, which included Dandy Spencer, the hidden strength he possessed. "I can believe that. You want a fight, I accept. Now, I pick how we fight and when. I see you have a pistol, so I choose pistols. And for the time and place; right here and now!"

With which, Quinton Praeger snatched a short-barrel, fifty-caliber pocket pistol— made by Deringer and Sons in Philadelphia— from inside his sash, cocked it and put a ball into the right elbow joint of Dandy Spencer. Dandy, whom fate had decreed to be left-handed, completed his draw in spite of the pain that flared up his opposite arm. Gritting his teeth, he swung the muzzle in the direction of Praeger and triggered a round.

His ball went wide. Quinton Praeger let his empty pistol drop to the tabletop and whipped out a second deadly Deringer. This ball he put between two ribs, low on the left side of the chest of Dandy Spencer. A stentorian roar came from the huge man, who absorbed the fatal shot with all the outward sign of having been bitten by a mosquito. His coach gun hit the floor and Dandy groped for another one.

"This one's a bit hard to finish," said Praeger in an aside to his companions. By then, they had come to their boots and drawn pistols to cover the rest of the room. Praeger took a third pistol from partway around the sash and brought up the barrel.

By then, the message sent by his body reached the tiny brain of Dandy Spencer and informed him that he was dead. Shot through the heart, he went slack-legged and flopped forward over the table occupied by the conspirators. Praeger returned the pistol to its proper place and hailed the bartender.

"I say, we need someone to remove this trash. And I'll stand a round for the house."

"Yes, sir, anything you say, sir."

Dawn found everything safe and sound. The Cheyenne did not attack. Accordingly, the column set out again on what could best be described as an uneventful journey. So confident had Lieutenant Colonel Danvers become that he urged Preacher to ride at his side. Preacher found that not at all a pleasant prospect. While they rode along, Danvers waxed almost eloquent. Waving a gloved hand at the fluttering grass on the uptilted prairie slope, he drew a deep breath and launched into his theme.

"Those Cheyenne did not attack us, as you can now see. They sat quietly and watched us, without any show of hostile intent. Perhaps they were curious. With their childlike minds, that could be expected."

Knowing it to be rude, and not giving a damn, Preacher interrupted. "Them 'childlike minds' you refer to have planned and carried off some of the slickest ambushes you'll ever see. As to their 'hostile intent,' Colonel, them braves had their feathers upright. Those feathers are symbols of their valor. They're fixed in a beaded disc, and are worn in different directions for different reasons. Down, toward their left shoulder, means they're lookin' for no trouble. Down, to the right, says they're lookin' to do some courtin'. Up, like they had 'em, means they're ready for war.

"The biggest mistake most whites make about Injuns is that since they live different from us they ain't got any smarts." Preacher cocked his head to one side. "Never fall into that pit, Colonel. It could be the death of you."

Danvers had a pensive look. Albeit he spoke stiffly, his tone lacked the icy sarcasm of earlier exchanges. "Believe me, I've learned that lesson already. I still can't find a reason why the Pawnee were so hotheaded."

Preacher sighed. To him it was entirely obvious. "Because the Blackfoot and Cheyenne are worked up. There's war talk— and raids all over the high plains. For all their lack of modern communication, word gets around the tribes mighty fast."

Danvers retreated to his orders for inspiration. "Our purpose in being here is to induce a calming effect."

Preacher shook his head. "Seems to me we're doin' jist the opposite." For a long time, he could not fathom the meaning behind the enigmatic smile with which Danvers answered him.

In the short term, Preacher soon found himself with a lot more to occupy him. By midmorning, the column had made ten miles, a new record since adopting the abandoned wagon train. It had been accomplished with no end of grumbling by the pilgrims. When Gus Beecher cantered up to the head of the column for the third time, Preacher knew he was in for more.

"Blast and damn, this pace is killing my mules," the burly blacksmith complained. "You have to slow down."

The colonel would not deign to address whining civilians. Instead he cut his eyes to Preacher in a silent order to the mountain man to handle the situation. Preacher sighed and made reply.

"We don't have to do anything of the sort. I can't see a reason to have to explain this again, but here goes. This is a military expedition. It is under orders to git along the trail at the convenience of the Dragoon Battalion Commander. That be Colonel Danvers here. He says we gotta make better time, we make better time. You may not like it, I may not like it. But we ain't got any say in it. I told you before, Mr. Beecher, to get rid of some of that heavy load yerself or do it at gunpoint. If I was you, I'd hightail it back to that wagon and start heavin' heavy things out as you go."

"You can't do this to me. I— I'll protest."

Finally, Danvers bestirred himself to partake in the exchange. "To whom?"

"Wh-why to the War Department."

"Go right ahead," Danvers challenged in a brittle tone. "I estimate the next post will run through here in about fifty years."

Gus Beecher muttered that he would hold a meeting, circulate a petition. Lieutenant Colonel Danvers put on a nasty smile. "Oh, you do that, Mr. Beecher. I *love* to read petitions."

Instantly deflated, Beecher uttered a muffled curse and turned away. He had ridden halfway down the column when, suddenly, a force of over a hundred Blackfoot braves in war paint rushed down on the cavalcade from one side and the rear. Women and children, out gleaning deadfall firewood along the way, dropped their bundles and ran, screaming in terror. Rifles cracked among the Indians and a slight-built boy of twelve went sprawling. At once a shrill howl of anguish came from the rear of a wagon.

"My boy! They've killed my Jimmy."

An arrow thudded into the tail gate in direct line with her body and she was violently thrust back out of sight. Nearly every Indian had a rifle, which they fired at once, with much enthusiasm, albeit little accuracy.

NINETEEN

Whooping and howling, the Blackfoot rode just inside range and loosed a flight of arrows. Commands had been shouted up and down the files of Dragoons and the troops immediately responded with a furious volley.

"Reload!" More order came to the troops as their unseasoned officers gained control. "Volley by Companies! . . . Company A, take aim . . . fire! Reload. Company B, take aim . . . fire!"

So it went, down the line of the four companies. Forty rifles crackling in answer. Then, yipping, the Blackfoot rode away. A final volley raced after them. A dozen rifles fired a parting shot from the rear of the column and the Indians departed. Silence returned to the cavalcade, except for the sobbing of the woman whose son had been killed.

Their respite lasted only a short while. The hostiles swarmed down on their white enemy once more. This time the discipline drilled into them by Iron Shirt and his closest followers dissolved when six warriors toppled from their saddles. Hooting and shrieking war cries, the braves turned their charge into a scramble for individual honors.

It became a pigeon shoot for even the most inept Dragoons, a source of deep disillusionment for the Blackfoot as one after another of the braves fell dead from their ponies. Time enough had gone by to calm troops and civilians alike. They now brought withering fire on the hostiles. Preacher took time, while reloading, to pose a question to Danvers.

"Might be none o' my business, but I wonder why you didn't put out flankers today."

For an instant, the colonel stiffened; then he forced geniality into his voice. "You're right, it's none of your business. The truth is, I grew overconfident. Are these some of your friendly Cheyenne?"

"Nope. Blackfoot, though I'm damned if I can come up with a reason for them to be so far east. Unless . . . that prophet of theirs got them all riled up and is out smokin' the war trail."

Danvers spoke darkly, as though privy to some secret. "That had better not be the case."

Dangerously close to the wagons, within twenty-five yards, the Blackfoot lost their nerve at last. They scattered up a red-orange slope, so many coppery leaves in a whirlwind. Bullets followed them, though only Preacher's, his companions', and BSM Muldoon's scored in flesh. Not to be daunted, Danvers issued fateful orders.

"First and Second Platoon, C Company, pursue the enemy. Lieutenant Brice in command. Move 'em out!"

"I woul—" Preacher made to dissuade the Dragoon commander, then cut off his words at sight of the wild light in the colonel's eyes. Stubborn man, Preacher thought, let him learn the hard way.

With a full platoon at left and right, Lieutenant Brice led the charge from the middle. The big, powerful Dragoon horses churned up the rise and hesitated only a fraction of a second before plunging down the reverse slope. They had barely gone out of sight when all hell broke loose.

Preacher did not wait for the realization to come over Danvers. Driving heels in the ribs of Tarnation, he shouted to Captain Dreiling. "Come on, Cap'n, bring the rest of yer company. Let's go get your men back."

With Danvers sputtering alone at the head of the column, the entire Dragoon battalion broke ranks and charged over the rise. In the lead, Preacher took encouragement from the continued crackling exchange. It had to be a small ambush to keep the troops alive so long. The big-chested, Morgan-cross, Tarnation, ate ground at a dazzling pace.

Preacher and the two remaining platoons of C Company slammed into the surprised Blackfoot war party before the Indians could react. The thunderous crash of Hall carbines drowned out their shrill war cries. To Preacher's right a Blackfoot swung around and fired his rifle one-handed. For all his lack of accuracy, the ball moaned past Preacher's head close enough for the mountain man to feel its wind. Preacher rode low now, the reins in his teeth, and the Hawken bucked in his grip. His shot hit the Blackfoot high in the chest, on the center line. Knocked to one side, the warrior disappeared under the hooves of his companions' horses.

With the Hawken dry, Preacher shoved it into the scabbard and pivoted at the waist to find another target. Plenty presented themselves. The Walker Colt spat lead and creased ribs on a youthful Blackfoot not yet out of his teens. Bone and meat flew in a welter of blood, and Preacher reckoned that the man-child would have a fist-sized depression on that side for the rest of his life. Preacher cocked the hammer as another Blackfoot swung his empty rifle at the head of the mountain man.

Powder smoke obscured the scene, so Preacher could not see the results of his hasty shot. The rifle butt did not meet his chin, so he rightly assumed he'd scored a good hit. Suddenly, the remaining Indians swung away from the onslaught of so many soldiers and rode swiftly out of range. Preacher took quick count.

Six Indian bodies littered the ground, and only one soldier had been killed. Seven had suffered minor wounds, though. Lieutenant Brice, his youthful face begrimed by greasy powder residue, dismounted and surveyed the scene. Then, Danvers cantered up, his saber drawn, and glowered at Preacher and Captain Dreiling.

"I demand to know who ordered that charge."

Dreiling cut his eyes to Preacher, who winked at him. "I do not know, sir. I did not. It . . . sort of . . . just happened."

Danvers surveyed the scene. "We'll not go after them. Mr. Preacher, your point about ambushes is noted and stored for reference." He turned to the Battalion Sergeant Major. "Sergeant Major Muldoon, return the men to the column."

Talking Cloud was decidedly unhappy. The medicine of Iron Shirt had deserted them. Of the number of warriors with which he had started— one hundred and seventeen— he had five hands killed and seven hands wounded. He directed the survivors to the big war camp to the west. There he went directly to Three Horses who listened to his complaints with obvious indifference. It only served to inflame Talking Cloud more.

"How could Iron Shirt's medicine have failed us?" Talking Cloud demanded hotly.

"They did not believe enough in the medicine, or they would be alive," Three Horses concluded about the dead. "Or they were not purified enough."

"You did not hear me. Twenty-five men killed, thirty-five wounded. Not that many could be impure or doubtful at the same time. That means we will not be able to guard our village from the Shoshoni this winter."

"Then take your people to the Bighorn Mountains."

Not satisfied in the least with this, Talking Cloud went in search of Iron Shirt. He found the visionary medicine man in the process of initiating a group of twenty-five Cheyenne. Talking Cloud viewed the proceedings with far less conviction than before. When the rite had been concluded and the mail shirt exposed, Talking Cloud took Iron Shirt aside. He wasted no time on diplomacy.

"Why is it that your rebirth in water and the gauntlet of coals did not purify the warriors killed so far?"

Iron Shirt cocked his head to one side, to show his disbelief. "You have had men die?" he asked in a chiding tone.

"Twenty-five," Talking Cloud shouted. "In one battle. They went down like aspen in a whirlwind."

Iron Shirt nodded thoughtfully, then gave Talking Cloud essentially the same answer Three Horses had given. After so doing, he suggested, "I think another Strong Heart ceremony is needed." He took on a cheerful expression. "Gather your men and we can do it while the coals are still hot. Then you will see."

That evening, when the nervousness and strain of the attack had eased, Eve Billings sought out Preacher, who sat with his companions, a plate of fatback and beans in his hands. She looked at the concoction with unease and forced a smile.

"You didn't come to supper tonight. I know Charlie relayed my invitation."

"Yep. That he did. An' nope, I did not. Too much good cookin' makes a man soft." He set the tin plate aside and pinched his flat, hard abdomen. "Why, I reckon I've gained five pounds spongin' off your generosity. I thought I'd take a day or two away from the delicious table you lay, so's not to make a habit of it."

Smiling, Eve reached out a coaxing hand. "I wouldn't mind if you made a habit of it. Matter of fact, I'd like that a lot."

Preacher sighed and roused himself. He joined Eve and they ambled off toward the southern edge of the large encampment. There they found the peaceful vista of a moonlit, rolling sea of grass that stretched out before them to the south, east and west. Eve sighed languidly and took Preacher's right hand in both of hers.

"It's so tranquil out there. You'd never know those savages are lurking out in the dark."

Preacher shrugged. "I don't reckon they are. They were Blackfoot. That means they were loaded up with that hokum of Iron Shirt's. When we killed a passel of 'em, they had to think the medicine failed 'em. They get spooked at that, so it's likely they'll go off an' lick their wounds.'

"I hope you're right."

They stood silently for a long while then. After the stillness grew strained, Eve started haltingly. "About the other night. The . . . kiss. It was— it was brazen of me. But . . . I— I think it was . . . wonderful."

She did a step turn and faced Preacher, her arms wide. He paused only a moment before he reached out and drew her into a firm embrace.

Iron Shirt stood before his lodge and scowled as Quinton Praeger and his two associates rode through the rings of lodges that made up this large encampment of Blackfoot, Cheyenne and some Pawnee who had left their country to the east to join in the battle against all whites. The Sioux would come to him soon. He believed that in his heart. Which intensified his displeasure at the return of these renegade white men.

"They should stay away," he confided to Bent Trees who stood beside him.

A ghost of a smile flickered on the face of Bent Trees. "We could *make* them stay away."

Iron Shirt put a restraining hand on the forearm of Bent Trees. "The time is not right to do away with them as yet, my friend. We must get the last of the weapons they promise, the powder and balls, the caps. Without them, we cannot win."

"I heard about Talking Cloud. Will he stay after the new ritual?"

"I do not know. If not, we lose eight hands of warriors. It would weaken us."

"The Cheyenne and the Sioux?" Bent Trees made the common plains sign of a slash across the throat to signify the Lakota.

Iron Shirt nodded. "They'll come. Not all, as we had hoped. Cloud Blanket has taken his people away."

Eyebrows elevated, Bent Trees pointed out the obvious. "If Talking Cloud leaves us, then we will be too weak for the final battle."

A sudden flare of anger darkened the face of Iron Shirt. "No we will not. We will drive the whites past the Big Water river. My spirit guide tells"— a shaft of reality pierced his mind when he reminded himself of the source of his spirit wisdom— "me this is true."

Bent Trees grunted. "Would that he told me the same."

Startled by this lack of faith, Iron Shirt blurted, "You doubt my vision?"

"No— no. Only I think you should fast and visit with your spirit guide again. *We* do not know him. We have not heard him speak. Our strength, our faith, comes from you."

Iron Shirt put a hand on his friend's shoulder. "Perhaps you are right. I will think on it. First we must impress on our white friends the need for more rifles."

After another three long, satisfyingly uneventful days, Preacher guided his fledgling soldiers to the spot selected by Lieutenant Colonel Danvers. It was situated on a nice promontory overlooking a deep valley and the ringing peaks of the Bighorn Mountains. Tents went up with many joyful sounds of relief. Even in their permanent situation, Preacher noted, the civilians kept to themselves, erecting their spare wagon covers for tents. A surveying crew set up and began to lay out the fort. Gus Beecher started to assemble his smithy, leaving his family shelter to his wife and daughters to prepare.

With the only direct, easy approach up a draw and along the wide, sloping finger of land that led to the site, the main gate would be there. Also the only stockade. That bothered Preacher. He left the details of their camp to Three Fingers Norris and Antoine Revier and went in search of Danvers. He found the commander with the surveyors, in shirtsleeves, gesturing with wide, emphatic swings of his arms. When Danvers completed his vehement discussion, he turned to find Preacher patiently waiting.

"Pardon me, Colonel. I figgered now was the time to remind you of a few things. You may want to put up a stockade all around this place. Look there, over my shoulder. That's a mighty high peak back there. I know it's kinda steep. Even so, hostiles could come sweepin' right down there and behind this wall. That'd trap you folks in back of your own device. Then there's the water. This spine is pure granite. I don't think you can dig a well. More likely a cistern would be the best you can do. A big pit, blasted out of the rock, an' covered over could give you a good supply of rainwater and snowmelt. But

not enough for year 'round. An' for trees to make buildings and yer stockade, you can see that outside that little
stand over there, the nearest are out of range of your
best riflemen. They'll have no protection.''

Lieutenant Colonel Danvers gave Preacher a long, cool
look up and down as though inspecting a tramp discovered in his back yard. "Your job with the Army is ended,
Mr. Preacher. I have these problems in mind and can
handle them adequately. If you so choose, you may
leave."

Preacher's eyes narrowed slightly, and he pursed his
lips to keep his true feelings from being spoken. "Is that
your final word on this?"

"It most certainly is. Now, if you will excuse me?"

"Well, then, b'god, I jist might pull out after all. Me
an' my friends."

Danvers hastily informed Preacher, "Oh, but there is
work for them if they wish to remain."

Close to loosing the iron grip on his anger, Preacher
responded tightly. "I think I can answer for them.
Thanks, but no thanks." With that, he stomped off.

Preacher felt duty-bound to explain his decision to Eve
Billings. He went to her and stood, hat in one hand,
over his heart, and informed her of his decision to leave
the next day for his favored country in the Colorado
Rockies. Eve's eyes went wide when she understood what
his rambling phrases meant.

"Oh, but you can't," she protested. "You have helped
us so much. We would never have made it without you,
dear, dear Preacher."

And that was part of it, too, although a small part,
Preacher told himself. He was beginning to feel entirely
too fond of this wisp of a girl. No, he corrected himself,
this stalwart young widow— and her children. Why, hell,

he had no use for children. Even those he had sired among the Indian camps mattered not a jot to him. At least not until they grew old enough to go hunting, trapping and fishing with him. Nope, the settled life held no appeal to him. Only how to tell Eve that in a gentle way?

"Er, the colonel don't want me around anymore. He as much as told me to pack my saddlebags and haul out of here."

"You are your own man, aren't you? He is bound to protect civilians within the range of the fort. You could . . . could join us and he would be obliged to put up with you."

"No— no, ma'am . . . er, Eve. I couldn't do that."

"And why not?" Eve spun on one heel and called loudly. "Charlie, Charlie Billings, come here at once." When the boy arrived, she gave him clear, quick instructions. "Go find Mr. Warner and Mr. Tate. Bring them here. Mr. Beecher, too. Tell them it is very important."

"Yes, ma'am," Charlie replied and scampered away.

Preacher tried to derail her juggernaut. "Now, Eve, there's no call to cause a fuss."

Eve gave him an impish, though determined, look. "It's not a fuss I'm figuring on. You must be convinced that we need you here, to teach us things to help us survive when we set off for Oregon Country again."

"Shoot, anybody can do that for you. Don't have to be me. The way I figger it, I've got about enough time to git back to the High Lonesome, stock up on supplies, then make it to my winterin' place and settle in."

Equally stubborn, Eve Billings put her hands on her hips and leaned toward Preacher. "Are you always this selfish? Don't you ever consider giving others a helping hand?"

Preacher bent even closer. "Nope. I al'ays had to make

do for myself. An' I've observed that those folks who get
ahead in this world have done the same.

"Why, that's awful. It's so un-Christian."

"I don't recall layin' claim to bein' a Christian."

Shocked by this admission, Eve arched her eyebrows.
"For shame, Preacher!" Then her mind exploded with
a realization. "Are we . . . are we having our first fight,
Preacher?"

Suddenly robbed of his self-defensive pique, Preacher
abandoned his aggressive stance and began to chortle.
"By dang, I think yer right. Looks like that's what it is."

Relaxed, and no longer feeling threatened, Eve joined
Preacher in his laughter. He reached out for her and
put one arm on her shoulder. They remained in a
chaste, semi-embrace when the wagon-train leaders
stormed up.

Beet-faced, Gus Beecher made the first complaint.
"What's so all-fired important to take me away from set-
tlin' in? I've my smithy to finish. We've a cave to dig,
and sod walls to put up, a sod roof to add." Then he
cocked a gimlet eye at Eve Billings. "Or is it that the
Widow Billings has chosen now to announce her engagement?"

Scandalized, Eve covered her mouth with one hand
for a moment before she spoke. "What stuff and nonsense, Gus Beecher. Preacher is talking about leaving."
She went on to relate what he had told her of the con-
frontation with Lieutenant Colonel Danvers and his decision to leave.

That changed the tone of the men, except for Gus
Beecher. "He can go any time he wants, for all I care."

Hiram Tate saw it differently. "Preacher, you can't
leave us like this. There's so much we need to learn.
And, how can we ever get along with Colonel Danvers?"

"I reckon much like porcupines make love— very carefully." Then Preacher blushed slightly and nodded to-

ward Eve. "If you'll pardon my language, ma'am. As to goin', I figger I'm free to do so when I take a mind."

Isaac Warner made an open plea. "You'll leave us helpless. Look at all you've done so far. We've learned how to make better time, how to effectively fight Indians, better ways to cook for the noonin'. Oh, so many things. An' there must be more. How to better track and take down game, what to avoid on the trail. Such things make you a gold mine to us. Please, at least take a day or two to think it over. We haven't much left, but we can pay you for your advice. Won't you at least give it fair consideration, Preacher?"

Erasing the scowl on his high forehead, Preacher spoke quietly. "I'll think on it some. No promises, mind, but I'll let you know."

TWENTY

By mid-morning the next day, the surveyor and his crew had driven stakes to set out the dimensions of the stockade and its headquarters. Also the corral and two outbuildings. Favorably noting this rapid progress, Lieutenant Colonel Danvers ordered felling crews to be detailed to cut down trees in the thick stands of pine down near the base of the finger-like promontory. Hearing of this, Gus Beecher came to the colonel and, toadying up as was his want, offered his services to forge hinges for the gate, along with bolts, spikes and other iron products as needed, at a reasonable price of course. To his credit, Danvers let his face show his distaste for the man, though he did hire him on a by-the-job basis.

The colonel learned of three men among the civilians who had sawmill experience. He interviewed them and, satisfied, hired them at once. "You are to inspect, set up and operate the portable saw that accompanied us from Jefferson Barracks. I expect a preliminary report by this afternoon." He soon learned the full extent of the bad news.

Shortly after two o'clock that afternoon, the three sawyers came to Danvers. The eldest, Tom Quigley, who had been a foreman, revealed the results of their studies. "The blade made it through nice as can be. Same for the other parts. The belts could stand a good oiling an' they'll be supple again. Only one problem."

"What is that?"

Quigley wiped a damp brow. "How are we goin' to power the saw? That blade has to be movin' a fair clip to cut through wood, especially green wood."

Danvers scowled at this setback. "I was given to understand that everything necessary had been included. Surely, you've overlooked something."

"Nope. Not a blessed thing. Oh, it's all there, disassembled and the parts numbered. Ya see, Colonel, this mill was designed to be run by a waterwheel."

Suspicion registered on the face of the colonel. "There was no wheel with the saw parts."

"Nope, we have to build it. The metal fittings are all there," Quigley informed him.

"How's it all operate?"

"Well, Colonel, there's this big ol' flywheel that attaches to the spline of the waterwheel, and a little one that goes on the shaft of the saw blade. The problem is we've got to have a water source to use it."

Danvers slapped the gloves he carried in his left hand against his outer thigh. "I am constantly beset with obstacles. Why is that, do you suppose, Mr. Quigley?"

Quigley ducked his head in embarrassment. "I wouldn't rightly know, sir', bein' I ain't been in the Army. But, from those I know what have been, it seems that's the way of it, Colonel. If it ain't one thing goin' wrong, it's six others."

Lieutenant Colonel Danvers produced a warm, genuine smile, the first, save those he gave to Eve Billings, he had ever given to one of the settlers. "Quite right, Quigley, quite right, indeed. That has been the bane of my existence since I attended the military academy. Not once has anyone put it so succinctly. But that's not my immediate problem. Why did those idiots in the Quartermaster Corps provide us with a water-powered sawmill when we were coming into this godforsaken country?"

Quigley shrugged. "It is mountainous, sir. Maybe they thought you'd find a waterfall, which would be dandy or this kind of mill."

Danvers grunted. "Those fools have never seen beyond the west bank of the Potomac, let alone the real West. Can you convert it to a treadmill?"

"Not easily, nor likely, Colonel. Best bet is we dam up that creek down below to build pressure and put the mill wheel in the spillway."

Danvers seemed doubtful. "Can that be done?"

"Easy as can be. Your engineer officer an' someone with knowledge of artillery could do the figgers and draw up what's needed. The surveyors could lay it out."

"Then, get to it. I'll assign the men you asked for to your supervision. We need that mill operative as soon as possible. By all means, long before winter."

Preacher decided to take one more look around at the operation Danvers had put in motion before making his final decision. What he saw only convinced him further of the folly of the entire project. The fellers had moved a good three-quarters of a mile from the site of the fort. Well out of range of covering fire, the only protection they had came from half a dozen Dragoons assigned to them. Already the detail assigned to limbing the logs and dragging them down to the area of the stockade had run into trouble.

Dragoon horses, unaccustomed to working in harness, rebelled against the strangeness of heavy loads that pulled against their necks. They clashed into one another, reared, whinnied and occasionally balked. For most of their journey, they remained out of rifle range from the fort as well. Preacher found Captain Dreiling watching the neophyte lumberjacks through field glasses.

Preacher addressed him in a low, confidential tone.

"Jist betwixt you an' me, Edward, this is one hell of a mistake. Those fellers out there are as exposed as a baby's bare bottom on birthin' day. You're all near a thousand miles from any other soldiers, jist about as far from any white man. Supply will be difficult, impossible in winter, and the colonel's plans for water are nonexistent, or plum silly at best."

Dreiling turned to Preacher. "Are you wound down now, my friend? For all the good it'll do, I agree with you absolutely. Putting a fort here, on this impossible plateau, in the middle of Indian country, is what I call downright suicidal."

Preacher shrugged. "I told the colonel he'd be wise to make a large cistern in the middle of the fort area. That'd give you a reliable supply most of the year. If he ran that stockade around the whole place, it would even be safe to draw water durin' an attack, too."

Dreiling brightened over that. "A cistern would work? Tell me about it."

For the next half hour Preacher enlarged his idea. Although in conclusion he returned to his main theme. "The smartest thing to do would be to get clear the hell away from here and set up somewhere else."

Later in the afternoon, Preacher had opportunity to point out to Lieutenant Colonel Danvers all he had discussed with Captain Dreiling. The colonel barely suppressed his irritation. He did make one concession.

"All right, Mr. Preacher. I'll agree with you on one point. I have been studying the approach routes to the site. I'm ordering other palisades to be erected along the south and west faces. I've come to the conclusion that without them we are entirely too exposed. I'm certain that the sheer walls to the east side will take care of any threat from that direction."

"I'd give that second thought, too, Colonel. 'Cause even if the walls are sheer, including being too steep to climb safely, unless they're completely concave, there won't be no such word as *can't* in the heads of Injuns fixed on climbin' up here."

"I'll consider it, but it won't be at the top of my list of priorities."

"Mayhap it had better be, Colonel. Because I'm sure it's on their minds." With a slow movement, Preacher raised his arm and, like the Specter of Doom, pointed a long finger at the figures of some forty mounted Cheyenne and twenty-five Lakota warriors watching in ominous silence from the hilltops in the near distance.

Eve Billings could not believe the emotions that surged through her. At one moment, a girlish giddiness flooded her. The next, she sank into deep shame that she could imagine such thing so soon after poor Howard's death, only to find herself awash with gloomy despair that she would never have what she so dearly wanted. Then euphoria surged again. She would hum old ballads, put a dance step in her walk, a sparkle in her eyes and a silly smile on her lips. Abruptly she broke off her self-examination to give Charlie's shoulder a hard squeeze.

"Charlie, sit still. I'm trying to cut your hair evenly all around."

"I don't want my hair cut," replied Charlie in a surly tone. "I want it to grow long so I can braid it."

Amazement washed over Eve's face. "Why, Charlie, whatever for?"

Charlie's lower lip came out in a pink crescent of pout. "Indian boys have their hair braided."

"Charles Ryan Billings, your hair is as auburn as mine, and your complexion as fair. You are not an Indian boy."

Conscious of having gone entirely too far, Charlie

could not meet her eyes. He inspected his feet, which in gratitude and relief, Eve saw were now covered. Although by moccasins he had acquired who knew where. "I wanna be."

"What put that notion in your head, son?"

"I've been thinkin'. Indian boys get to ride and hunt and fish and swim whenever they want to. Preacher's told me so." Then he cut his dark eyes to his mother. "Preacher also told me that Indian boys' folks don't spank them."

Eve studied her son, conscious that he had aged beyond his years, yet remained emotionally a little boy. "Have you done something you think you might be spanked for?"

Shock registered on Charlie's face. "No! Yes. Er . . . I mean, I don't know."

"Do you want to tell me about it?"

"I can't. I promised. It's a secret. Between him an' me." Whenever Charlie Billings suffered from guilt feelings, he spoke in short, incomplete sentences.

"Who? Preacher?"

"No, Mom. Not him. Someone . . . secret."

One hand on her hip, Eve shook her head in resignation. She would learn about it sooner or later, she knew with a mother's certainty.

A week went by with the logging detail required to go farther from the rudimentary fort each day. The present party of eighteen, twelve loggers and six guards, had only ridden out of sight when Preacher heard the thin, high keen of a war cry, followed by the muffled pop of gunfire. Quickly, he ankled his way across the crudely marked-out parade ground. He went directly to the large tent located in the center of an area that would become the future headquarters.

He brushed past the sentries and strode straight to the desk behind which sat Lieutenant Colonel Danvers. "Sorry to bother you, Colonel, but from the sound of it, your loggers are gettin' attacked."

Voice almost a squeal, Danvers bounded from his chair. "What! That's impossible. They have an escort."

Had the situation not been so serious, Preacher would have laughed out loud. "I don't think that means much to half a hundred Cheyenne."

Before Danvers could work up a reply, a mounted man thundered up to the tent. He shouted through the canvas. "Colonel— Colonel, we're under attack. Injuns are swarmin' all over us."

"Here?" Danvers mouthed rhetorically.

The wild-eyed Dragoon, his face slicked with fear sweat and mottled with dust burst through the flap. "It's the detail, sir. There must be a hunnerd Injuns."

Surprising to Preacher, Danvers responded quickly. "Borden," he snapped to the commander of Company A. "Assemble your men. Form a relief column. Extra cartridges for all. Be ready to ride in five minutes. Mr. Preacher, will you scout?"

Preacher stifled a groan. "I reckon so, Colonel."

Dust and powder smoke boiled up from beyond the near swell on the breast of the Bighorn Mountains. Preacher ignored the rough trail already cut into the soil and took the most direct route. Streaming behind him in a column of twos, Preacher noticed with satisfaction, the Dragoons pounded hard over the ground. Seven minutes later, they came upon the rear of the left flank of a two-sided Cheyenne attack.

Startled Indians in the grass turned at the sound of pounding hooves. Two of them started to swing their rifles into line as Captain Borden bellowed; "Echelon left and right, draw carbines . . . aim . . . fire!"

Four warriors went down before a scythe of lead. Three others took wounds that disabled them. Preacher noted that a Dragoon sergeant had learned his lessons well. He skidded his mount to a halt and covered the injured Cheyennes with his revolver. Preacher faced front in time to drive the buttplate of his Hawken into the face of a snarling brave.

"Pour it on, boys! Help's come," sang out the voice of Lieutenant Gresham of Company B.

Gresham had been in charge of the logging detail, Preacher recalled. Quickly he cut his way toward the stalled wagons, his hand filled now with a Walker Colt. Gresham reared up and fired at a warrior who lunged from the back of his pony toward Preacher. Preacher's .44 ball reached his attacker at the same time as Gresham's .54-caliber Hall carbine round. In the next second, the complexion of the battle changed entirely.

With a hundred-twenty Dragoons rushing down on them, the forty-three remaining Cheyenne warriors lost interest in their no longer easy prey. They abandoned the attack and raced through the waving grass, to disappear down a draw. Odd, Preacher thought to himself, he could swear he had seen some Blackfoot among them. The two tribes had been enemies for hundreds of years. Preacher would have never believed he would see them fighting side by side.

The Cheyenne might listen to the message of Iron Shirt, but Preacher could not believe even such a powerful prophet could weld a lasting alliance. Yet, he felt certain he had seen a Blackfoot pattern on a shield and in the decoration of a feathered lance. When the last warrior had left the field, Preacher trotted Tarnation over to Lieutenant Gresham.

"You lose any men?"

"No, thanks be. Not that they didn't try damned hard. We're going to have to take a larger escort."

"It'd be smarter if you didn't go out at all. I've talked myself blue in the face tryin' to get Colonel Danvers to see that. Don't do much good, but I'll try again."

"I wish you luck. And . . . ah . . . thanks for gettin' the relief here so fast."

"You're welcome. Ain't your fault you've got yer neck stuck out a mile. Next time, you might not be so lucky."

Back at the fort, Preacher stormed directly into the headquarters tent to confront Lieutenant Colonel Danvers. So exacerbated had he become, his face bore the likeness of a thundercloud. He found himself forced to stand in impotent silence while Danvers dallied over an inconsequential report. When at last the colonel glanced up indifferently, Preacher used every bit of will to curb his temper.

"Colonel, according to what those fellers in Washington City writ to me, I was to advise you in all matters regarding the frontier, including Injun fighting techniques and the habits of the tribes. For the last two months, that is what I've been tryin' to do. Only you seem determined to ignore what I say.

"Now, unlike me, these boys has got to do as you say." Preacher paused, then delivered his suspicions in clear and cogent speech. "What I wonder is why you remain so blind to the formidable danger everyone is being subjected to? Don't you care? My point is, we have hostiles where there were none when I left for Jefferson Barracks. That could be exceedingly costly in the lives of these young men."

Put off balance by Preacher's erudite delivery, Danvers gaped a moment before he waved a hand in easy dismissal. "They volunteered for the Army, every man jack of them. As for my lack of surprise, I must say that after all, I didn't expect the savages to come down and greet my troops with open arms. I learned that from you on the way out here. It is something we all have to take in stride, or get out of the game. Now, is there anything of importance you have for me?"

Preacher bit off his furious reply. "I want to scout that raiding party, see where they're goin' and what they're up to."

"That's quite all right with me. Be ready to make a complete report when you return. And leave at least one of the other scouts for duties around the fort."

An hour later, Preacher and Antoine Revier left the fledgling fort. They traveled light, with only what their saddle- and possibles-bags could carry. Once clear of the finger of land and out of sight of the fort, the wilderness swallowed them. To some, the silence and vastness would be intimidating. Not so the mountain men, for Preacher and Antoine, a welcome blanket of tranquillity settled over them.

They picked up the trail of the fleeing Cheyenne easily and began to follow it. Conscious that they were being watched every inch of the way, Preacher had an intense itching sensation between his shoulder blades.

TWENTY-ONE

Preacher and Antoine trailed along behind the war party at a leisurely pace. That way it took two days to catch up. Preacher saw the first sign of the hostiles. The point and part of the shaft of a feather-decorated lance seemed to float on the horizon. Within a few strides, a mop of black, braided hair rose into view. A single eagle feather protruded upward from the back of the head. Preacher made a sign to Antoine Revier and they reined in their mounts.

Preacher cupped his chin in one hand. "We've found 'em, right enough. Now what are we gonna do with them?"

"I figger you've got an idee or two up yer sleeve, Preacher. Me, I could use a nice snooze between now and full dark."

"Right. We eat now and wait 'til nightfall to move in closer."

After staking out their horses to graze, the two mountain men leaned against their saddles, which they propped against the thick trunk of an ancient oak. They gnawed on strips of softened jerky. Cold biscuits and a pot of beans, provided by Eve Billings, filled out the meal. Preacher's jaw continued to work as, with a slender wild onion he had pulled from a bunch that grew nearby, he pointed in the direction taken by the Cheyenne.

"Them fellers ain't gonna throw out a welcome blanket for us. So, I figger we need to get in real close tonight and find out what they're talkin' about. Get the lay of the land, so's to speak. Then we can decide what to do."

Antoine washed down beans with cold water from the creek. "Suits. I ain't exactly anxious to go mix in with them. How's yer Cheyenne?"

"Good enough, though a mite rusty. I reckon I can make out what they're sayin' among themselves."

"Good. How's it feel to be away from those soldier-boys an' on yer own for once?"

Preacher heaved a long sigh of relief. "I ain't felt this good in three months. Jist about got the stink of white folks out of my lungs. Why is it there's so many of them has such an aversion to keepin' clean? A good Injun nose could smell 'em comin' a good quarter mile away."

Antoine snorted, amused at the image he had created. "Can you imagine the mess it would make in a crick if all them soldiers, an' the pilgrims, took a bath every night?"

Preacher wrinkled his nose. "Never thought of it that way before. Might be you're right. All that soap and stench floatin' downstream would tell an Injun jist where to look. No matter, it's good to be out here. Now I'm gonna pull me a tomcat and catch a few winks."

Only the pale, frosty light of the stars broke up the black blanket of a moonless night later on when Preacher and Antoine fastened their horses to ground anchors and eeled through the tough, wiry grass to within twenty feet of the Cheyenne camp. Low, small lodges had been set in a semicircle around a large, central fire. Preacher extended his spyglass and swept the rows of seated men.

Sure enough, he was not pleased to note, there was more than one Blackfoot among the Cheyenne. One of them stood before the assembly and harangued them in

their language. His Cheyenne was imperfect, and
Preacher found it hard to understand. What he did make
out alarmed him.

"When Iron Shirt and our people join you and your
cousins, the Lakota, it will be easy to kill all the white
men on the bluff. Then we will sweep across the plains
with rifle and firebrand and drive the rest out of the
country of our brothers forever." He paused to strut
proudly in front of the rapt Cheyenne.

"In two sun's time, all of the Iron Shield Society will
join us here and the massacre will soon follow. Those
who died in the attack on the wagons did not have strong
enough faith in the medicine of Iron Shirt. Look about
you. The faces you see are of those who, like you, believed. With strong hearts like yours, we cannot fail."

Preacher had heard enough. He tugged at the sleeve
of the hunting shirt worn by Antoine Revier. When Antoine cut his eyes to Preacher, the latter motioned for
them to draw back. Cautiously they began to move away
from the Cheyenne camp. They made it halfway to their
horses without incident. Then, as he crawled past a large
sage bush, Preacher found himself looking at five pair
of coppery knees.

Slowly he raised his gaze to take in the warriors, all of
whom competently held modern rifles, pointed directly
at him. He froze and sucked in a deep breath. From
beyond the obscuring brush he heard the soft voice of
Antoine Revier. "Preacher, dang me, but I think we're
caught."

Preacher's heart rate increased rapidly, driven by the
fight or flight reflex, as adrenaline pumped into his sys-
tem. Suddenly he lashed out at the nearest pair of legs.

Thrashing sounds across the sage told Preacher that
Antoine had chosen to resist also. Preacher had the

Cheyenne warrior off his legs in no time. He snatched up the dropped rifle and used it clublike to knock the knees from under another brave. Then the other three jumped him.

Preacher fought silently, and with a controlled fury that left one Cheyenne with a broken jaw. Another warrior came at him from the front, prepared to do a kick to Preacher's face. Preacher dodged and slapped the leg to the side. Then he came upright and split the upper lip of the unprepared Indian. Grunts and the soft impact of fist against flesh told him Antoine was holding his own. A knee to the groin toppled the bleeding Cheyenne.

Preacher started to follow up with a knockout punch, only to have his arms grabbed from behind. A sturdy warrior held him tightly while the last of the group kicked him in the belly. Stomach juices burned their way up Preacher's throat. He gagged and retched while he struggled to free himself.

It did little good. The next instant, blackness washed over him and pain erupted in his head from a blow with a rifle butt. His knees went slack and he hung from the grasp of the Cheyenne who held him.

Preacher and Antoine Revier came to in the center of the Cheyenne camp. Spread-eagled and staked to the ground, they had been stripped of their clothing and moccasins. A tidal surge of pain churned in Preacher's head. Through it, he vaguely heard a stirring beyond his bare feet. A blurred figure came into view and Preacher tried to blink his eyes into focus.

When the image came clear, it turned out to be a man Preacher recognized. "Swift Bear," he grated rustily in Cheyenne. The effort caused him another tsunami of pain.

"It is truly you, White Ghost?"

"Yes, it is, Swift Bear. Yer warriors caught me fair and square." With that admission, Preacher set out on a plan that had only begun to form in his mind. It was one he hoped would save their lives. After another hard swallow, he began to bargain.

"You know me, Swift Bear, an' you know I do not lie."

"That is so. What is it you wish to talk about lying there on the ground?"

Preacher stalled a moment. "Glad you mentioned that. I would feel better about it if I was sittin' upright, so I could talk like a man, instead of a deer laid out for dressin'. Could you do that, Swift Bear?"

After due consideration, the Cheyenne war chief nodded in agreement. "Since it is you, I shall allow it. Release his arms."

Now he was getting somewhere. When the rawhide thongs had been severed, Preacher flexed his fingers to restore feeling, and levered himself up into a sitting position.

Preacher made a nod of his head and proceeded politely. "White Ghost thanks Swift Bear. Now, what you've got here is two fellers who have been friend to the Cheyenne for many winters. Why, I even took me a Cheyenne wife, had two sons by her. 'Cept she got took off by sickness."

"The white man's curse," Swift Bear provided.

"Yep. Smallpox. Nothin' could be done about it. But, my boys are being raised as Cheyenne in the band of Cloud Blanket. It is as the Great Spirit sees best. What I'm gettin' at is that since we're friends, more or less, maybe you would cut us loose and let us go on our way?"

"We are a war party. And I have a band of my own now. I no longer listen to the words of Cloud Blanket."

Preacher cocked a brow. "You two at odds? That's a shame. What happened?"

"Cloud Blanket turned away from the Iron Shield Society."

"What is that?"

"A new warrior society, with powerful medicine. It was brought to us by a Blackfoot shaman."

"Oh, yes, Iron Shirt." Preacher cocked a brow and continued shrewdly. "But Iron Shirt does not speak for the Cheyenne, now that I know for a fact. An' I don't think he speaks for Swift Bear."

Swift Bear curled his lower lip outward a moment before replying. "We follow him in the great battle."

"What fight is that?"

"To rid our land of the white men. Iron Shirt leads us in that."

"But he doesn't tell you what to do with a friend."

"No. That is so. True though it is, I cannot simply release White Ghost. You were spying on a war camp."

Preacher put on an unhappy expression, then brightened with a show of hope. "There is a way, though, isn't there?"

A brief smile showed Swift Bear followed Preacher's logic. "You could . . . fight your way free."

"You mean, take on the whole mess of you?"

Swift Bear shook his head. "No. If you could fight your way past ten warriors, you could go on your way in peace."

"What about my friend? He looks a mite worse for wear. Could I fight for his release, too?"

Considering that a while, Swift Bear finally made answer. "You would have to better four hands of men for that." At Preacher's unhappy expression, he added. "Or you could fight one man to the death."

"I would have to fight any man you send against me?" At the nod from Swift Bear, he went on. "If I win, me an' my friend go free and unharmed?"

"That is so. And if you do not defeat my choice, let us hope you both die like men."

"What weapons will we use?"

"That will be decided by the council tonight."

Preacher had another, vital question to ask. "Who will I fight?"

Swift Bear remained silent, let his gaze roam over the gathered warriors. Then he made a gesture that summoned an important-looking Blackfoot. The two spoke too quietly for Preacher to hear. When they had decided, Swift Bear turned back to Preacher.

"I have asked my brother, Three Horses, who he thinks should uphold our honor. He has suggested that it would be fitting for Tall Bull to claim your scalp. Tall Bull is a Blackfoot, one who has taken the way of Iron Shirt and is immune to the weapons of the white man."

By the slightest value of intonation, Preacher managed to keep sarcasm out of his voice when he replied dryly, "Well, then, I don't think pistols would be a fair choice for weapons. I need at least a little chance to win."

"You will learn of our decision tomorrow. When the sun is high, the fight will begin."

Preacher and Antoine spent an uneasy night. In the chill mountain air, they soon found themselves stiffening and had to clench their jaws to keep their teeth from chattering. Tied to the trunks of a pair of saplings, they could not even lay out full-length to sleep. When morning came, their muscles had grown knotted and sore.

Thoughtfully, Swift Bear had ordered them cut loose and, while food was brought to them, they worked out the kinks. They were kept under control by rawhide tethers around their waists. Preacher ate with his usual appetite; a stew made of some sort of meat he could not identify. Then he began to exercise lightly.

Relentlessly the sun climbed the sky while Preacher continued to stretch, bend and run in place. All the while, he tried to think through a strategy to insure he won. When he worked up a light sheen of sweat and his muscles seemed as smooth in operation as usual, he stopped and sat beside Antoine.

Lacking tact, Antoine brought up one of several old acquaintances who had undergone such a challenge. "Remember ol' Kip? He had to fight for his life one time like this. Against the Arapaho, I believe. Too bad it kilt him."

"Now, that's a fact. How about French Jake, though? He came through it missin' only three fingers of one hand. Gives a feller real inspiration, that does."

Antoine had more encouragement. "How about ol' Jim Bridger? Seems he ran afoul of some excitable Paiutes. They was fixed to torture him and burn him alive, only he talked them into a fight, best man wins all. Now, you know the Paiutes is sneaky. He had to fight three men before they kept their word. Killed all three Jim did. With only a couple light cuts on his arms."

"Not to mention a slice on one cheek that near tooken out one eye."

Antoine cut a slantways glance at Preacher. "You sound like you're regrettin' this fight already."

Preacher slid his gaze to the whiskered face of his companion. "Now that you mention it, maybe I am."

"You want out of it?" probed Antoine.

"I want out of here. An' the only way to do that is go through with a fight."

Antoine offered a crumb of hope. "You coulda said no."

"An' we'd been killed on the spot. Nope, that's not for this child. I plan on livin' a whole long time after this affair."

"We've had some good times, haven't we, Preacher?"

"You goin' softhearted on me, Antoine?"

"Not me, *mon ami*. I was . . . only thinking."

"About what?"

Antoine sighed heavily. "We both know of more men that failed to get through such an ordeal than those who did. I feel responsible in a way. It is as though if I had not been along, you might have gotten away."

"Nonsense, my friend. You did not cause this. I failed to keep careful watch. They found us and nabbed us, an' here we are. But I think I've figgered a way out for us. It would be crazy to expect that I'll not get hurt some in the process."

Sincerity radiated from the respectful expression Antoine wore. "By *le bon Dieu,* Preacher, you have more sand than any ten men I know. God go with you."

Preacher swallowed hard at the lump that had suddenly appeared in his throat. "Thank you, Antoine."

Before they expected it, the time arrived for the mortal combat. Down the slope a way, the Cheyenne and their tenuous allies gathered in a large, loose circle around a bare spot of ground. Swift Bear and four of his warriors came for Preacher. Two of them escorted Antoine Revier while the other pair accompanied Preacher. To muttered insults, Preacher's captors shouldered a path through the crowd and delivered him to the center. Then they released the tether and stepped back.

A loud clamor rose as Tall Bull stepped through the ranks of spectators. His name suited him to perfection. He towered well over six feet, with thick muscles and tree-trunk legs. His hands were the size of a grizzly's paws and his head would not fit the largest hat size. He had Preacher by five inches and a good fifty-five pounds. Swift Bear came forward and handed each man a knife and a tomahawk. Relief coursed through Preacher when he found that the weapons were his own. Then the Cheyenne chief stepped back and motioned for the contestants to face him.

"This is a fight to the death. You will use no other weapons than those given you. If you lose both, you may

use hands, feet, and teeth. It is in the hands of the Great
Spirit, and up to your skill, to decide who will win."

With that, he melted back into the inner ring of onlookers and raised his arm. "Let the fight begin."

TWENTY-TWO

Warily, the two fighters circled, intent on studying each other's strengths and weaknesses. Tall Bull, with the advantage of size and weight, struck first. His tomahawk whistled loudly in a roundhouse swing. Preacher lithely sprang out of the way. Instantly he retaliated with a flick of his left wrist.

The keen edge of his Greenriver knife bit into flesh over the left eye of Tall Bull. A sheet of blood washed over the lid and obscured his vision. In the instant of hesitation that caused, Preacher lashed out with his war 'hawk and lightly nicked Tall Bull over the left hipbone. A heavier stream of blood flowed down the Blackfoot's leg. The spectators raised an angry roar.

Tall Bull stumbled twice, then flexed his knees and coiled his body for another attack. He came in straight, tomahawk whirring in a silvery blur before his face. Knife held with the edge up, he feinted for the proper opening and drove the blade forward. Preacher jumped high in the air and brought his 'hawk down on the haft of the one in the hand of his adversary.

Sharp pain radiated up the arm of Tall Bull and he nearly dropped his tomahawk. Then he shifted his weight and spun in a full circle. When he saw the hated white man again, he let out a howl and swung his knife with all his force. The stroke split Preacher's buckskin shirt from his left hip to his right shoulder. A thin ribbon

of blood oozed from the chest of Preacher. Off balance
from his effort to avoid the deadly steel, he stumbled
over his own feet.

Down Preacher went, but not before Tall Bull charged
forward and sank the sharp edge of his tomahawk into
the thick muscle of Preacher's upper chest. By immediately going slack the blade did not cut through bone or
pierce a lung. Preacher hastily rolled to one side. He
recovered before Tall Bull could follow up his advantage.
Panther quick, Preacher smacked the Cheyenne in the
gut with the flat of his blade.

Groaning, Tall Bull doubled over. Preacher sacrificed
a chance to get in another blow to return to his feet.
Slowly, a plan began to form in his mind. Swinging rapidly in a figure-eight, Preacher made the blade of his
'hawk a continuous blur between them. Inexorably he
edged Tall Bull backward, toward a large, old tree. Eyes
fixed over the shoulder of Tall Bull, Preacher gauged
his distance. When he had the Blackfoot in the proper
position, he feinted to his left, then whirled right and
ran around the slower-moving Tall Bull.

Seeing an opening, Tall Bull rushed in. His arm raised
above his head, he was prepared to split Preacher's skull.
The moment his opponent committed himself to the
blow, Preacher dropped flat on the ground. Unable to
arrest his motion, Tall Bull buried his tomahawk in the
tree trunk up to the haft. Swiftly, Preacher cut a line
across the exposed belly of Tall Bull, which released a
river of blood.

Tall Bull choked back a howl of pain while he struggled to free his weapon from the wooden vise. Suddenly
aware that Preacher was on the way up, momentary panic
seized him. Unable to free his war 'hawk, Tall Bull abandoned it for his knife, which he changed to his right
hand.

Making a shrewd surmise, Preacher tossed away his

own 'hawk and shifted to his Greenriver. This gesture
brought the first sound of appreciation from the spectators. Preacher stepped in and began to circle. Awkward
and uncertain, his reservoir of cunning and strength
bleeding out through his wounds, Tall Bull did likewise.
Grimly, the fight went on.

Steel clashed on steel as Preacher parried an overhand
thrust. Pain flowed through his chest like fire. Both men
danced back and circled again. Tall Bull moved slower,
his shoulders drooped and his head canted forward. He
gasped in great drafts of air and vigilantly sought an
opening. At last he sensed a flaw in Preacher's defense.
With a deep grunt he lunged forward on his right leg
and drove the tip of the blade toward Preacher's belly.

All at once, the knife in Preacher's hand showed up
where it should not be. It deflected the blade of Tall
Bull as Preacher spun away out of danger. Loss of his
target sent Tall Bull stumbling to one side, bent over and
vulnerable. The wound in Preacher's shoulder stung
mightily as he tried to reverse his swing and plunge the
Greenriver into the soft side of Tall Bull.

Having missed his lunge, Tall Bull knew the cold lone-
liness of desperation. Slowly he calmed his racing emotions. In sudden inspiration, he bent lower and snatched
up a handful of dust and pebbles. Recovering his balance, he turned and hurled the contents of his hand into
the face of Preacher.

Blinded, Preacher dropped low and did a forward roll.
After two turns he crashed into the legs of the onlookers
and, before Tall Bull could close on him, snatched a
remembered gourd of water from between the nearest
Cheyenne's legs. Quickly he poured the contents over
his head and blinked his vision clear as he came to one
knee. He managed it in time to keep from having Tall
Bull's knife buried in his back.

Slowly Preacher yielded to the relentless pressure of

the heavy, muscular warrior who had crashed into him. He shifted his feet and used the momentum of Tall Bull to throw the Blackfoot over one hip and send him crashing into the Cheyenne spectators. Immediately, Preacher regained his equilibrium and lashed out a foot.

His kick caught Tall Bull in the side of the head. Instantly groggy, Tall Bull momentarily lost sight of his opponent. Seizing his chance, Preacher dove in and made a quick slash that cut the throat of Tall Bull, who dropped to the ground, where he died before the gasping Preacher. A long, stunned silence followed.

Frowning, Two Moons stepped forward to clasp forearms with Preacher. "You have won fairly, White Ghost. Take your friend, your weapons and horses and ride out in peace. You will not be harmed."

Preacher and Antoine made the return trip to the fort in a day and a half. They paused only to dress Preacher's wounds and to rest their mounts. Preacher had grown feverish by the time they came in sight of the partly erected palisade. He rejected the suggestion made by Captain Dreiling that he see Major Couglin. Like most mountain men, he was wary of the medical profession.

"You never hear a pill-roller say he's *doing* medicine. They're all the time *practicin'*, which says to me they ain't got it right yet," he growled at the Dragoon officer's repeated insistence. Instead, he sent Antoine Revier and Three Sleeps Norris to find some special moss, leaves and spiderwebs.

When Eve Billings heard of his condition she came at once to the lean-to where Preacher lay. His forehead was dew-slicked with perspiration, and he had sunk into an uneasy sleep. His dry lips parted and he muttered unintelligible words. Eve knelt at his side and dabbed his

mouth with a water-soaked cloth. Preacher moaned and
shuddered reflexively.

Gibberish spilled from his tongue. "Ubbajubba."

By that time, his companions had returned with their
shopping list filled. Eve looked up at them in an appeal.
"Why didn't he go to the Army doctor?"

Three Sleeps answered her. "Stubborn fool won't have
no truck with a doctor. Says a Cheyenne medicine man
can cure a feller faster. An' a shaman won't cut anything
off."

Secretly, Eve agreed. She saw as hopelessly medieval
the popular assumption that amputation was the solution
for nearly everything that would not respond to bleeding.
Yet, Preacher obviously had an infection. The inflamed
skin around the wound, the steady ooze of yellow matter
from the broken scab pointed to no other possibility.

"We brought the things Preacher wanted." Antoine
Revier offered the reed basket to Eve for her inspection.

What she saw made her nose wrinkle. "Do you know
how to mix these?"

Revier, the half-French, half-Delaware mountain man
answered eagerly. "Yes, ma'am. More or less that is. If
Preacher was awake, he'd know the exact amount. We'll
jist add a dab of this and a drop of that until it starts to
pull the pus outta that wound."

A bullfrog croak came from the supine Preacher. "I
am awake, damnit. Now listen." He went on to give the
proportions of each ingredient.

Antoine mixed them while Eve hovered over Preacher.
Then the jaunty son of a *voyageur* grew serious while he
poured whisky over Preacher's wound and scraped away
all of the scab with his knife. Next came the poultice,
which Antoine packed deeply into the cut. Finally, while
Three Sleeps lifted Preacher's shoulder and Eve held his
head, Antoine bound the wound with a folded strip of
cheese cloth he had purchased off Hattie Honeycutt,

then wrapped a thin, thoroughly wet strip of well-boiled buckskin over that.

"There," he pronounced over his ministrations. "That should start to draw right nicely by this evening. Tomorrow, he'll be up and sassy as ever."

Not at all convinced, Eve asked, "Are you sure?"

Antoine considered it. "By noonin' time, at least."

Decidedly uneasy, Eve made an offer. "If you don't mind, I'll watch over him part of the evening, give you two a rest."

"Fine with me," Three Sleeps agreed. "I'm sure Preacher would rather wake up lookin' at your face instead of one of ours."

Regardless of the assurances given by Three Sleeps Norris, three days passed before Preacher awoke from his septic delirium and made conscious note of his surroundings. He forced a delighted smile, though too weak to sustain it long, when he found Eve Billings dutifully at his side with a damp cloth ready to salve his fevered brow. That his mind had not suffered became immediately clear.

"How long?" he asked.

Eve fought back the tears of joy and relief that formed in her hazel eyes. "Three days. You . . . you were very sick."

Preacher made little of it. "Weren't nothin'. A li'l bout of sweats is all."

"Preacher you nearly burned up with fever. Dr. Coughlin wanted to bleed you. I told him I'd take a shotgun to him if he tried."

Lips curled in a feeble smile, Preacher expressed his gratitude for that. "An Army sawbones is good for only one thing. Makin' a feller worse off." His voice gained

strength and a gentle warmth. "Thank you for lookin'
out for me, Eve. I'm much beholdin'."

"No thanks needed. Call it . . ." Go on, say it, her
mind told her. "Call it a labor of love." Then she stumbled on. "Your friends took turns with me, watching
over you." Eve reached out and wiped Preacher's brow
a final time.

A week went by before Preacher walked abroad un-
aided in the fast-growing compound. The first floor of
the headquarters had been completed, along with a long,
low, warehouse sort of building for the quartermaster.
First to go up, Preacher had pointed out to him by Antoine Revier, had been the sutler's.

"He has some near quality whisky," Antoine advised.

"Beer," Preacher corrected. "One beer is about all I
think I can handle."

"*Très bien!* Then let us go and get it now, before you
change your mind, or your nursemaid comes along and
forbids it. *Allez vite!*"

Two more weeks went by before Preacher pronounced
himself as fit as before the fight. He looked back on the
duel with Tall Bull as he surveyed progress on the fort.
He had not intended to kill the big Blackfoot. He had
used the ploy of throwing aside his 'hawk in furtherance
of that. But a Blackfoot was a Blackfoot. When Tall Bull
threw the dirt in his face, Preacher knew he might not
leave this circle of warriors alive. So, all bets were off.

Old news, Preacher thought as he discarded his reflec-
tions and watched the last of the split logs being ham-
mered into place on the second-floor roof of the
headquarters. Somehow, panes of glass had survived the
arduous trek to this promontory and amateur glaziers
were gingerly fitting filled sashes into the lower floor's

windows. The front stockade had been completed, Preacher saw with relief.

It consisted of a double palisade of foot-thick pine trunks, sharpened on the tops with a two-foot space of rammed earth between. Running the length of it, a five-foot-deep battlement had been installed, to provide for firing from the wall. The huge gates had been hung and now moved ponderously on thick iron hinges. Fully a third of the outer defenses extended along the west face. Some ten feet inside the main gate, a pounded ramp of dirt and granite boulders provided access to a platform of the same material at the top. The battalion's three-pound field piece could be hauled up there to give covering fire. It stood now beside a flagpole which had been erected in front of the headquarters building in a circle of white-washed rocks. More of the chalky stones marked out the parade ground and walkways to and from the buildings.

"Danvers must have these poor devils working day and night," Preacher observed to Eve.

"Yes, he does. I overheard some of the soldiers talking. They said the colonel was setting a record in minor infractions' punishment. The men who break minor regulations receive extra duty details after retreat— whatever that means."

Preacher turned an amused smile on her. "I think that's when they fire off the little cannon and haul down the flag."

Perplexity lined Eve's brow. "Oh, yes. But, why do they call it 'retreat'? Isn't that running from the enemy?"

Preacher shrugged. "Same word, diff'rent meanings. That's the Army for you." They laughed together.

"You're coming to supper tonight?" Eve asked.

Chuckling, Preacher spread his hands in submission. "A team of a dozen mules could not keep me away."

* * *

Something had gone decidedly wrong with the alliance between the Blackfoot, Cheyenne and Sioux, as it often did in such meldings of one-time enemies. The Cheyenne had been slow in coming in. Three large bands, including that of Cloud Blanket, had refused to join at all. The Sioux had sent only token numbers from the Brule, Oglala and Teton subtribes. Notable among those absent were the members of Red Cloud's band. As a result, the planned great uprising did not happen on schedule. Iron Shirt fumed over it. At last he decided to take out his anger on the nearest whites.

Accordingly, he stormed into the lodge occupied by Praeger, Gross and Reiker. He studied them in silence a moment, smelled their sudden outbreak of fear. What puny creatures, he thought to himself.

"Where are your wagons of rifles? Where's the powder?"

"On the way, Iron Shirt," Praeger managed calmly.

Iron Shirt spat into the fire. "That is not good enough. We hold back and waste our energy in races and gambling. This war cannot begin without the weapons you promised. When will they be here?"

Coldly Praeger responded. "I don't know any more than you do. Besides, the other tribes have not come in as you expected. When the warriors get here, the guns will be here also. What you need is another show of big medicine. I think I might have just the thing."

Intrigued, Iron Shirt leaned toward the broad-shouldered, lean white man, his eyes fixed on the knife scar. "What is that?"

"Give me time to get everything rigged up. Then, tonight at the dances, tell everyone that you are going to do a most potent dance. A spirit dance that will do wondrous things, like nothing they have ever seen. Use the dance you worked out last month, the one you were going to use as a victory dance when the white soldiers are destroyed."

Plentifully shrewd for all his lack of sophistication, Iron Shirt's eyes held a gleam of anticipation. "What is it I am going to make happen?"

"Tell them that you will make stars rise from the ground up into the sky."

Uncertain, Iron Shirt blurted, "Can I do that? I mean, what are you going to do to make it happen?"

Praeger gave him an enigmatic smile. "Wait and see. I promise you it might even have you wetting your loincloth."

Praeger and his associates, along with Soures and three henchmen spent the rest of the day well beyond the large encampment of Blackfoot, Cheyenne and Sioux. They had the last tube in place shortly before dark.

Praeger headed for the rear of one wagon. "We'll fix something to eat out here. No sense in going back and drawing attention to ourselves, then having to come back after dark. Someone might follow and spoil the whole show."

"You've got it all figgered out, Mr. Praeger," Blake Soures said, sincerely complimenting his boss. "Those Injuns'll think the world's comin' to an end, sure enough."

Morton Gross raised a cautioning hand. "We do not want to terrify them into running away. This exercise is merely for the purpose of reinforcing the magical powers of our great prophet, Iron Shirt."

Aaron Reiker added his own praise. "Still, it was inspired of you to have ordered these pyrotechnics and to have had them shipped out here."

Praeger fought back a smirk. "We'll soon see, won't we?" He began to take food from a large woven reed basket and pass it around.

Two hours after darkness fell, Quinton Praeger roused himself. "Better get ready. That's the drum beat for Iron Shirt's fancy dance. It'll take about twenty minutes, then we let go the first shell."

When the time came, Praeger touched the glowing tip of a length of slow match to the short fuse near the bottom of a fiberboard tube. With a dull thud, a whoosh and a hissing roar the projectile leaped into the night sky. It burst when it reached the apex of its arc, showering the sky in smoky red streamers. By then the second star shell was on its way.

This one erupted in green and white, with bright spots at the end of streamers of smoke that crackled and popped as their internal fuses burned down to the small charges. Most of the fireworks Praeger had arranged for consisted of three-pound star bursts. For the finale, he had something special. Following a simultaneous discharge of six star shells, he and his associates ignited and launched five aerial reports.

Discs of white appeared one after another in the sky, each followed by a violent blast and an accompanying shock wave. When the awesome sound of the last one rolled away across the hills, Quinton Praeger heard the cackle of Blake Soures.

"That'll have them savages dribblin' in their drawers for certain sure. What a hell of a show, Mr. Praeger. I'd call it brilliant."

Those in the camp did not share the enthusiasm of Blake Soures. Unable to contain them, the guards stood helplessly by while the pony herd stampeded. Many of the warriors abandoned their immense pride to hide, shivering under their bison robes. Some fell to the ground, stupefied, in superstitious veneration. The

Great Spirit truly spoke through Iron Shirt, others exclaimed to their neighbors.

Slowly the pandemonium subsided. Shaken to his core by the dreadful display, Iron Shirt had no words for those who gradually came to reaffirm their allegiance. He could only grip their forearms and nod and mumble. The coldly analytical part of his mind eventually asserted itself. Whatever the white men had done, it had restored his power over these fractious tribes.

He turned, smiling, to his most trusted subordinates, Two Moons and Bent Trees. "Trust me, my friends. With this great medicine, the mighty battle really will come."

TWENTY-THREE

Preacher had become downright itchy-footed. Another week had gone by and still no major attack by the hostiles. There had been skirmishes against wood and water details, the fellers had been shot at from a distance and the newly erected sawmill had been thoroughly riddled with .54 caliber balls on two occasions. Preacher considered the damming of the swift little creek and the locating of the mill on its banks below the obstruction to be the height of stupidity.

"Even dumber than buildin' this fort out where it's exposed to ever'thing," he had been heard to opine frequently. At least one of his worries seemed to have somewhat worked its way to a solution.

Every day, more of the pilgrims settled in to rest and wait out the year at the fort. Spring, they declared, would suit them fine to move on. They had listened to his tales and those of his companions about winter in the high country. None among them felt hearty enough to endure exposure to the elements in wagon boxes. Well and good, Preacher figured. It gave him more time to ponder on why the Blackfoot and their allies had not attacked in force.

An exception to the settling down of the immigrants was the subtle campaign still waged by Eve Billings and Isaac Warner to get Preacher to commit to leading them through the wilderness. It manifested itself again that evening at a supper presided over by Eve and Rebecca Warner. After a satisfying meal featuring roast venison, Isaac Warner sopped the last of a rich brown gravy from his plate with a delicate, yeast-raised bread roll, leaned back and patted his fledgling potbelly.

"Yessir, I've come to see spring as the ideal time to move on. We can learn a lot in the meantime, and the animals will certainly be more fit."

Preacher accepted a cheroot from the wagon captain which he tipped toward his benefactor before he lighted it. "Couldn't do a better thing. By then, it might be this fuss with the Injuns will be ended."

Isaac touched a burning ember to his own cigar. "Only one thing is left undone, then. We will still be in need of a guide, competent scouts, that sort of thing."

Preacher tried to be evasive. "When word gets around about this fort, there'll be all sorts of folk drop by. You can find someone easy."

Warner was not to be put off so easily. "Fact of the matter is, myself and the committee are set on it bein' you and possibly your friends, Revier and Norris."

"Nope. Ain't possible. Soon's this Injun ruckus is over with, I'm on my way to the Shinin' Mountains."

"We can pay well. If not all in advance, then when we reach the Oregon Country."

Shaking his head, Preacher made to leave. "Sorry, Mr. Warner. I ain't in the guide business. I leave that to them that enjoys it." He gave his thanks for the good meal and walked away.

Eve excused herself and quickly followed. When she caught up to Preacher she scurried around his broad-shouldered frame and halted in his path. Every bit the auburn-haired image of determination, she came right to the point.

"Preacher, for the life of me, I don't know what you have against leading us to the Northwest. Mr. Warner said we could pay well. Forgive me for being far too bold, brazen even, but let me tell you this. Along with the monetary reward we can give you, there can be other, more pleasant rewards, if you agree."

Stifling a groan born of inner turmoil, Preacher put his big hands on her tender shoulders. "Eve . . . Eve, what's a body to do? By jing, the truth is, I'd plow an' plant a garden for one of your smiles. For a kiss, I'd do handsprings from here to the Grand Tetons. If . . . if I heard you right, for that, I'd take on those Blackfoot single-handed and whup them all. But I can't— I won't let myself be harnessed up and put in charge of a wagon train. I'm sorry. I know I'll regret it tomorrow. Only it's jist the way I am."

Disappointment registered in Eve's hazel eyes. "That's the longest, and most eloquent, speech I've ever heard you make. I'm sorry over your stubborn refusal, but I think I can understand. You've always been a free soul. Any sort of harness, and I'm afraid that includes matrimony, would only chafe. But, now that I've said it, Preacher dear, the offer remains open. Good night."

Five double hands of Lakota warriors had set up a camp near their Cheyenne cousins. In spite of their earlier promises, they had failed to join with the Blackfoot for a large raid on the soldier-place. Iron Shirt went to visit them, his patience at an end. They welcomed him warmly enough and, after the customary meal, got down to serious talking.

"We are coming. It has been decided, and we will be there," Spotted Horse, the Lakota's principal war chief stated patiently.

Iron Shirt barely held his impatience in check. "Yes, but when?"

Spotted Horse made a gesture of indifference with his

bead-decorated turkey-wing fan. "When we get there. Why are you in such haste, Iron Shirt? Going to war requires deliberation and careful planning."

That loosed a spill of heated words. "The planning is done; there is nothing difficult about it. We must not let this soldier-place be built. Like all white men, once they come, they never leave. Do you want all of your bison killed? The soldiers will do that. They shoot them for trophies. As you know, I have three tame white men in my village. They tell me this is a true thing."

Spotted Horse nodded sagely. "I have been told they scratch the ground, tear up the grass to put in seeds."

"Yes, they plant for food, like the Navajo," Iron Shirt spat in disgust. "We must attack this evil place and burn it to the ground."

Spotted Horse pursed his full lips, then nodded curtly. "It is agreed. We will come at the next moon."

Exasperated, Iron Shirt sprang to his feet. No! It must be now. We leave for the soldier-place with tomorrow's sun. Meet us there."

For want of something to do, Preacher rode out with Lieutenant Judson of Company C the next morning on the water detail. The youthful officer, Preacher was willing to bet he did not shave more than every other day, had matured considerably since their encounter with the Pawnee. Lines had appeared on his forehead and cheeks, where none had been before. He didn't talk as loudly, nor move with nervous energy like a youngster in his teens. Privately, he shared Preacher's opinion of the water situation. With construction nearly complete at the fort, he felt secure in bringing up the subject to the mountain man.

"Our engineering officer, Major Vickers, has completed his tests for building a cistern. I for one will be glad when we don't have to come out every day to water the horses.

For some reason, I can't shake the prickling sensation that Blackfoot eyes are watching my every move."

Preacher chuckled deep in his throat. "That outlook'll keep you alive a whale of a lot longer than some others I could mention."

Vickers read Preacher correctly. "Colonel Danvers certainly does have an optimistic attitude. Not that I'm criticizing, of course."

"Ain't for me to be bearin' tales, Tom. Right now, I'm jist an unemployed scout."

"Then why do you take these risks like the others?"

Preacher rubbed his square chin. "Keeps my edge keen. Fastest way to get yourself kilt in the High Lonesome is to take to thinkin' you're nice and safe."

"Is it really that wild out here, Preacher?"

"It is at times. Thing is, you never know for certain when those times have come around. Injuns is moody, and changeable. The closer you are to them, the more they give you cause to play guessin' games."

Lieutenant Judson cast a nervous glance around the hillside above the creek bed. "And we're mighty close to them down here."

"Yep. There's three Cheyenne watchin' us now, right up in them pines." Preacher jutted his chin to indicate the direction of the observers.

Tom Judson jerked as though wasp-stung. "I'd better alert the others."

A restraining hand went to his arm as Preacher drawled in a low voice. "Nope. I wouldn't get all stirred up and make 'em think we're the hostiles. If they had any thought to lift our hair, they'd not let me get an eye on 'em."

Judson cut his eyes to Preacher's face. "How can you be so sure?"

"I ain't. But I've jist never seen warriors sit their horses right quiet like that an' then attack."

"What should I do then?"

Preacher did not even hesitate. "We'll jist mosey right slow along the crick, tell the watering detail as we go. No hurry. Them Cheyenne ain't gonna leave until after we do."

Half an hour later, Lieutenant Judson heaved a heavy sigh of relief as the watering detail rode away from the creek. He reported their discovery to the Battalion Sergeant Major upon their return. BSM Muldoon doubled the number of the second detail to take horses out for water.

"It's Injuns now, is it?" Muldoon developed a faraway look in his blue eyes. With a limited supply of old John Barleycorn, his nose had lost much of its ruddy glow. He had leaned down some, also. Preacher noted the changes approvingly. Fat might be all right for a politician, but a man on the spare side moved faster in a fight.

"Three Cheyenne. One of them was a mere boy."

"But Mr. Judson said he never laid an eye on them, sure an' he did."

"*I* saw them, that's all that mattered, Muldoon."

"Right ye are, Preacher."

Preacher changed the subject. "Judson says the engineer is about ready to blast out a cistern."

"That he is. By all the saints, they're goin' at it backward as usual. What I mean is, what are we to do with all these winders in place? One mistake in the amount of blasting powder an' we'll have glass flyin' all over the inside o' this room, we will."

Preacher laughed. "Board them up, Sergeant Major."

Muldoon cocked his head to one side. "Ye ever see how fast a chunk of rock moves with a big bang behind it?"

"Ummm. You've got a point. All you can hope for is none of them powder men has got three thumbs."

"You goin' out with the new detail?"

"No. I've had an invite to take nooning with Eve Billings. She's promised something special."

Merriment twinkled in the eyes of BSM Muldoon.

"Sure an' ye've the sound of a man that's been already caught."

A twinge radiated from the area of Preacher's heart. "Not in the least. I've been alone, on my own, for too many years to change my ways."

Laughing, Muldoon turned back to his paperwork. "Now, that'll be the day, it will."

Bored by lack of something destructive to do, Blake Soures and three of his henchmen decided to pay a visit to the sutler's store at the new fort. They had a hanker to try out some of the whiskey the government-contracted civilian merchant had in stock. They rode inside the stockade shortly after noon the same day, having noted the watering detail on the way.

"Somebody's mighty stupid around these parts," opined Eden Dillon. Yellowed, snaggy teeth made an unhealthy slash in the lower part of his mouth. "They ain't gonna git no water outta rock."

Blake Soures nodded agreement. "The thing for our Indian friends to do is catch them out in the open, watering horses. Be a regular slaughter."

They dismounted at a freshly built, raw, yellow pine tie-rail and looped reins. With his accustomed swagger, Soures led the way into the saloon side of the sutler's store. There, the first thing he saw was a large sign in bold, black, capital letters.

HARD LIQUOR SALES PROHIBITED
TO ENLISTED AND NCO
PERSONNEL
(OFFICERS and CIVILIANS ONLY)
by Order of
Lt. Col. Danvers, Commanding.

Soures pointed it out to his subordinates. "Well, lookie here. Aren't you glad you didn't sign on to wear one of those pretty blue uniforms?"

Pete Price leaned toward Blake Soures. "I betcha we found out who thought up puttin' this place on a finger of rock."

"It ain't natural, that's what." Dillon was put out. "Not right to get between a man an' his whisky. Downright barbarian."

From behind the bar, a jovial-faced man urged them toward the planks. "Seein' as how none of you gentlemen are soldiers, step right up and enjoy a drink."

While the four outlaws settled themselves at the bar, the barkeep poured into large, fish-eye shot glasses. With a deft flick of his wrist, he distributed them to his new customers. "You're new here, so first round is on the house."

Soures answered him with a big grin and a hearty voice. "Now, that's mighty nice. Much obliged, my good man." He had listened intently to the conversations of Quinton Praeger and his associates and now often made a conscious effort to mimic their speech mannerisms when he addressed strangers.

With a good-natured smile, and a wink, the barkeep informed them, "The next one'll cost you double."

Soures eyed the man over the rim of his shot glass, which he had raised to his lips. "Sounds like a place I know of down in the French Quarter of New Orleans."

Entermann, the sutler, gave Soures an expression of innocence. "I've never been in N'awlins."

They shared a laugh and Soures downed his whisky. A moment later, Preacher entered the saloon. He came up short on the threshold and eyed the strangers with immediate suspicion. To the best of his knowledge, there wasn't a white man within two hundred miles. Except, of course, the ones rumored to be with Iron Shirt.

Preacher broke his momentary freeze and crossed the plank floor to the far end of the bar.

From there, he could keep an eye on all four hard-faced men. For their part, they wasted little time before turning cold, killer's eyes on Preacher. Their threatening demeanors sent warning jangles along the arms of the mountain man. Ordinarily, he did not wear his pair of Walker Colts inside the fort, only he'd had no time after returning from the water detail to remove them, because of his noon invitation from Eve. Sight of these four set his fingers itching to close around the butt of at least one .44. When they had made clear their awareness of his presence, Preacher seized the main chance.

"You fellers is new around here. Might I ask what brings you to Fort Washington?" Recently, Danvers had grandiosely named his small compound after the Father of His Country.

Constantly on the prod, Pete Price made a snotty reply. "You might ask, but you won't get any answers. So, butt out."

Even more on guard, Preacher tried calming words. "Now, now. That's hardly the way to answer a polite question. Seein' as how I'm the unofficial welcoming committee, I only sought to make you feel at home."

"We don't need a welcome," snapped Soures. "Who are you to be pokin' your nose into our business?"

"Folks call me Preacher."

Thought of the thousand dollars in gold bonus for killing the mountain man named Preacher galvanized Blake Soures. His hand sped to his sash and the butt of a .60-caliber pistol while he shouted to his underlings.

"We got us a thousand dollars, boys! Get him!"

With his outside holsters, Preacher beat all four easily. A Walker Colt filled his right hand and he had the hammer falling before the speediest, Pete Price, could clear the barrel of his long single-shot pistol from his belt. A

thunderous clap announced the detonation of the powder load in one chamber of Preacher's Colt.

A powerful fist slammed into the lock plate of Price's
pistol and rammed it painfully back into his gut. He
doubled over painfully and his finger reflexively
twitched. An accomplished shootist, Pete Price had
cocked the cumbersome firearm before drawing it clear.
As a result, another loud blast filled the room and Price
blew a fist-sized hole in his left thigh. He went down
shrieking in agony while blood spurted from his femoral
artery. Now, Preacher had only three to contend with.

Hot lead cut a painful path across the top of Preacher's
left shoulder. An instant later the Walker spoke again.
Its message went to a wooly-faced hard case with mean
little pig eyes and a smoking pistol in his left hand. He
had fired too soon, Preacher noted. The muzzle was still
high. He learned of his mistake when the messenger of
death split his breastbone and ripped a hole through his
left lung.

Preacher went to one knee, the .44 Colt erupting a
third time. Glass tinkled when the ball shattered the
chimney of a wall-mounted coal oil-lamp, after it exited
the back of the head of surly Eden Dillon. Preacher cut
his eyes to Blake Soures, who had taken refuge behind
the bar.

Intent on making the perfect shot, Soures did not recognize the dreadful image of the Grim Reaper crouched
before him in the person of Preacher. A fourth ball fluttered through the air with the leathery rustle of the
death angel's wings. The lead pellet smacked through
the bar front and ended in the hinge of Soures' right
elbow. With a howl and a curse, he propelled himself
backward, fumbled left-handed with the pistol in his
waistband and drew it.

By then, Preacher had the fourth piece of frontier

trash to deal with. Their weapons fired as one. Preacher immediately flattened out on the floor.

"You got him! You got him, Earl!" Soures shouted as he came full upright in time to hear the bad news.

"No, I didn'," Earl gargled out through the blood welling in his throat. "He . . . got . . . me."

Horrified, Soures cut his eyes to the floor. He focused at once on the black hole that formed the muzzle of Preacher's Walker Colt. Flame blossomed in that darkness, then a stunning agony seared through the chest of Blake Soures. He fired his pistol blindly. The slug put a shower of splinters in the face of Preacher, who fired his second Colt into the exposed gut of his would-be killer. Soures died before he hit the floor.

"Damned unfriendly fellers, I'd say," Preacher offered to a bug-eyed Hyman Entermann.

"B'God, Preacher, you are faster than a scalded cat."

"I've worked at it a mite. Now, I think I'll have me a beer. Gun-fightin' gives me a thirst."

A moment later, the Provost Marshal, Captain Preston, and three of the afternoon guard detail rushed into the sutler's store. "What's going on here?" the officer demanded.

"Nothin' now," Preacher answered laconically.

"How did these bodies get here?"

Preacher took a pull on his beer and made a sour face. "Preston, I swear, you don't have a sensible question to ask. What you should be findin' out is who started the shootin'." His annoyance rang in his voice.

"Well . . . who did start the shooting?"

Nodding toward the jumble of broken and spilled bottles and the body sprawled among them, Preacher spoke simply. "That one there did."

With almost a simper in his prim, disapproving voice, the Provost Marshal declared, "Brawling is prohibited in this establishment or anywhere at Fort Washington. Brawling with firearms is a flogging offense."

"You won't be floggin' this mother's son."

Captain Preston gauged the man he addressed. "Oh? And why not?"

"Take a look around you, Captain Preston. There's four of them here. An' they were ready for me. An' I've got five loads left for this revolvin' pistol here."

Hyman Entermann interrupted. "It was self-defense, Captain. This one back here said they would be paid a thousand dollars gold for killing Preacher. Then he went for his gun. Preacher beat him. End of story. Now please have your men remove this filth from my establishment."

Preacher beamed at the bantam rooster attitude of the sutler. "Yer a good man, Brother Entermann."

"There'll be an investigation," Captain Preston grumbled darkly. Then he made a curt gesture to the guards.

Preacher had the last word. "Don't count on it."

Three days later, Preacher awakened as usual an hour before dawn. He pulled on a long-sleeved flannel shirt against the morning chill and stretched out the kinks. He struck flint to steel, ignited the hat-sized fire he had laid out the previous night and put on water to boil for coffee.

He was working on his second cup in the pearly light of a peaceful dawn when the Blackfoot, Cheyenne and Sioux attacked.

TWENTY-FOUR

Lieutenant Brice had the water detail for the Company horses. He kept in mind everything Preacher had told his friend, Tom Judson. For one thing, he never looked directly at anything in the shadows of the trees that grew along the gorges that formed the watershed for Goose Creek. Although he could not put a name to it, Brice had a particularly active itch between his shoulder blades.

It came as no surprise to him, then, when his roving gaze picked out feathers where there should be none. Neatly trimmed feathers at that. Controlling his urge to draw his Dragoon revolver from the saddle holster and fire, he brought up the nose of his drinking horse and ambled over to his platoon sergeant.

"Sergeant Meaney, pass the word quietly for the men to prepare to draw and fire a cylinder load into those trees over there on my command. Then we get these horses the hell away from here."

"May I ask what it is, sir?"

"Indians, Meaney. Too damned many of them for us to hold off on our own. I have me an itch that tells me they are all around the fort."

Sergeant Meaney nodded his understanding. "I have a sore gut that tells me the same, sir."

"Very well. Be careful about it, don't let the savages suspect we know they are there."

Throughout their exchange, Lieutenant Brice used all his will to keep from looking at the spot where he had seen the feathers. Now he rode with a tense back to the location, expectant of an arrow at any second. He reached the far end of the formation, told Corporal Grange about the hostiles and then looked back over the detail with every show of boredom.

To his satisfaction, he saw every man had his hand near or on the sheepskin covers of his pistol's holster. "All right, men . . . do it now!"

His own Dragoon pistol came free, and he had the hammer back before the muzzle centered on the area where the feathers had been before. "Fire!"

A thunderous roar swelled up in the creek bed, as twelve Dragoons emptied six rounds each from their pistols. Immediately they smoothly changed weapons. Lieutenant Brice stood in his stirrups.

"Back to the fort at the double. . . . Hooo!"

With exceptional skill, the platoon had the entire company's horses on the move and up and out of the creek bed before the hidden Blackfoot could recover from the blazing curtain of lead delivered by the Dragoons. They came on soon enough. Whooping and yipping, all of the Indians broke from concealment and splashed across the creek. In the lead, Red Elk, a Cheyenne, raised his rifle and fired blindly.

His bullet cracked over the heads of the trailing soldiers. It only served to move them faster. Thinking quickly, Lieutenant Brice put Sergeant Meaney at the head of the string of horses and turned back to hastily form a rear guard. The crackle of their pistols drowned out the war cries of the Blackfoot. The sudden, unexpected conflict triggered a premature opening to the battle.

While the Dragoons raced for a small sally port near the corral inside the stockade, a long line of Blackfoot warriors whipped their horses to a gallop on the long, steep slope beyond the fort to the west.

Fully a hundred Blackfoot warriors swept down the steep slope to the west of Fort Washington. An equal number of Cheyenne charged toward the main gate. Behind them loomed the Sioux. Frantically, the sentries labored to swing closed the gates. A bugle blared hysterically. Dragoons on fatigue details dropped their brooms and pitchforks and ran for their Hall carbines. Others spilled from their tents, drawing suspenders over their long-sleeved underwear. Half a dozen ran for the cannon. Preacher made for his lean-to to recover his rifles.

"Knew they would be comin'," he shouted to Three Sleeps Norris, headed in the same direction from their cookfire.

Three Sleeps spat a quid of tobacco from his mouth. "Damn right. Jist a matter of time."

Lieutenant Colonel Danvers's adjutant stood in the middle of the parade ground and bellowed orders. "Companies A and D to the west wall. Companies B and C to the north wall. Get that cannon moving!"

Dust boiled up inside the compound as Dragoons dashed back and forth, uncertain as to whether they should dismount and man the walls or form as skirmishers for a future counterattack. Gradually the officers calmed and directed them. Rifles crackled from outside.

Return fire started at once. Preacher heard Captain Dreiling's firm voice steadying his troops. "Hold your fire until they're well within range. Hold fast, men. Take careful aim. Ready . . . fire!"

A swath of lead balls flung thirty-five Cheyenne warriors from their saddles. "Reload . . . take aim . . . fire."

* * *

Two Moons had the contentment of a man whose dream had come true. He fully believed again in the medicine of Iron Shirt. Now that they traveled down the long-promised warpath to drive out all whites, the Blackfoot war chief banished all doubts. His warriors would be in the second wave to dash down the high mount. They had been given the honor of scaling the wall and fighting the soldiers hand to hand. The first surge, made up of braves from Iron Shirt's band, who were supposed to give covering fire, had already ridden half the distance to the high, pole barricade. Two Moons reflected on the past moon of difficulties.

It had taken a lot more effort than Iron Shirt's white men had expected. Not an easy task to get a warrior, proud of his individual feats of bravery, to work as part of a *team*. Even now the white man's word tasted strange in the mouth of Two Moons. What was a *team*, and what made it a better way to fight? Why was it superior to the way we have fought since the ancestor days? Where is the honor to be won if everyone holds back to shoot at the enemy from behind rocks and from the protection of gulley banks?

There was little glory in counting coup on a dead man. That was for boys beginning their seasons as warriors. Two Moons recalled the time when his sap ran fresh and hot. He had gone on a raiding party against the Cheyenne. They had stolen horses and ridden away without a scratch. The Cheyenne followed them. When the Red Top people came up to them, they offered challenge. A younger Two Moons had ridden out ahead of the line of his Raven Society brothers and shouted insults at the Cheyenne. He had exposed his manhood and waved it in the faces of the enemy while he told them what he would do with it when they had been conquered. Then he had charged directly at them, an arrow nocked and ready. The Cheyenne stared at him as though frozen.

Two Moons shot one Red Top warrior in the chest, then struck another with his bow. Two perfect coups, and right in front of his brothers! A line of fire ran across the point of his shoulder as a Cheyenne lance barely grazed him. He whirled and rode back, then all the Blackfoot charged.

The Cheyenne fought like Dark Spirits. One of them had a white man's fire-stick— no, a rifle— the older Two Moons corrected himself. With it, he killed two of the Blackfoot. Yet, when the fighting ended, Two Moons and his brothers rode away victorious, dripping scalps tied to their bows, and with more Cheyenne horses than they had started with. Now, the Red Top people fought with them, not as enemies. How the world had turned upside down. Two Moons shook his head in wonder.

From the tree line north of the fort, Spotted Horse could hear the solid thuds when the high gates swung together. The soldiers would be protected now, he thought. How foolish, the Lakota leader thought, for a man to lock himself inside a small place to fight. Only the clear, open plains suited a warrior's soul. Beyond him, on the narrow shelf that jutted out from the base of the foothills, the Cheyenne, led by Red Elk, raced toward where the soldiers waited. The *Sahiela*— the Cheyenne— our cousins, are brave and they fight well. Yet, only our braves can match the ferocity of the Blackfoot. Spotted Horse spat as he thought the word for their traditional enemy. How is it that we come to fight beside them?

Because of the medicine of Iron Shirt, he acknowledged unwillingly. He had seen with his own eyes men who died, even though they had been given the protection of Iron Shirt's medicine. Not all of our people agree, he recalled, mindful of the young hothead, Red

Cloud. He had maintained that the medicine was fake. He had agreed with Cloud Blanket of the Cheyenne, and strangely, the elders agreed and stayed out of this fight. He himself had only changed his mind at the last minute. Gunfire erupted along the wall before him and the two sides joined. Spotted Horse readied his pony. Their time would come soon.

Red Elk pushed his pony to a full gallop and loosed one arrow after another at the high wall of the fort. Never had they fought against such a thing. He doubted that arrows would do much damage against the thick forest of lodge-pole pines that had been lashed together across their path. What a strange way to fight, he mused. Who would want to hide behind a barrier three times the height of the tallest man?

Where was the honor in that? From beside him, one of the rifles given them by Iron Shirt barked, and as the smoke cleared, Red Elk saw a white soldier rear up and fall backward. Maybe they had a chance after all. It would be their job to keep the blue-coats busy while their cousins, the Lakota, rushed forward and scaled the walls. Such a strange way to fight. Yet, Iron Shirt had assured them all that it had come to him in a dream. One small thought nagged at him: the Blackfoot have been our enemies since the grandfather times: why do they share their medicine with us now? He would soon see how it worked, of that he was certain.

From his vantage point outside headquarters, Battalion Sergeant Major Muldoon could see little of the hostiles. Here and there feathers and painted faces revealed frantic action beyond the walls. Farther back, more ranks of savages could be seen on the slope that overlooked the fort.

He turned to the young headquarters lieutenant next to him. "Sure an' it's just like Preacher said it would be. Th' heathen devils have got themselves up on that hillside and can look right down in here. If they knew a jot about artillery, we'd all be dead ducks, we would."

A tightening of jaw muscles gave clear indication of the effect of those words on the youthful subaltern. For all *he* knew, the Indians might well have a battery of field pieces. So far, none of the savages they had engaged conducted their battles like Indians were supposed to fight. For some reason, they used standard military tactics. That made it downright scary. From the next words spoken by Muldoon, he might have been reading the lieutenant's mind.

"Of course, when they be pressed too hard, they have always fallen back on their every man for himself ways and flung themselves at us with total disregard for their lives or those of their unit. That's when the advantage falls to us. Ye'll be sein' that here, I've no doubt, sor."

Shouted curses came from the parapet behind the wall and the rate of fire increased. "There's more of 'em coming!" Arrows sailed over the defenses to land harmlessly on the parade ground.

BSM Muldoon touched the edge of the shiny black bill on his cap in salute. "If ye'll excuse me, sor, I must go and take a better look at what's makin' up. Th' darlin' colonel will need to know."

A surge of relief passed through the lieutenant, and he made no offer to accompany Muldoon. "Right, you do that, Sergeant Major."

A flight of twenty-five arrows slammed into the ground all around, their colorful fletchings so many evil blossoms. Muldoon did not even flinch from them, instead he strode through their pattern with a light word on his lips. " 'Tis a fine day for a stroll through the flowers, it is."

Not being paid to defend the fort, the immigrant men armed themselves and formed a protective screen around their portion of the inner compound. Not surprisingly, when the call for the men to rally had come, Charlie Billings had taken up his light rifle and started off. Eve caught her son by the scooped back of his overalls.

"Where do you think you are going, young man?"

Talking over one shoulder, Charlie explained himself. "They called for all the men to arm themselves. There's Injuns out there attacking the fort."

"That did not include ten-year-old boys. You can do your best service by staying here and reloading for me, if the Indians get inside."

Charlie's face clouded. "Aw, Mom."

"No arguments. The matter is closed. Besides, I thought you liked the idea of being an Indian."

His stubborn streak flaring, Charlie answered hotly. "That's different. These are bad Injuns. *Hostiles.*"

Eve would not be swayed any more than her son. "I want you to watch your sister in the meantime. And," she added to soften her refusal, "I think it would be wise for you to carry your rifle with you while you do."

Charlie brightened. "Sure, Mom."

When Charlie and Anna departed for the soddy that had been built for the family, Eve lifted her eyes to the heavens. "Dear God, don't let anything happen to them."

Preacher and Three sleeps reached a portion of the revetment over the gate before the Cheyenne came into range. Both shared in the dismay of the lieutenant.

Never had they seen such control and order among charging hostiles. Someone had found a way to train them and make it stick. At least for the present. Pick off a couple of war leaders and that would quickly change, he reasoned.

"There's hundreds of them, Preacher."

"Yer right, Three Sleeps. And more yet to come. D'ya notice they're fightin' like soldiers?"

"Yes, and I don't like it."

Three Cheyenne had ridden well inside range. Preacher took aim on one, Three Sleeps sighted on another. They fired a fraction of a second apart and the targets left the backs of their ponies for the Spirit World. Quickly, the mountain men reloaded. Preacher popped the last one at forty yards. Some twenty-five yards from the stockade, an irregular line of broken rocks and fair-sized boulders had been left behind by the Dragoons when the fort grounds had been cleared.

Preacher had cautioned Lieutenant Colonel Danvers about this slip in planning and had, as usual, been ignored. He pointed them out now to Three Sleeps as Cheyenne braves, who had ridden double, slipped from behind their friends and taken cover in this manmade barrier. "I told the colonel about those rocks. They'll hide a Cheyenne right enough."

An increased rate of fire from the west told Preacher of the arrival of even more hostiles. He took a quick look over the parade ground and saw the six Dragoons still trying to get the cannon in place. He shook his head.

"Ain't any of those dummies ever heard of a horse? That's half a ton of metal they're tryin' to carry on their backs. A couple of horses would pull that gun up the ramp in no time at all."

"There's a right way, and a wrong way, and—"

Preacher's sigh cut off Three Sleeps. "Yeah, I know, the Army way."

From the tree line came the foulest of Lakota curses. *"Hu ihpeya wicayapo!"*

Preacher's scowl held a bushel of misery. "Aw, damn, the Lakota have got in this thing, too. Well, one thing certain, they ain't gonna use *me* like a woman."

"Not this chile, neither," Three Sleeps readily agreed.

Eighty-five Lakota warriors, painted and ready for war, rode out of the trees. Three Sleeps saw a brown shoulder between two large rocks and snapped a shot. A howl answered him and the now bloody shoulder disappeared. While he reloaded, he offered his observation to Preacher.

"It don't get much nastier than this."

"Right as rain, Pard. An' I got a feelin' it's gonna get worse before it gets better."

Being senior, by time in grade, Captain Dreiling commanded the defenses over the main gate. He watched with even greater trepidation than Preacher when the Sioux showed themselves and began the charge down the length of the promontory. Protectively, the Dragoons on the parapet had crouched down when the Cheyenne had taken positions in the rocks and begun a sniping duel. Now he found himself forced to go along the double rank of defenders and whack rumps with the flat of his saber to get the troops up to fire at the new hostiles.

"All right, ladies, this is not a quilting bee. Get loaded, get up and prepare to fire by volley. The Sioux have come to pay us a visit." Funny, he did not feel the least bit sarcastic. At the bottom of it, he knew himself to be every bit as scared as the greenest Dragoon out there.

There had to be one in every unit, and Private Finney was the one in Company C. "But, Cap'n, if we do that, those other Injuns will potshot us for sure."

Captain Dreiling ground his teeth. "Why do you think

there are two ranks of you? The kneeling rank covers the rocks, the standing one fires on the approaching hostiles. Make ready, men, they are almost in range."

How vastly different from exercises in tactical defense of fortified installations taught at the Academy, Edward Dreiling mused as dust and powder smoke drifted across the ground below. There had been no bullets or arrows snapping past then. If anyone received serious injuries it was due to carelessness or stupidity. These red men swarming out there wanted to kill those in the fort.

From what he had been told they would not stay their hand if appealed to for quarter. The Indians knew no such civilized concept as taking prisoners for exchange. This day there would be many deaths.

Will I be ready for it? his mind mocked him.

TWENTY-FIVE

By noon, two heavy, concerted charges by the hostiles had been repulsed. Preacher munched on a wedge of cornbread, passed out by the women of the sheltering wagon train, and examined the powder-smeared faces of the young Dragoons. To his relief and satisfaction, he saw only expressions of determination. They had gotten over their initial fear. Some of them had even gotten up a game of mumblety-peg. Now, if luck held, the Injuns would not think of the concave wall to the east of this finger of land. Preacher lifted a gourd pitcher to his lips to wash down the cornbread with water. It had tasted good. Someone had thoughtfully cooked bits of bacon into it.

Years of fighting Indians and living in the wilderness had conditioned Preacher to take advantage of food whenever the opportunity presented itself. He ran the tip of his tongue across his teeth and reached for one of two flaky biscuits that remained on his tin plate. When he lifted it, a pink-centered slice of roast venison appeared beneath. He nodded at his plate and spoke to Antoine Revier.

"Maybe we ought to fight Injuns ever' day. Those folks are sure feedin' us nice."

"The venison came from *you know who,*" said Antoine, who gave Preacher a poke in the ribs.

"Aw, git off my back, Tony."

A sudden stir broke out at the junction of the north and west walls. "They're comin' again!" BSM Muldoon bellowed. "Dragoons, stand to your arms."

Iron Shirt had lost his patience. So many warriors should have overrun that small number of soldiers long ago. They had followed orders well, at least until the volume of fire had rained down from those cursed walls increased to a steady roar. Then they forgot what they were supposed to do and went back to the old ways. He decided that a display of courage was needed. Taking up lance and rifle, he gathered his closest, most loyal followers and set out to lead the next attack.

First he harangued the warriors. "We must take this fort before the sun goes to sleep in the west. We cannot fail. Do you see that small knoll? If we do not carry the walls this time, I will be on the top, to make medicine and renew your spirits. One way or another we will kill all of the soldiers before darkness."

Revived, the Blackfoot, Cheyenne and Sioux formed new lines and made ready to attack. At the signal from Iron Shirt, they threw themselves at the walls again. For many, it took supreme effort to blank out the images of their dead brothers and friends, men who were now supposed to be protected from the white men's bullets.

Battalion Sergeant Major Muldoon had worked through the noon hour. At his direction, two sets of compound pulleys had been rigged at the top of the pounded earth ramp. Muldoon strung ropes through them and attached one end of each piece to the carriage of the three-pound cannon. The other ends, he gave to mounted Dragoons.

"Bend them around the pommels of yer darlin' saddles, if ye will. When I give the word, set off at a walk toward the stables."

Private Mallory scratched his chin. "But the stables ain't built yet, Sergeant Major."

One thing that had not changed during the journey here had been the woeful lack of intelligence on the part of Mallory. His patience already frayed by rampaging hostiles, BSM Muldoon got right up in the face of Mallory. "Sure an' they ain't gonna get built, ye idiot, unless we get this darlin' cannon into action and drive them hostiles off. Now, *do as I say.*"

Wooden pulleys creaked and taut ropes thrummed as the weight of the cannon came on them. Step by persistent step, the half-ton weapon rolled toward the base of the ramp. The lines vibrated wildly when the wheels started up the incline. Then one cord, which had been exposed too long to sun and heavy dewfall, snapped with a loud report.

Like a whiplash, it hummed through the air and viciously struck the rump of the horse ridden by Mallory. The animal uttered a very human squeal of pain, reared and dumped its dull-witted rider to the ground.

Muldoon exploded. "Damn yer black heart an' empty head, Mallory. Ye come a thousand miles and still can't keep yer seat. Harris, git over here with that horse an' another rope."

After another twenty minutes, the small field piece had been dragged into place. Quickly the crew milled around it, rammed home a bag of powder, a wad and a fist-sized ball. They all stepped back smartly and stood rigidly in a position of attention.

"Prick . . . prime," the gun captain commanded. Then he lowered a slow match over the touch hole. The little cannon went off with an ear-splitting roar.

The small, round projectile screamed through the air, to burst ten feet above a cluster of Blackfoot. Hot, smol-

dering shrapnel slashed into them and their horses.
Shrieking, they went down together in a heap.

"Reload."

Out came a water-soaked brush, to clean the bore, then
the loader placed another bag in the muzzle and the
rammer drove it down to the breech. Next came a cloth
patch, and another ball. The gun crew stood back and
the piece barked again. Shrieking, the ball lobbed over
the wall slowly enough to be almost visible from the side.

It burst above another clutch of Blackfoot warriors.
The defenders' volume of fire increased, and confusion
washed over the stunned Indians.

Although Lieutenant Colonel Danvers thought it better to have one of the mountain men on each of the
completed walls, Preacher did not agree. If left together,
their disciplined fire and superb, long-range marksmanship would have a devastating effect on the hostiles. Accordingly, he took Three Sleeps Norris and Antoine
Revier to the west wall, where the Blackfoot had concentrated.

They began knocking riders from their horses at seventy yards. Perplexed, the Blackfoot soon gave evidence
of their doubt. The medicine of Iron Shirt had failed
them. Only twenty-five of the seventy who were supposed
to do so ran forward to throw braided horsehide ropes
over the barricade. Almost at once, three of them stumbled and went down from the well-placed shots of
Preacher and his companions.

Preacher made an observation about their stubbornness. "They's still got it in their heads that our bullets
can't hurt them. We've gotta make them think otherwise."

Norris nodded. "You know, once an Injun's got somethin' in his head, it takes billy-be-damned to knock it out of there."

By then, six of the attackers had scaled to the top of the wall. Preacher reached out and smashed one in the head with the butt of his Hawken. The Blackfoot fell away without a sound. Then the little cannon opened up.

Its first round stunned to immobility fully a hundred of the enemy. Seven of them died along with their horses. None of them had ever experienced anything like it. The second detonation ignited fear in the hearts of many of the more prudent among the Cheyenne and Sioux. Wisely, they broke off their attack.

When the third projectile killed one and wounded seven Sioux, a general exodus began. Warriors streamed from the field, eyes wild with open fear that not even their enormous pride could suppress. Within ten minutes, not a single warrior remained within rifle range of Fort Washington.

"Well, that looks like it put the fear of the Almighty into them," opined Preacher. When he reported to Lieutenant Colonel Danvers, he summed up with an ominous statement. "They'll be back. Maybe not today, but give 'em time to whup up some more medicine an' they'll be on our doorstep bright and early tomorrow."

Preacher kept his plans to himself. He had a strong hunch that Lieutenant Colonel Danvers would strenuously disapprove of what he had on for tonight. Accordingly, he, Antoine and Three Sleeps left the fort quietly, by way of the sally port near the corral, well after dark. Lights out had been sounded by the trumpeter and the fort had settled in for sleep. Out on a small knoll to the west, a big bonfire blazed.

Preacher correctly judged that Iron Shirt would be

whipping up more medicine. He'd have to, the mountain man reasoned, after the disaster of today's attack. The heartbeat throbs of the big medicine drum reached Preacher's ears as they headed toward the first target, their aim to create confusion and dread among the allies of the Blackfoot. For that purpose he had selected the Lakota encampment first.

With the soldiers bottled up in the fort, and their cousins the Cheyenne close by, the Sioux had not bothered with a night watch. Only the usual herd guards had been placed to prevent their ponies from straying. Preacher found one of them easily. The youthful Brule sat quietly on his pony, eyes fixed on the stars. His lips moved silently.

No doubt he's making a poem for a gal friend, Preacher speculated as he crept up close to the unaware sentry. He had approached from downwind so not even the piebald animal gave warning as Preacher raised up in the tall grass and swung with the flat of his tomahawk blade.

A soft clang came as fine steel met hard head. The teenaged Sioux slumped forward onto the neck of his mount and twitched slightly. Preacher sprang forward and dragged him from the pony. With rawhide thongs he bound the youth, gagged him and left him in a shallow draw. Quietly, he moved on in search of another guard.

Three Sleeps Norris all but blundered into the first of the herd watchers on his side. He surged up out of a gully and found himself not three feet from the broad, bronze back of a Sioux warrior. He recovered quickly enough and brained the warrior with a pistol barrel.

One less to worry about. Gliding on moccasins through the grass, Three Sleeps continued to skirt the horses. He

had nearly completed his third of the circuit when he
came upon another guard. This one showed wide-eyed
surprise at suddenly being confronted by a white man.

"Wa— " he blurted a moment before Three Sleeps silenced him with a hard fist to the jaw. The brave went
slack, then heaved himself upward from the ground.

Three Sleeps rapped him back into quiet with the flat
of his tomahawk. In no time he had the Sioux bound
and gagged. Then he started back, to cover the same
ground and make certain he had gotten them all.

Antoine Revier slithered, belly down, through the
grass. A chubby, moon-faced youth lounged against a tree
trunk. His hand went constantly to his mouth and Antoine
realized he was eating something. The French-Delaware
cut to his right to circle the herd guard and came upon
him from the rear. In the end it became all too easy.

Gnawing on the hind leg of a roast rabbit, the drowsy,
fat, young man could not have heard the last trump due
to his sensual absorption with food. Antoine's left arm
circled his neck and choked off the air. Surprise caused
the Sioux to suck fragments of flesh into his lungs. He
began to choke and thrash.

Antoine silenced him with a doeskin bag of damp sand
taken from the creek. The hapless sentry would have a
lump the size of his fist on his head the next morning,
provided he didn't strangle on his meal. The brave tied
tightly and dragged out of sight into some brush, his
assailant ghosted away into the night. There would be
at least one more, Antoine thought grimly.

By prearrangement, the trio of mountain men met
back at the spot where they had separated. Each had
taken out two of the young watchmen. Being careful not

to raise an alarm, they started to cut out ponies from the herd. When they had what Preacher estimated to be between twenty and thirty, they eased them away from the rest and headed toward the Cheyenne camp.

When they had come a safe distance, Antoine Revier whispered softly to Preacher, "I can understand, you bein' right friendly with the Cheyenne, why we'd not do any permanent damage, but why spare them cutthroats. The Lakota are bad news."

Preacher answered him readily enough. "Also they are allies of the Cheyenne, and considered to be cousins from sometime in the far-off past. No sense in riling them too much. Thing is to get them to break this alliance with the bloodthirsty Blackfoot."

"Well and good, Preacher, but for me, I'd as soon kill 'em all," Three Sleeps offered.

Preacher tendered his assurances. "I think we'll have us some fun this way."

When they drew close to the Cheyenne camp, Preacher and his friends slipped onto the backs of three ponies and whipped the others up into a gallop. Whooping and caterwauling, they soon turned the gallop into a stampede. Jolted out of their ruminations on lush sweet grass, the animals bounded toward the camp.

Pounding in among the lodges, the ponies created havoc. Warriors, dopey with sleep, struggled into loincloths and stumbled out into the path of the horses. Meanwhile, Preacher, Three Sleeps and Antoine overturned several hide tents and set more afire. Only a few stray arrows challenged them. Howling with laughter, they rode well beyond the Cheyenne village to where they had left their own horses.

Dawn brought back the warriors, boiling with anger this time. After a night of medicine dances, their faith had been restored in Iron Shirt and his Iron Shield ritual. The insults the Sioux and Cheyenne had endured at the hands of Preacher and his friends had not turned them from the alliance. Rather it had stiffened their resolve. They hurled themselves at the stockade with total disregard for personal safety. Braided horsehide lariats snaked over the pointed poles of the outer wall and found purchase on some.

"They're comin' up the walls!" shouted a nervous lieutenant in Company D.

"Shoot 'em off," Preacher grunted.

Fire arrows joined the arsenal of the Blackfoot. The smoking, flame-tipped, shafts whirred over the palisade and thudded into the ground. Two landed on the roof of headquarters, only to be extinguished quickly by the soldiers stationed there, at Preacher's suggestion, for that purpose.

Three Sleeps pointed in the direction of headquarters. "Those fellers are gettin' riled some."

Preacher inclined his head. "Let's hope they don't have too many of those."

With the scalers repulsed, the hostiles drew back a little and the battle became a protracted exchange of gunfire. Using all the speed they could, the Blackfoot and their allies reloaded and fired at the men on the walls.

Lieutenant Colonel Danvers called together the company commanders of Company A and D. "We can sweep them from in front of the gate with a counterattack."

Captain Bronston of Company D scratched at a bald spot on his head. "Do you think that's wise, sir? Once we're exposed, the massive force on the west could flank us and roll us up right smartly."

"Mr. Preacher assured me that when something went wrong for the savages, they would break off an assault and scatter. I'm confident they will do the same now."

Bronston had a ready reply. "Yes, sir, but haven't you noticed that they are fighting in a disciplined manner for once. It is as though someone has introduced them to tactical concepts. If that's the case, they will attack."

"We need to find that out, don't we? Prepare your companies for a counterattack, gentlemen. The gun crew has come up with grapeshot loads from fifty-four-caliber balls we have in reserve. We can cover you with the cannon."

"Yes, sir. Sabers, sir?"

Lieutenant Cal. Danvers considered Captain Bronston's suggestion a moment. "Yes, I think so. Leave your carbines behind."

It had been a facetious offering and the response took Bronston by surprise. Still, he replied quickly. "But the Halls offer us our best firepower."

"Your men cannot hold both in their hands at the same time. You'd only get off two shots at best. Pistols and sabers, Captain Bronston." He turned away.

Ten minutes later, the sally port swung open and the two companies charged out and around the flank of the Cheyenne and Sioux positions. Sabers gleamed in the sun as they descended on the unsuspecting hostiles. Only a few reared upward and fired their rifles at the fast-approaching Dragoons. Pistols barked, and those who resisted died where they stood.

Keen edges flashed deadly light as the Dragoons hacked and slashed their way through the massed forces of warriors. Faster than Captain Bronston imagined, the flank turned back on itself and Indians fell to both sides, wounded or dead. Word of the attack raced through the warriors. It took little time to rally the Blackfoot to come to the aid of their allies.

By that time, the Dragoon charge had come level with

the main gate. With a roar of encouragement for the beleaguered, the Blackfoot swarmed around the corner of the stockade and rushed toward the soldiers. Arrows and rifle balls flew toward the mounted troops. Still they prevailed. With a sharp roar, the cannon detonated. Thin shrieks filled the air as the insubstantial leather sheath stripped from the improvised grapeshot. The balls rippled as they passed in front of the Dragoons. At once, some of the men among the Blackfoot began to scream in agony.

Captain Borden, who commanded the counterattack, raised his saber above his head. "Turn about! To the rear . . . Hooo!"

Back through the disorganized hostiles they rode. More of the Cheyenne and Sioux suffered from the pistols and blades in the hands of the Dragoons. Ahead of them, the sally port swung open and the troops streamed toward it.

Fighting dragged on into the afternoon. Preacher offered his opinion of the counterattack. "They lost eight Dragoons kilt an' another eleven wounded. Damn waste of time, I say."

Around three o'clock, nature intervened to disrupt the plans of Iron Shirt. Huge towers of black thunderclouds billowed up in the northwest. They moved swiftly across the Bighorns. Lightning flashed and crackled through the heavy air. The first sheet of rain swept over the finger of land toward Fort Washington at three-ten.

In seconds it turned to a solid downpour. Visibility shrank to mere feet. The three-pounder became inoperative. Already short on ammunition, the hostiles hunkered in the chill deluge and engaged in only desultory return fire. Another benefit the way Preacher saw it, the drencher softened the bow strings of the warriors, which rendered them useless.

Silently, they began to stream away from the walls of Fort Washington. Disappointed in this reversal, the Blackfoot, Cheyenne and Sioux did not even cast glances back at their relieved enemy. When the last of them plodded out of range, a shrill, worried voice came to Preacher's ears.

"Anna! Anna! Charlie, have you seen Anna anywhere?"

"No, Mom," Charlie Billings called back, sudden guilt burning his face red. "Where was she?"

"I . . . I don't know. I left her at the cave with you. When the storm came up, I thought she would surely stay."

"She's not here now."

Eve Billings saw Preacher on the wall and hurried to the stairs that led upward. Worry creased her brow when she approached the mountain man. "Preacher, Anna is missing. I can't find her anywhere."

"We'll look." Preacher grated the words out.

Twenty minutes later, every corner and nook of the fort had been searched without results. Preacher brought Eve the bad news.

"I don't know how, or why, but somehow Anna has gotten out of the fort."

"Oh, my God. You have to find her."

Despite the visions Preacher had about the appeal of a sweet-faced, blond little girl to a Cheyenne or Sioux warrior, he spared Eve that torment. "I'll do ever'thing I can. Don't you worry. It may take a while, but I'll turn over mountains to find her."

TWENTY-SIX

Not until Preacher passed well beyond the ground churned up by the Indians did he find any sign of Anna Billings. He suspected that she had become terrified of the constant fighting and later the crackling lightning and the boom of thunder. Somehow, in the midst of the furious storm, she had managed to slip away. The small door in the sally port had been found partly open. It stood to reason that the eight-year-old had drawn the latch and left the fort by that means. Preacher's major concern centered around the very good chance that she had been seen by some of the stragglers among the Indians and taken captive.

He found it encouraging when he came upon her small shoe prints in the mud, at a right angle to the direction traveled by the retreating hostiles. It did not eliminate the possibility of her capture. She could have escaped from her captors, Preacher speculated. If so, they would be coming after her. The wind diminished slowly as he followed her sign. Preacher quickly recognized the terrain. Her trail led down into the valley where Goose Creek ran through, made swift and turbulent by the dam and water wheel.

Preacher swung Tarnation northward to stay with her steps as they led toward the mill. He surmised that the small building there had been her goal. Ahead of him now, he thought he saw a frilly, lace-trimmed collar and flaxen head. He urged Tarnation to a faster pace. Satisfaction glowed in Preacher's chest when he pushed through the tall grass and saw Anna on the bank of the treacherous stream.

Calmly, she went about unlacing her shoes. She was going to cross, Preacher realized. The creek bank looked insubstantial and slippery. He drummed heels into Tarnation's flanks. The hooves squished noisily in the sodden turf, the thump of their impact muffled. Not enough, though.

Anna looked up wide-eyed at picking up sounds of the rapid approach. Unable to recognize Preacher in the low light from an overcast sky, she saw only a huge horse looming over her, remembered the charging Indians, and panicked. With only thought of escape in her mind, the girl sprang to her feet and took a step toward the water. A second later, the saturated soil of the bank gave way under even her slight weight.

With a thin scream, Anna Billings toppled forward into the stream fully clothed. Swollen by the rain, Goose Creek ran swiftly. Anna wailed in terror as the current swept her quickly downstream.

Preacher shouted encouragement as he skidded Tarnation to a halt. "Anna! Hold on. I'm coming."

He took time only to shuck his heavy holsters and Walker Colts, his hat and moccasins. Then he dove into the roiling water. Anna's fair hair formed a dim halo on the surface as she was whirled away.

"Get on your back," Preacher shouted. "Try to float."

Anna tried, failed, and went under. She came up sputtering. "I can't. My dress pulls me down," she wailed. "Please help me."

Preacher drew closer with powerful strokes. "Take off your dress."

A deeper look of horror came on Anna's face. "I c-can't. I don't have a petticoat."

Preacher was barely over an arm's length from her. "Do it anyway. That thing could suck you under for good."

Small fingers tugging at the stubborn buttons, Anna undid her dress far enough to allow its sodden weight to drag it free from her body.

Two more strokes and Preacher reached her. He slid an arm under both of hers and across her bare chest. "Now we've gotta get out of this current."

One-armed, he pulled at the turbulent water at an oblique angle to that of the stream. It soon became hard work. Preacher strained until the cords in his neck stood out like whitened ropes. To his gratitude, Anna did not try to fight the water. He noted progress when a large rock flashed past. Preacher recognized its shape and knew it to be close to the near-side bank.

A few more stout pulls, legs scissoring to provide thrust, and Preacher felt mud and sand beneath his toes. He relaxed and stood upright. Gasping for breath he sized up their situation. Anna clung to him like a monkey. Staggered by the rush of water and his burden, Preacher made unsteady progress to a bar of pebbles and sand that extended into the creek. Once there, he put the girl down.

"You've only one shoe. Best that you take it off 'stead of limpin'."

Tears welled in Anna's eyes. "Thank you, Preacher. You saved me."

Preacher looked down, embarrassed. "It was me scared you into the crick in the first place."

"Did . . . did your horse run away?"

"No. He'll stay where I dropped the reins. We'd best be movin', get you a blanket."

When the naked Anna was wrapped warmly, Preacher handed her up onto the back of Tarnation, then mounted behind her. The girl gave not even a single backward glance at the stream that had come so close to claiming her life.

* * *

On the way, Preacher swung Tarnation down into a gully to keep off the skyline. They rounded a bend in the ancient, eroded riverbed and came face-to-face with five grim-visaged Cheyenne warriors.

"Oh-oh, missy, it looks like we've jumped into some trouble," Preacher told Anna calmly while he lifted and shifted her to one side to put her behind him.

Correctly reading Preacher's intention to fight, the Cheyenne raised their weapons. Preacher tensed and drew both of his Walker Colts. His intention was to weaken the Cheyenne enough to crash through and make a run for it. The fight was about to begin.

Then, at the last moment, an older warrior drifted down the shallow bank. He raised his right arm in a commanding gesture and called to his fellow Cheyenne.

"Hold! Do not attack this man. I know him well. He is a friend."

He trotted forward then and greeted Preacher. "Ho, White Ghost, it seems that you are always helping little children."

Preacher recognized him at once. "Cloud Blanket, you look the same as when I last saw you."

Cloud Blanket turned in his saddle so the other Cheyenne could hear his words. He spoke in his own tongue. "I made you my brother when you rescued my little son and daughter from that bison stampede on our hunting grounds that summer long ago."

Preacher smiled and replied in the same language. "I remember it like it was yesterday."

Cloud Blanket gestured to the five warriors. "These men scout for my band. I am moving far to the east because of the unrest among our people."

"If you are talking about the fightin' at the fort, I can

understand. What's your fix on what's gotten the tribes so stirred up."

Cloud Blanket scowled. "It is the doing of one man. Iron Shirt. I will come and talk about it with you over coffee."

It all started with a misunderstanding at the main gate. Private Masters, on sentry duty, saw Preacher approaching with an Indian at his side. He drew the obvious conclusion.

"Corporal of the Guard, Post Number Two. Chief scout returning with a prisoner. Looks like he's found the girl, too."

When Lieutenant Colonel Danvers received word of that, he left his office hastily and went to meet Preacher. Two privates and a nervous Corporal Penny stood around a mounted Indian, weapons leveled. Before Preacher could explain, Danvers burst onto the scene.

"Corporal Penny, escort the prisoner to the guard-house."

"Yes, sir."

Preacher protested at once. "Now, hold on a minute. This man is my friend. He's not a hostile."

"He's an Indian, isn't he?" Danvers replied.

Eve Billings, tears of relief on her face, came up then to relieve Preacher of Anna. She stopped short, astonished at the figure who sat his horse in front of her. "Why, that's the Indian I told you about, Preacher. He's the one who watched us from a distance." To Danvers, she added, "He's friendly right enough. He smiled and waved to me every time."

It was time for introductions, Preacher felt. "His name is Cloud Blanket. This is Miz Billings. An' this is . . ."

Charlie Billings came forward and raised his right hand in the sign of greeting and peace. "*Heyota,* Cloud Blanket."

Shock registered on the face of Eve Billings. "Charles Ryan Billings, you . . . you *know* this Indian?"

"Oh, sure. He's my friend, but it's supposed to be a secret. Back in the other mountains he came to me and taught me how to track game. That's why I always done so good."

"Did so well," Eve corrected automatically.

"He gave me these moccasins, too." Charlie beamed with pride in his friendship.

Lieutenant Colonel Danvers interrupted the domestic scene. "He is still a hostile prisoner, and I want him removed to a secure place at once."

Preacher's dander rose. "An' I say hell no. 'Fore you lock anyone up, Colonel, we'll all jist ride out of here and leave you to the mercy of the real hostiles."

"You can't do that. It's desertion in the face of the enemy. I'll have you shot for that."

Eyes narrowed alarmingly, Preacher pinned Danvers with a burning gaze. "You may try, Colonel, but you'll have a damn hard time doing it." He raised himself in the saddle. "Antoine, Three Sleeps, grab yer gear. We're gettin' out of here," he shouted.

After two tense minutes, the mountain men appeared with their horses loaded. The Arapaho warriors came with them. Without another word, Preacher and Cloud Blanket in the lead, they left the fort by the open main gate. After they departed, Danvers looked around and spotted BSM Muldoon.

"Sergeant Major, take a horse and follow them. I want to know every detail of what they are up to."

"Yes, sir."

Beyond the ridge that overlooked Fort Washington, Preacher halted the small party and made a fire for coffee. While it brewed, he listened to what Cloud Blanket knew of Iron Shirt. His conclusions, arrived at over the first cup of heavily sweetened brew, surprised Preacher.

"I believe that there is more behind this than a moon-struck holy man. There are three white men who go wherever Iron Shirt goes. They do not have kind faces. They are the ones who bring the rifles."

"I'll have to look into that. A while back I thought I had run into the whites that was supposed to be runnin' with Iron Shirt." He went on to relate the run-in with Blake Soures, including a description of the outlaw leader.

Cloud Blanket nodded thoughtfully, then brightened at the portrayal of Soures. "That is the man who brought the wagons with the rifles. He is like the rattlesnake."

"Was, Cloud Blanket. I killed him."

"He will not be missed by me or any of my band."

"I'm gonna have to go get a look at these other whites you tole me about."

"You are not going back to the soldier lodges?"

"No. Let that damned pompous Danvers sweat a bit. The others can go back in a couple of days, if they want. That'll help some."

"While you are gone, my braves and I will not be able to protect the foolish soldiers, but we will try."

They drank another cup of coffee and Cloud Blanket described to Preacher how to find the war camp. They parted as friends.

BSM Terrance Muldoon and his three-man detail returned to Fort Washington to report. They remained unaware that they had been allowed to get close enough to hear what was being discussed. Nor, after hearing Preacher speak in Cheyenne, did Muldoon wonder why the conversation had been in English. Doubtless he

would have been furious to learn that it had been done
that way for his benefit.

"So, Mr. Preacher is going off to look for some nonexistent white renegades who are supposed to be aiding
the hostiles that attacked us? Do you suspect, Sergeant
Major, that he intends to join them?"

BSM Muldoon bristled. "Certainly not, sor, an' that's
a fact. Preacher may be a lot of things, dependin' on
how ye see him, but he's not disloyal, not a bit, sor."

"I want a detail sent off to trail our Mr. Preacher.
Lieutenant Judson will lead it. I know how you dislike
garrison duty, Sergeant Major, so I am sending you
along as ranking noncom."

"And the purpose of our going after him, if I may
ask, sor?"

"I want you to bring him, and the others who deserted
us, back here."

Muldoon raised an eyebrow. "To be punished, is it,
sor?"

"No, to tell us what we need to know to defeat these
hostiles."

"Ye think they'll be comin' back, do ye, Colonel, sor?"

"You can count on it, Sergeant Major. As soon as they
lick their wounds and get in a proper frenzy." Then he
turned his attention to a dispatch he had to write to his
superiors back East.

After a three-days fast, hard journey, Preacher and his
friends, none of whom seemed eager to return to the
fort, reached the war camp deep in the Bighorn Canyon
region. It had been up and down mountains all the way.
Mostly up, as Preacher saw it. At noon of the last day,
Preacher reined in and pointed to the crisp-edged im-
prints of iron wagon wheels.

"There's no question that there's white men with that

biggest Blackfoot band. They're close, too. I think we need only get close enough to take a peek, then git on back."

"Sounds right," agreed Three Sleeps.

Antoine cast one eye at an odd angle. "You reckon the colonel will thank us for what we find out?"

Preacher ran long fingers through his long, dark, sandy hair. "I doubt he knows the words, Tony. We'll ease up on these-here hostiles after dark and see what we can see."

Late that night, what they saw, though they had no names for them, were Praeger, Gross and Reiker. Preacher watched their activity for a while, then came to the conclusion that the Blackfoot and their allies were making preparations to return to Fort Washington. He nudged Three Sleeps in the ribs and whispered in his ear.

"I think we got what we came for. We'll ease our way out of here and head back in the morning."

Except for Lieutenant Judson and BSM Muldoon, the detail that followed Preacher consisted of men so inept that they made their presence painfully obvious. So lulled did they become, that they had not the slightest awareness of being watched. Early the next morning, they blithely walked their horses directly into imminent danger.

When the large war party of Blackfoot attacked, they took the Dragoons entirely by surprise.

TWENTY-SEVEN

Arrows flew in a dark cloud out of the grass along the trail left by Preacher. Three Dragoons died before a one could fire a shot. The hostiles, who had left early to return to the fort, had come across the sign of white men and decided upon an ambush. The sight of the Dragoons had been entirely too tempting.

Lieutenant Judson acted correctly and promptly. "Dismount. . . . Form a circle with your horses. Every other man, return fire."

The only trouble was they saw nothing to shoot at. Another flight of deadly shafts rose from the concealment of waving grass and thick brush. Instinctively, the Dragoons aimed at the places where the arrows first appeared. Several cries of pain rewarded them. Mounted warriors came from a tree line along one ridge and charged toward the circle of horses. Had the Blackfoot waited only a short while longer, they could have caught all of the birds in their nest.

It turned out not to be so. From a distance, Preacher and the men with him heard several muffled reports. The mountain men cocked their ears and concentrated a moment.

"It sounds like carbines to me," opined Preacher, who pronounced the word *car-bines*.

Three Sleeps agreed. "That it does. Now, what you suppose?"

"Figger Colonel Danvers sent some people after us."

Antoine joined in. "An' they got theyselves in trouble." He ended with a cackle.

Three Sleeps Norris turned to Preacher. "Should we go help 'em out?"

Preacher pretended to ponder that a moment. "I don't see why not."

The Arapaho in their wake, they set off at a brisk canter. From the faintness of the sound, Preacher reckoned they had a good twenty-minute ride.

A lot can happen in twenty minutes. Terribly outnumbered, the eighteen-man patrol died by ones and twos. Blackfoot swarmed around the improvised shelter, the horses targeted indiscriminately, along with the Dragoons. One beast, shrieking in pain from a neck wound, broke the grip of the soldier holding it and ran out among the charging hostiles.

That opened a gap which allowed a dozen Blackfoot to dash through. With lance and tomahawk, they began to slash at the Dragoons from terribly close quarters. BSM Muldoon saw Lieutenant Judson go down, a lance rammed through his belly. The unfortunate Private Mallory died a second later, his body draped over that of his officer.

"Poor, stupid lad," Muldoon said aloud as eulogy for them both.

Then his ears heard something he could not believe. Gunfire! And coming from beyond the press of savages. It could only be Preacher and those he had taken with him. Relief flooded Muldoon as he shot a screaming Blackfoot full in the face from two feet away. Another of

the Dragoons died while he cocked the hammer to take
out a hostile.

Three mountain men and six Arapaho warriors
charged down on the backs of the triumphant Blackfoot.
Their rifles cracked at the best possible range and nine
Blackfoot died. Preacher unlimbered one of his Walker
Colts and shot two more before the hostiles could react
and turn to face this new threat.

Wounded, one of them thrashed in the grass. Preacher
aimed at a fourth target. He knew his chances to be good;
he hadn't missed yet. His evaluation of his marksmanship
proved accurate. His .44 ball slammed into the skull of a
warrior who swung a war club at the head of BSM Muldoon.

Preacher's action did not prevent Muldoon from being
hit, but turned the strike into a hard, glancing blow.
Believing the spirits had turned on them, the surviving
Blackfoot fired a few final arrows, those without mounts
were hoisted up by comrades on horseback and the warriors streamed off over a notch in the ridge to the south.

Stunned by the rap on his head, Muldoon looked
slowly around himself to discover he had come out of
the fray as the sole survivor. "Jesus, Mary an' Joseph,
sure an' I'm glad to see you, Preacher, that's a fact."

Preacher also totaled the grim score. "How'd this happen to you?"

"Devil take it, lad, they got us entirely by surprise,
they did. Didn' know there was any heathen about 'til
they shot arrows at us from the grass, an' then more of
the spalpeen bastids come out of the trees, shootin' better rifles than we have. It was a terrible slaughter, it was."

Preacher tried for understatement. "I can see that."

"All me poor lads. Even lame-wit Mallory, an' our darlin' lieutenant. The colonel's not going to like that, he's not."

"No doubt. Tell me something, Muldoon, you seemed to put a note in your voice when you mentioned the colonel. Was it the knock you got on your head, or something else?"

Muldoon's grimace of pain turned to a sour expression. "You've got the heart of it, Preacher, sure an' you do. I've not seen nor heard anything certain, but I do have some worries about the darlin' colonel, I do. He's been writin' a lot of dispatches of late. Only they aren't to Gen'ral Ferris, or the War Department. I've yet to see to whom he addresses them, but it's certain sure it's not anyone in our chain of command."

"There's more?" prompted Preacher.

"Aye, that's the big an' little of it. It's about his attitude toward the men, Preacher. The way he sent us out here, an eighteen-man patrol into hostile country, with not a fare-thee-well. An' orderin' that counterattack back when the heathens had the fort surrounded. It's almost as though he wants us to get killed off to the last man jack of us, it is. But, a commander leads his men, inspires them, an' protects them, too. It can't be."

That awakened dark suspicions in the mind of Preacher, although he had to put them aside for the present and look into it all later. Muldoon had suffered a hard, messy blow to the head, which cut his scalp and raised a knot. Time that was taken care of.

"You know about those things more than I, Sergeant Major. Now, let me get a good look at that wound of yours." After some gentle probing and prodding, Preacher satisfied himself the skull remained intact and pronounced his verdict. "You'll recover. But with your patrol wiped out, and no way to get back alone, it might be best for you to ride with us."

BSM Muldoon's eyebrows elevated. "Yer not goin' direct to the fort?"

"Nope. This ambush tells me we haven't finished our business here. We need to get a look at this Blackfoot messiah, Iron Shirt, up close and personal. Find out what hold he has on these Injuns."

"When will that be?"

"Tonight," promised Preacher.

Preacher's little band made careful observations of the routine engaged in by Iron Shirt. In this case, two large bands of Northern Cheyenne, won over by news of the near success at the fort, prepared for the ritual. Late that night, after the immersion, fire-walking, feasting, drumming and singing ended, would be ideal for what Preacher had in mind, he told the others.

Once they had pulled back far enough from the camp, Preacher revealed his intentions. "Antoine an' me are gonna go in there and stir 'em up some. Leave some real scary things for Iron Shirt. If we're lucky, he'll begin to doubt his own medicine."

"Such as what?" BSM Muldoon asked.

Preacher brushed off the question. "Oh, some things we gathered up earlier today."

The hearty band had ridden west of the ambush scene to avoid any contact with hostiles that might happen by. Preacher and Antoine had hunted during part of the afternoon, using bows with all the skill of an Indian. Part of what they took, they ate. Some portions of the animals had been put away for later use. Preacher knew exactly what he wanted, and had used the last hours of daylight to paint plains-Indian pictographs on strips of rawhide. He took those, and the animal parts, with him when he and Antoine slipped away to the Blackfoot encampment at around two o'clock in the morning. A heavy overcast made the ground a pool of ink.

They entered the sleeping war village silently. Only the soft scuff of moccasins on hard soil indicated their movement. Preacher worked his way to the center of camp, then located the ideal spot.

With Antoine standing guard in front of the entrance to the lodge of Iron Shirt, Preacher placed a headless skunk on the ground. Next came a fresh deer heart, to which he affixed one of the pictograph strips. Those were the symbols for Iron Shirt's name, he had explained when he painted them. Beside that, he left the severed testicles of the same deer, with signs on the rawhide for White Wolf takes these from Iron Shirt.

Satisfied with his nocturnal display, Preacher signaled to Antoine and the mountain men slipped out of camp. Once beyond any chance of apprehension, they both threw back their heads and made the wailing sounds associated with the spirits of those who had been blinded and mutilated and could not journey to the Other World. Not too surprisingly, no one stirred in camp until daylight.

Shortly after the uproar that heralded the discovery of Preacher's handiwork, the hostiles broke camp and rode off to the southeast, in the direction of Fort Washington. Preacher's stalwart band followed at a discreet distance.

Over the next several nights, Preacher continued to pay ghostly, taunting visits to the band of warriors. On the fourth night, he edged in close to two teenaged boys, along as apprentice warriors and assigned as herd guards. After a round of ordinary talk about which girl in their village they thought the most beautiful, one lad brought up a subject that Iron Shirt's fury prohibited from being talked of openly.

"My older brother has seen the bad medicine that appears in camp these last nights. This White Wolf has powerful medicine. My brother thinks maybe more strength than Iron Shirt. Men have tried to kill White Wolf before, yet he lives, while our warriors die by the white man's bullets. My brother is thinking of taking me and returning to our village."

The other boy agreed. "Yes, that is a wise thing."

From his careful observation of the furtive glances the warriors made in all directions when they left their low war lodges, and now this indication of unrest, Preacher decided that an aura of bad medicine and even fear hung over the entire camp. His work had been well done.

A quick count of those in the war camp the next morning informed Preacher that some twelve or more had abandoned the cause. Earlier that day he had watched the three white men in camp set off southeast with Cheyenne guides, well ahead of the rest. Cloud Blanket had been right, and Preacher would tell him so. A big stir came when Iron Shirt learned of the defections.

He called the warriors together, most of them already mounted to continue the ride. "They are women! They shame the name Blackfoot. I have had a vision. We will make a mighty raid on the soldiers we have fought before with our Cheyenne and Sioux brothers. This time we will be victorious! I have strengthened the medicine that protects you. Nothing of the white man's can harm you."

From his vantage point, Preacher grinned at the craftiness of this fraudulent medicine man. As if he did not plan all along to go back to the fort. He decided upon one more visit to this uneasy war camp that night.

They came in the darkest part of the night. Preacher and his companions burst into the gathering of lodges from ten different points of the compass. Whooping ferociously, a torch spluttering in one hand, Preacher bent low to set fire to a six-foot-high lodge. Then he made for another one.

Not far away, one of the Arapaho, Gourd, overturned another and shot the occupants. Three Sleeps Norris trampled mounds of supplies and set them ablaze. Antoine Revier hurled cases of ammunition and bundles of arrows into the central fire. The enemy swirled all around them, unwilling to fire their rifles for fear of hitting a friend.

In the mad gyration of the swift raid, Preacher eventually came face-to-face with Iron Shirt. Preacher's right-hand Walker Colt bucked first and the ball smacked into the chest of his enemy. Iron Shirt went down in an eye-blink. Elated, Preacher signaled for the others to leave. They had accomplished much more than he had expected. Firing their weapons behind them, the mountain men, Arapaho, and BSM Muldoon quickly faded into the dark.

TWENTY-EIGHT

To Preacher's astonishment, the warriors did not disband after the death of Iron Shirt. Nor did they take time to mourn the loss of their leader and elect a new one. Rather, some set out immediately, with Cheyenne braves acting as guides, in search of those who had done the damage. The rest continued toward the fort.

Preacher soon learned the reason. Iron Shirt was alive! Obviously sore as hell, he moved slowly and sat his pony warily. Surrounded by a hundred Blackfoot warriors, the medicine man was unreachable. Knowing where the hostiles were headed, Preacher urged all speed to the fort. Muldoon concurred.

Mid morning remained markedly cool two days later, when the sentry's voice rang out from the gate. "Corporal of the Guard, Post Number Two. Visitors at the gate."

Bustling over on sore feet— he'd joined the Dragoons to ride, not to walk— Corporal Collins found three men confronting the guard. They were dressed like dandies. Nevertheless, he addressed them politely enough. "Good morning, gentlemen. May I inquire as to your business at Fort Washington today?"

Quinton Praeger took the lead. "We must see your commanding officer at once."

Collins blinked. "What about?"

"It is a matter of great urgency."

Following regulations, Corporal Collins did not give an inch. "If you tell me what it is, I can convey the information to Colonel Danvers."

His patience growing short, Praeger put heat in his words. "It is a matter of life and death."

Amused by the man's pomposity, Collins let his eyes go wide. "Oh, that's what it is, eh? The colonel will want to hear that, I'm sure."

Praeger flared. "Damnit, man, the country west of here is full of roving bands of hostiles. Tell him that, and tell him that Quinton Praeger and two associates are here to see him at once."

Corporal Collins scratched one ear. "I reckon you fellers didn't see the bullet scars on the wall. We've done whipped the savages and sent them running."

Praeger regained his control and fixed the insolent corporal with a frigid stare. "No you didn't. Because all the Indians we saw were headed this way. Tell that to your Colonel Danvers."

"Uh . . . yes, sir, right away, sir."

When Lieutenant Colonel Danvers learned of their presence, he had the three men ushered into his office. He waited a moment to insure that no prying ears lingered beyond the door then turned on Praeger, Gross and Reiker with a face suffused by hot fury.

"What in the name of God are you doing here?" he demanded.

Praeger took a step forward, asserting his control. "The whole thing is coming apart. Preacher is alive."

"I know that. But he's gone now, I dismissed him and he went away."

Praeger's words struck Danvers like lead pellets. "He went right to the war camp of Iron Shirt. He's worked some sort of savage mysticism that's nearly driven Iron

Shirt out of his mind. He told me after the first little
gifts were left that Preacher wants his balls. It's true what
I told your corporal. The Blackfoot, Cheyenne and Sioux
are on the way here. But if we don't get a war started
soon, it will all blow up in our faces."

Danvers fumbled for words. "That's . . . terribly dis-
turbing. What do you expect me to do?"

"I want you to have these Dragoons attack the peaceful
Cheyenne at once, the ones who did not join Iron Shirt.
That's sure to bring about the desired reaction and sat-
isfy our friends back East." He paused, looked around
the headquarters and at the palisades beyond.

"Apparently you did too good a job on this fort. By
now I expected to find all but you dead. The troops are
in much too good shape. Looks as if they could fight
their way through any number of Indians."

Instinctively Danvers stood up for his men. "My Dragoons had to fight their way out here. Naturally they
gained experience."

Praeger closed with Danvers in two rapid steps. He
tapped a long forefinger on the colonel's chest. "Let me
remind you that *they* are the ones who are supposed to
lose. The whole program is poised to fall into place.
But . . ." He raised the finger and tapped Danvers again.
"It will take a massacre and an Indian war to clear the
land of the savage vermin."

Choking on his anger, Lieutenant Colonel Danvers
turned partly away. Why had he ever thrown in his lot
with these insufferable scoundrels? Desperately he tried
to disassociate himself from this distasteful part of their
plot. "I am only taking orders. I am not a participant in
anything beyond the military involvement, of which, I'll
remind you, I took no part in the planning. I suggest
you leave forthwith, before any fighting begins, if you
value your hides so much." With that, he showed them
out of his office.

* * *

Preacher's valiant band arrived at Fort Washington the next day. The Blackfoot, Cheyenne and Sioux came right behind. Once more, the fort was very active. From the round-top knoll where he had made medicine, Iron Shirt observed the frantic activity within the walls through a brass telescope given him by Quinton Praeger. He could not mask his surprised reaction when he recognized three particular faces. He lowered the glass and turned to Two Moons.

"The Great Spirit smiles on us. The man Praeger and his nurselings are inside the fort. We can now sweep all of our enemies away in one battle. Then all the plains will burst out in flame."

For his part, Two Moons would have preferred to be spared Iron Shirt's rhetoric. Cunning and intelligent, Two Moons had long ago accepted that the great medicine of Iron Shirt was a fake. Men died at the hands of the whites not because they had lost faith, but because they had been shot. What sat foremost in the mind of Two Moons was the swiftness with which Iron Shirt had turned against their benefactors. Praeger, who wanted to be called Star Child, had brought them the fine new rifles, the barrels of powder and boxes of caps. For that he deserved praise, not death. He kept all that to himself as he replied to his leader.

"We have them trapped right enough. Why have they come here?" Two Moons inquired.

"Why do the white men do many stupid things?" Derisive laughter followed that suggestion.

"Iron Shirt, since they know of our plans, it cannot be for protection. It may be they came here to betray us."

Iron Shirt's face darkened at that. "Then they shall die slowly."

* * *

Quinton Praeger withdrew into a dark rage when he learned of the death of Blake Soures. He took his fury to the saloon in the sutler's store only half an hour before the Indians swarmed down the length of the narrow finger of land to the stockade that surrounded Fort Washington. There he observed the three, buckskin-clad men who had ridden in earlier in the day. They gulped down prodigious drafts of beer and wiped their lips with the backs of their hands. When the Blackfoot and their allies appeared, the sutler spoke from behind the bar to one of them.

"Well, Preacher, looks like you brought us more company than we wanted."

"I coulda told ya they were on the way, if you'd've asked," came the reply. "Boys, we'd best be gettin' to the walls. Those Injuns ain't here for a bison feast."

Jolted by this revelation and driven by a blind desire for revenge on Preacher, Praeger went in search of Heck Driscoll, one of Soures's lieutenants, who managed the wagons. He found him near the stables.

"Driscoll, I have a job for you. I've located this troublemaker, Preacher, and I can point him out to you. I want you to kill him. Do it up on the wall, so it will look like the savages did it."

Driscoll hitched his belt and produced a confident grin. "I can handle that all right." With that, they set off to find Preacher.

Like a cataract's roar, gunfire greeted them as they approached the wall. From outside came the challenging reports of Praeger's nice new rifles. Praeger winced involuntarily at the thought of being shot at by them. He quickly located the lean, broad-shouldered man in buckskin and pointed him out to Driscoll. The renegade gave a curt nod and moved off toward the access stairs.

* * *

Preacher first became aware of Driscoll when the
mountain man moved abruptly and a tomahawk blade
swished past his ear. The haft struck his right shoulder
and Preacher turned, expecting to find a warrior had
scaled the wall.

Not so. He faced another white man, one he vaguely
recognized. His carefully planned blow gone astray, Driscoll sought to recover. Before he could lift the 'hawk,
Preacher hit him in his exposed gut. Driscoll dropped
the tomahawk and bent double. Air rushed from Driscoll's lungs, to be quickly stopped when Preacher kneed
him in the face.

Dazed, Driscoll went to one knee. The fighting around
them had grown so intense that no one noticed as Driscoll slid a knife from its sheath. Concerned with holding
off the Indians, Preacher did not have time to play by
the rules. He simply drew a .44 Colt and blew a hole
through the head of his assailant. Heck Driscoll did a
backward half gainer off the parapet.

Then enlightenment settled on Preacher. The dead
man had been with the others in the Blackfoot war camp.
He'd handed out rifles and ammunition from the rear
of a wagon. That meant the other whites must be here.
He knew them by sight, and vaguely recalled that someone had given him names: Praeger, Gross and Reiker.
Behind him, the firing slackened and the first assault by
the hostiles broke off. Preacher went in search of the
men behind this uprising.

He found Quinton Praeger with surprising ease.
Shunning the hypocrisy of fighting his Indian allies,
Praeger had returned to the saloon. Preacher came upon
him there.

Arctic chill coated the words Preacher spoke in a slow
drawl. "I reckon you're the one they call Praeger. You're

responsible for stirrin' up this Injun ruckus. An' I reckon you know who I am. For what it's worth, yer errand boy didn't get the job done." Preacher's lip curled in contempt. "I hate a stinkin' white renegade more'n I hate a Pawnee. Are you going to do it the easy way an' give up?"

From outside they heard sound of renewed attack. This time it came from the west. Praeger responded with a bravado he did not feel. "That'll be the day."

Preacher had come willing to oblige. "Do you want it inside or out?"

Praeger did not reply. Instead, he fired with a concealed pistol from under the table. The sneak's aim was off because of the extreme angle, so all that hit Preacher was a shower of splinters. The flattened ball moaned past. Responding in a manner totally unexpected by Praeger, Preacher dove over the table at him.

They spilled out of the chair together. Preacher rammed Praeger's head against the floorboards repeatedly until a small cloud of dust hung around the battered renegade. Drops of blood from Praeger's split scalp formed a halo around his head. His eyes glazed and Preacher eased up, came to his feet.

He soon found that Praeger had more than one card up his sleeve. Lightning quick, Praeger grabbed for the butt of another of his short-barreled .60 pistols. He found himself not fast enough.

Preacher filled his hand with a Walker Colt and shot his enemy in the right shoulder. The Deringer went flying. His gun hand made inoperable, Praeger made a try with his left. To his surprise, he got the pistol free and fired a shot that creased the outside of Preacher's right thigh. That did not prevent Preacher from shooting the corrupt land speculator through the heart.

Hyman Entermann stared at Preacher a moment. "There's another of them out back in the chicksale."

Preacher nodded his thanks and left the saloon. He found Morton Gross at the outhouse. The chubby renegade fumbled to button his fly as he exited the small building. Preacher's words froze him.

"I killed Praeger not a minute ago. I'd gather you are the one called Gross. It sorta fits," he added parenthetically.

"I . . . I don't know who you mean. My name is Pembrook." His slight hesitation over the name put the lie to his words.

Preacher took note of it. "I don't care what you call yerself. You rode in with a piece of renegade white trash named Praeger, who's been stirrin' up the Blackfoot, Cheyenne and Sioux. I'm here to take you to justice in front of Colonel Danvers, or bury you. The choice is yours."

In the next tense second, Morton Gross made the biggest mistake of his life. Instead of surrendering, he grabbed for his pistol. He cleared it of his coat and had the hammer back when Preacher drew and fired his Walker Colt. The .44 ball struck Gross in a rib, which flattened it and deflected it from his heart, though it did terrible damage to his left lung. Eyes wide, he blinked slowly and sagged to the ground. Preacher stepped close and kicked the gun away.

"Where will I find Reiker?"

"I . . . don't know. You must be Preacher, right?"

"That's what they call me."

"I know . . . I'm going to die. I . . . just want . . . to do something . . . on the plus side of . . . the ledger . . . before I do."

"Go on, I'm listenin'."

Blood bubbled in pink froth on the lips of Morton Gross. "Watch out . . . for your Colonel Danvers, Preacher. He's in on . . . this thing of Praeger's."

Preacher bent close. "You're sure of that?"

A breathy word answered him. "Yes." Then Morton Gross shuddered and died.

"Dang. That went too fast. I sure would like to know where Reiker is," Preacher said over the dead man.

"He's right here." The voice came from behind Preacher, like the crack of a whip.

A violent crash and a rumble came from beyond Aaron Reiker. Unlike the previous time, the Blackfoot warriors did not try to scale the wall. Instead, they rode forward, attached several ropes to a series of spike-topped lodge-pole pines in the palisade and rode fast away from the wall. With as many as eight horses per upright, the log barricade strained and at last gave away. The rammed earth behind cascaded down from sheer gravity.

Preacher tensed and made ready to spring to one side. He fully expected to get a bullet in the back at any second. Instead, Reiker started toward him, talking as he came.

"I saw Quinton's body. And now I see you have disposed of Morton as well. Saves me the trouble, I suppose. I should be grateful and let you go. Our Indian friends will finish you readily enough." Reiker paused and sighed. "But then, coward that he was, I imagine Gross told you more than you should know. You've more lives than an alley cat, Preacher, and you might get away from the Blackfoot. So, you see, I don't have any choice."

While the overconfident Reiker rambled, Preacher's expectations soared. Braced for evasion, he used flexed knees to power his next move. With a loud, piercing yell, he jumped straight into the air and spun, bringing a Walker Colt ahead of him. Lacking the precise position of Reiker, his first shot missed.

Lithe as a cat, Preacher came down on the balls of his moccasined feet as he eared back the hammer. Reiker's ball caught Preacher by surprise, and burned like hell's fire along the left side of the rib cage. Had he been standing still, he would have died. It put Preacher's second shot off so that it only cut a chunk off Reiker's right hip-bone.

Reiker stumbled to his left, to the protection of the outhouse. A stench came from the interior that told of much frequent use. A fastidious man in dress and decorum, Reiker wrinkled his nose. Over it all, though, hung the coppery odor of violent death. Cautiously he peered around one corner.

Surprise puckered his lips when he saw no sign of Preacher. Where could he have gotten to so quickly? Reiker searched the entire area behind the sutler's with his eyes. Confident that Preacher had left, there being no hiding place, he came from behind the small structure and started back toward the saloon. The door to the outhouse creaked on leather hinges at his back.

"Behind you, Reiker."

He made a valorous try, spun from left to right, so his pistol would come in line first. Preacher let him complete his turn before he pumped a .44 ball into the center of Reiker's chest. Gagging, Reiker sank to his knees. His pistol discharged. The ball punched through the door of the toilet. Feebly he reached for another pistol.

Preacher shot him again. This time the ball put a black hole at the top of the bridge of Reiker's nose. Preacher stepped into the clear.

"Got to remember to tell Entermann to do something about that smell," he muttered. He sighed and set to reloading his Walker Colt. With this accomplished, all he had left was Iron Shirt and the aroused Indians.

TWENTY-NINE

With the wall almost breached, Preacher busied himself in an effort to get some of the young Dragoons to pull the three-pound cannon to the top of the dirt platform. Lieutenant Colonel Danvers confronted him there.

"Do you mind telling me where Mr. Praeger and his associates happen to be?"

Mincing no words, Preacher told him. He concluded with a fateful remark. "An' before one of them died, he told me you are mixed up in this dirty little business."

Danvers's eyes went wild. Froth formed at the corners of his mouth as, heedless of his condition and surroundings, he drew his Dragoon revolver. "That's a damned lie. Soldiers! I'm arresting this man as an Indian sympathizer. Disarm him and lock him up in the guardhouse."

Moving swiftly, Preacher knocked both privates aside and pulled his Walker Colt. Danvers had already triggered his Dragoon pistol. The shot went somewhat wild, to punch a hole through Preacher's left shoulder, which caused him to drop his Colt. Danvers took aim again.

In the next instant, a Cheyenne lance split the heart of Lieutenant Colonel Danvers. It had been hurled by Cloud Blanket, who dropped from the roof of the headquarters building to land beside Preacher. They embraced in the Cheyenne manner.

"Now all we have to do is kill Iron Shirt and this first-cousin-to-a-skunk alliance will fall apart."

Cloud Blanket appeared saddened. "Yes. I always knew it would come to that. Though I will not be the one to spill his blood. Here, that shoulder needs caring for."

While Cloud Blanket bound Preacher's shoulder, he offered advice on the best means of finishing Iron Shirt. Preacher listened intently. Around them, the battle raged on. Once the cannon had been moved into place, as Cloud Blanket packed the wound with a poultice, the assault on the weakened portion of the wall ended quickly.

Little respite came for the defenders. No sooner had the Blackfoot withdrawn from the west stockade than the Cheyenne and Sioux flung themselves at the north face. They used the same tactic of tearing down the wall. Another section broke away and the dirt buffer rumbled into a loose ramp. Up it plunged the Sioux warriors.

With the fortifications about to fall, the desperate young Dragoon gunners manned the cannon, firing in a flat trajectory now. When they ran out of prepared grapeshot, they dumped loose balls down the barrel and double wadded it. Preacher reappeared on the parade ground with his French Le Mat sporting rifle. Aching from wounds in both shoulders, he fought his way through a group of Sioux who had breached the wall and now swarmed onto the parade ground. BSM Muldoon saw him coming and helped clear a path with some well-aimed shots. After a solid smack to the kidneys of one warrior, which sent torrents of pain through Preacher's body, he gained the parapet.

Eyes straining against the haze of smoke and dust, Preacher at last located the Blackfoot prophet. This was going to hurt him almost as much as it would Iron Shirt, he thought as he knelt and put the buttplate of the rifle to his shoulder. True to his word, Iron Shirt made medicine on the little round-top knoll. His body twisted and jerked in the gyrations of his ritual dance around a blazing fire. Taking careful aim, Preacher touched the set trigger, then put a fingertip on the release tang.

The Le Mat let go with a terrible bark at the front end and a ferocious bite at the back. Preacher's face screwed up in a response he could not suppress. Two long seconds passed; then Iron Shirt looked up sharply as the ball cracked over his head. Moving like an aged weakling, Preacher reloaded. Again he took aim.

With another punishing report, the Le Mat fired again.

Iron Shirt staggered, sagged, toppled. He hit the ground and lay there, his limbs twitched in agonized reflex for three long minutes, then he lay still. A gusty sigh of relief came from Preacher.

It had worked as he'd expected. Although much smaller, the .36-caliber ball had markedly more velocity and better sectional density than a .54 round so that it cut through the links of chain mail and pierced the heart of Iron Shirt. Word of the messiah's death traveled fast. Suddenly, the allies fell silent on the battlefield. Cloud Blanket appeared at Preacher's right. He raised his bloodied lance to command attention.

"My brothers, your false prophet, Iron Shirt, is dead. His medicine was not good against the long gun of White Ghost, who took his life. Stop the fighting and go home. Live there in peace with the white men, who will leave this place in the Moon of Painted Leaves. There will be no fort in this place."

Slowly, his message sank in. Their heads bowed in perceived defeat, the warriors turned away from Fort Washington and began to leave the area in small groups. Within an hour they had all passed out of sight

* * *

After the warriors had left the field and order had been restored, Eve and her children came with some of the others to where Preacher sat under a single oak that had been spared by the builders, deadening the ache of his wounds with a jug of good rye.

Not one to defer to any man, Eve spoke what they had on their minds. "Preacher, we were wondering what you had in mind for the next few months?"

Preacher took a long pull and smacked his lips. The liquor probably was not good for the healing process, he knew, but by the time he got well into the second jug, he wouldn't give a damn. "Well, I'm gonna write a report on what happened here, to go with that Captain Dreiling. You know, the one whose gonna lead these soldier-boys back come September. My friends, Antoine an' Three Sleeps, will scout for them."

Eve pushed him further. "Yes, but what about you?"

"Me? I'm gonna take myself off somewhere quiet, where I won't see no Injuns or pilgrims or soldier-boys for a long, long time, an' jist plain heal up."

Eve's expression revealed that he had just slammed a door on what she wanted so desperately to know. Gathering her resources, she relented for the moment. "Actually, I wanted to ask you about a more immediate future. I would be pleased if you would take supper with my children and myself."

Preacher beamed up at her. "Well now, I think that could be managed. I'm tired of all this backslappin' that's gone on over me shootin' Iron Shirt. A little quiet supper sounds fine."

After the meal, with Charlie and Anna asleep for the night, Preacher and Eve talked earnestly and quietly for a while. Then they took a stroll to the small cabin set aside for Preacher.

* * *

Early the next morning, Preacher emerged from the low log structure. He yawned and stretched as much as his wounds would allow, then glanced back through the open door as he made his way to the nearest cookfire and pot of coffee.

He had a big grin plastered on his face as he made an announcement to the unseen person within. "Well now, I'll allow as how I jist might find that quiet place I want to rest up in somewhere in the Northwest Territory."

William W. Johnstone
The *Mountain Man* Series

__Pride of the Mountain Man	0-8217-6057-2	$4.99US/$6.50CAN
__Journey of the Mountain Man	0-8217-5771-7	$4.99US/$6.50CAN
__War of the Mountain Man	0-8217-5610-9	$4.99US/$6.50CAN
__Code of the Mountain Man	0-8217-5944-2	$4.99US/$6.50CAN
__Pursuit of the Mountain Man	0-8217-6011-4	$4.99US/$6.50CAN
__Courage of the Mountain Man	0-8217-5058-5	$4.99US/$6.50CAN
__Blood of the Mountain Man	0-8217-5324-X	$4.99US/$5.99CAN
__Fury of the Mountain Man	0-8217-5364-9	$4.99US/$5.99CAN
__Rage of the Mountain Man	0-8217-5361-4	$4.99US/$5.99CAN
__Cunning of the Mountain Man	0-8217-5362-2	$4.99US/$5.99CAN
__Power of the Mountain Man	0-8217-5363-0	$4.99US/$5.99CAN
__Spirit of the Mountain Man	0-8217-5191-3	$4.99US/$5.99CAN
__Ordeal of the Mountain Man	0-8217-5373-8	$4.99US/$5.99CAN
__Triumph of the Mountain Man	0-8217-5551-X	$4.99US/$6.50CAN
__Honor of the Mountain Man	0-8217-5820-9	$4.99US/$6.50CAN
__Battle of the Mountain Man	0-8217-5925-6	$4.99US/$6.50CAN
__Vengeance of the Mt. Man	0-8217-5681-8	$4.99US/$6.50CAN

Call toll free **1-888-345-BOOK** to order by phone or use this coupon to order by mail.

Name _____

Address _____

City _____ State _____ Zip _____

Please send me the books I have checked above.

I am enclosing	$_____
Plus postage and handling*	$_____
Sales tax (in New York and Tennessee only)	$_____
Total amount enclosed	$_____

*Add $2.50 for the first book and $.50 for each additional book.
Send check or money order (no cash or CODs) to:
Kensington Publishing Corp., 850 Third Avenue, New York, NY 10022
Prices and Numbers subject to change without notice.
All orders subject to availability.
Check out our website at **www.kensingtonbooks.com**